P9-CMT-832

Also by Sarah Price

The Amish of Lancaster Series
#1 Fields of Corn
#2 Hills of Wheat
#3 Pastures of Faith
#4 Valley of Hope

COMING SOON: Plain Fame

The Adventures of a Family Dog Series
#1 A Small Dog Named Peek-a-boo
#2 Peek-a-boo Runs Away
#3 Peek-a-boo's New Friends
#4 Peek-a-boo and WeeWee

Other Books
Gypsy in Black

Find Sarah Price on Facebook and Goodreads!
Learn about upcoming books, sequels, series, and contests!

Hills of Wheat:
The Amish of Lancaster Series

By Sarah Price

The Pennsylvania Dutch used in this manuscript is taken from the Revised Pennsylvania German Dictionary (1991) published by Brookshire Publications, Inc. in Lancaster PA.

Contact the author at sarahprice.author@gmail.com or visit her weblog at http://sarahpriceauthor.wordpress.com.

Chapter One

On top of the hill, surrounded by growing shoots of winter wheat that waved gently in the late-March breeze, a young woman stood by herself. She wore a short-sleeved blue dress, covered with a plain black apron. Her brown hair was barely visible as it was tucked neatly beneath a white heart-shaped prayer cap. Her eyes were shut as she felt the wind against her face, already brown from working outside. But on this day, she did not have to work. It was Sunday, a day of rest. Instead of relaxing inside the house with her family, she had felt drawn to the outdoors. Again. It was where she always retreated when she had a few spare moments. It was where she felt the closest with God.

She lifted her arms into the air, letting the breeze touch her skin. It brushed against her like gentle feathers. She smiled and began to spin around, slowly at first. The sun warmed her face while the breeze cooled it down. A laugh escaped her throat, a laugh of pure joy and happiness. Spring had almost arrived, the time of year when life was reborn on the farm. New plants, new flowers, new crops.

In just a few weeks, the winter wheat would change to a creamy light brown in color. The low rolling hill would be covered with shimmering wheat. It would glow like gold in the sun. Then, later in the summer, in the early morning hours, she would help her father and brothers plow the field, working to collect the sheaths behind the harvester, pulled by two mules, as it cut them down. The smell of the freshly cut wheat, the warmth of the sun, and the sweat of honest labor would greet her every day during that time. Her family would create neat rows of shocks to let the wheat dry before bringing them in for market. It was her favorite time of year.

But now, just now, as she stood among the growing wheat, she felt the birth of spring. The warmth, the sun, the upcoming harvest. She knew what it meant. For the Amish, it was a time of renewal. But for the girl, it meant much more. It was a rebirth, not just of her senses but also of her entire soul.

He was lost. That was the one thing he knew for certain. Beyond that, he did not know anything other than the fact that he was lost in Lancaster, Pennsylvania. Once he had turned off the main road, everything began to look the same. The roads were long, weaving through miles of fields and farms. Each farm stood next to an even larger barn and windmill, looking like picturesque paintings against a backdrop of green fields. Silos completed the picture, hovering over the barns and casting long shadows onto the fields.

Cows dotted the fields, most of them black and white Holsteins. Occasionally, he would drive around a bend, hoping to find a street sign or some type of indicator as to where he was. But each bend brought him further away from the main road and further into the heart of farmland.

He glanced down at the paper in his hand with the handwritten address. But, he couldn't even read his own writing. Frowning, he looked up in time to see the two children walking along the road and up the hill. The boy wore a straw hat and the girl a black bonnet. They had lunch pails in their hands and one was on a scooter. Both were barefoot. His old pickup truck was headed right for them. Cursing silently, he swerved, more on instinct than by need. The children didn't even notice and continued walking.

The truck wobbled and he felt a bump followed by a loud rattle noise. He could hear the too familiar thump-thump of a problem.

"Aw come on," he mumbled as he slowed down the truck.

He pulled off onto the side of the road, parking halfway on a grassy hill and opened the door to his pickup. As expected, he had a flat. He knew that he should have changed the tires before he left on his journey.

"Just what I need," he said to himself, as he ran his fingers through his dark, curly hair and looked around, hoping to see another car or some inkling of civilization. But all he saw were the farms, pastures, and cows. Lots of cows. But no people and certainly no cars. He also didn't even see telephone lines. His cell phone battery had died less than twenty minutes after he had crossed the state line earlier in the day. This was a bad idea, he thought to himself, not for the first time that day.

With a deep sigh of resignation, he set to work changing the tire. It had been a long day, a day filled with long highways and deep emotions. Leaving Connecticut behind would begin the healing, he knew that. But it didn't hurt any less as he left the only home he had ever really known for new, unchartered territory. He knew that he needed the change, needed the fresh start. Still, he hadn't counted on the forlorn sense of closure that increased with every mile of the journey. And now, with only a few minutes left, if he could ever find the house, the flat tire was like a slap in the face.

The sun was overhead but there was a cool breeze. He wiped the sweat from his brow and glanced at the sky. It was clear, the perfect spring day. The air was sweet, occasionally carrying a hint of the cows in nearby pastures. But he didn't find the odor offensive. Indeed, he was looking forward to being around the farms, away from the city and rat race he had called life. If only he could be at the house, unpacking the truck and getting situated before nightfall. Instead, he was stuck on the side of the road, battling with a lug wrench and rusty lug nuts.

As he turned back to the wheel, he noticed a motion out of the corner of his eye. Standing up, he leaned against the truck, shielding his eyes with his hand. Despite the blinding sun, he looked in the direction where he thought he had seen something move and, indeed, there was the most unusual sight.

In the middle of the hill, a young woman stood with her arms stretched out and her face turned toward the sun, the warmth caressing her cheeks. She wore a blue dress with a black apron covering the front. The white covering on her head completed the picture. Amish, he thought. Yet, even from this distance, he could tell she was a pretty girl. She was lean, which made her look taller than she actually was. And she was smiling to herself, unaware that she was being observed.

The moment struck him as one of peace. He was drawn to it. He hadn't had many moments of peace in the past few years. That was what he was seeking: peace and tranquility. He needed to find that type of peace again. Somewhere along the way, it had disappeared. He thought he knew the reason why it was gone and he definitely knew the moment when it had vanished. The search for peace was the very reason he was here, on this road, lost with a flat tire. It was the reason he was watching the young woman spinning slowly on the hill that was covered with what he suspected was a growing crop of wheat.

Without being aware of his own actions, he stepped away from the truck and took a few steps toward the hill. In the distance, he saw the farmhouse and barn with surrounding pastures filled with cows. A dog barked in the distance but he couldn't see from where. Perhaps behind the barn or by the farmhouse. He imagined that was where she lived. What he couldn't understand was why she was here, all alone, in the field of the growing wheat on the hillside. While he admittedly knew very little about the Amish, he did know that Sundays were usually a day of worship and time spent with family.

He stood on the edge of the hill, watching her. The wind caught her prayer cap and it flew behind her. For the briefest of moments, she didn't seem to care. It lay at her feet and she continued to spin, her face tilted toward the sun. But then, after a long moment, she dropped her arms to her sides and took a deep breath. That was when she turned to pick it up and saw him.

He could tell that she was startled by the way she quickly glanced over her shoulder at the farm behind her. It was as if she was contemplating a quick retreat. But she hesitated long enough for him to smile, wave, and point toward the road where his truck was parked.

"I'm sorry," he called out. "I didn't mean to frighten you. My truck...it has a flat."

She quickly put the prayer cap back on her head and, once again, glanced over her shoulder toward the farm. She averted her eyes, trying not to look at him as she took a step backward. "You need help, ja?" she asked, her words thick with a Pennsylvania Dutch accent and her voice carried in the breeze, despite the soft tone.

Cautiously, he took a step toward her. "I think I got it fixed. Just the tire." He glanced around the field and back toward the road. "But, perhaps you could help me try to find my way?"

"You lost, then?" she asked, an inflection on the last word.

He ran his fingers through his hair and looked around. "I'm afraid so. I know I'm close but these roads don't have street signs." He met her gaze, his blue eyes sparkling. "And they are so winding. My GPS system doesn't seem capable of keeping up."

"Where you looking to go?"

"Musser School Lane?"

She smiled. "Then you aren't lost at all! Your truck is on it!" There was something genuine about her smile. It lit up her face and caused her eyes to crescent in happy half-moons.

"Really?" He laughed, looking over his shoulder at the truck again. "I wonder how that happened?"

An awkward silence fell between them. He took advantage of the silence to study her. Despite being Amish, she was, indeed, a very pretty girl with a natural beauty. Her skin was tan and clean, a healthy glow on her cheeks. As he watched her, a flush covered her face, the blush from his scrutiny too apparent. She took a step backward and glanced back at the farm again. Off in the distance, he could hear the gentle musical rhythm of a horse's hooves clip-clopping against the macadam. There was nothing more to say.

"I should be going," she finally said. She turned and walked down the hill, her pace quick and light. It wasn't often that Amish women spent time alone in the company of men, especially non-Amish men. She wanted to be back in the safety of her world and away from his questioning eyes.

He watched her as she walked away, carefully crawling through the fencing into the cow pasture. When she finally disappeared into the barn, he turned and headed back to his truck. He wanted to finish that tire and get to his final destination in time to unpack the truck and settle in for the night. He knew he had some long days ahead of him and plenty of time to learn more about the Amish.

Chapter Two

The markets were crowded. Sylvia took a deep breath and closed her eyes, saying a silent prayer. She disliked market days. Oh, it was nice to see some of her friends and she loved the smell of the foods. Homemade cheeses and breads, pies and meats. The smells were gloriously powerful and she could stand there for hours, imagining the women who had spent afternoons making such good food.

But once the doors opened, it was too busy with too many staring eyes, silly questions, and sneaky strangers. At least twice each day, she would find some tourist trying to steal a photo of her, despite the signs that told the customers NO PHOTOS. But it was inevitable. After all, she thought disdainfully, rules don't apply to the Englischer. When it did happen, the only recourse that Sylvia had was to turn away quickly. She was too embarrassed for the tourist to scold them and too shy to protect herself.

Today, the aisles were crowded with people slowly strolling past the vendors. Each of the little booths offered different culinary experiences: jams, cheese, bread, salads, and root beer. Everything was homemade on an Amish farm from within a ten-mile radius. During different seasons, there would be beautiful displays of tomatoes and corn or pumpkins and squash. People would drive for miles to attend the Amish Farmers Market at Bird-in-Hand, Pennsylvania. During the winter, the market was only open on Fridays and Saturdays but starting in mid-March, it was also open on Wednesdays. Sylvia was just glad that she only had to work there on Wednesdays and Fridays.

"Excuse me, miss?"

Wearily, Sylvia forced a smile at the woman on the other side of the food display. "Yes ma'am?"

"I'd like to buy some of that jam," the woman said, pointing to the small pyramid of jam jars. Sylvia started to pick up the jam to show to the woman. "You make that jam at your own farm?" She asked.

Sylvia took a deep breath. The questions. Now it was time for the questions. It was almost as bad as the picture thieves. "No ma'am. I just work for the farmer who does make it."

"You people really don't use electricity?"

Sylvia shook her head, hurrying to put the jar into a brown bag. "That will be five dollars please."

The woman took her time rummaging through her purse. "I can't imagine! No electricity!" She handed Sylvia a five-dollar bill. "How on earth do you wash your clothes?"

Sylvia took the five-dollar bill and handed the woman her bag. "Have a good day, ma'am." She quickly turned away, hoping that the woman would just disappear. She hated the questions from these complete strangers. It was always the same thing. First about the electricity then about schooling. If they really got carried away, the next question would undoubtedly be about how large Amish families are. It amazed Sylvia how these people were so curious about the Amish, yet demonstrated their complete ignorance of the culture by always asking their brazen, probing, and predictable questions.

She longed for the day when she could just stay at home. She loved the peaceful days at her father's farm, working in the fields inbetween the morning and evening milking. She didn't even mind helping her mother in the kitchen or when she went to help her brother Emanuel's wife with their small farm in Ephrata. But Jacob Zook needed help. His wife was ill with the cancer and his oldest daughter needed to stay at home to tend to her needs. Until the situation changed, one way or the other, Katie Lapp had volunteered her youngest daughter, Sylvia, to step in to help at his stand at the Farmers Market. No one had asked her if she minded. And Sylvia knew better than to complain.

A man lingered near the display. "May I help you, sir?" she asked as she took a step forward. When he looked up, she frowned, trying to recall where she knew this man's face. She couldn't place it. She only came into contact with Englischers at the market. But the only Englischer men tended to be tourists. Yet, there was something so familiar. Then it dawned on her.

He was the man from the hill. She remembered his curly brown hair and dancing blue eyes. There was something rustic about him that had made that brief encounter stick in her memory. A blush covered her cheeks and she shifted her weight. It was unusual for her to know any of the people who came to the market as buyers. Instead, she took comfort in knowing the other vendors, people like her, who would prefer to be at home on the farm but did what was needed for the family and the community.

She knew at once that he had recognized her when he smiled and leaned forward. He rested his arms on the top of the glass case between them. "I know you," he said softly. She didn't reply, not quite certain what to say. He solved that problem by reaching out his hand. "We didn't properly meet last weekend, did we? My name's Jake Edwards."

Sylvia stared at his hand, not moving to shake it. She

looked as uncomfortable as she felt. "I...I..." she stumbled over her words. "Sylvia Lapp, Mr. Edwards. May I help you with something?"

"Well, for starters, you can call me Jake. Mr. Edwards sounds so old...reminds me of my father," he said, his voice light and teasing.

She wasn't certain how to respond. When she glanced up, her eyes met his. For a long second, too long for her comfort, he held her gaze. Yet, she couldn't tear her eyes away. She had recognized that he was handsome from the encounter on the hill. But, now that she was up close and indoors, she saw how handsome he truly was. When he smiled, his face lit up with such sincerity that she felt as if she knew this man. But their acquaintance had only been for a few minutes on top of the hill just a short week ago. And, clearly, he was not Amish.

"May I help you with something?" she repeated, her voice barely a whisper as she avoided the issue with names entirely.

Seeing that he wasn't getting past the wall, he sighed and ran his fingers through his hairs. His curls fell back onto his forehead, casting a slight shadow over his eyes. "I'm new around here, Sylvia. So, perhaps you could help me by pointing out the best vendors for some basic supplies. I need to outfit my house and want to acquaint myself with the local farmers." He smiled again. "I figured that would be a great way to get to know my new community."

"I see," she said, her voice soft and her eyes darting around the market.

"Perhaps you could help?" He followed her gaze around the market.

She chewed on her lower lip, not quite certain what it was that he wanted. But he waited for her to speak. He wasn't going anywhere and Sylvia knew that she had to reply. Cautiously, she said, "I suppose the first thing to know would be that Englische men don't usually shop here."

"What do you mean?" He laughed, looking over his shoulder at the hoards of people wandering throughout the market. "I see plenty of men here!"

"Ja," She said as she leaned forward, lowering her voice as she certainly didn't want anyone to overhear. "But they are *tourists*," she whispered as if it was a dirty word. "If you want to get to know your new community, you won't do it here."

Now it was his turn to look uncomfortable. For the past week, he had been working and trying his best to get organized, settled down. He had seen the sign for the Farmers Market and thought that he would give it a visit on his next trip into town. "Well, where does one go then? I haven't found much of anything around here, outside of the tourists traps at Intercourse."

"Well," she began slowly. Her hesitation caught his attention. "If you remember Musser School Lane, there is a local store on one of the back roads near there. You can get everything you need, I suppose."

He raised an eyebrow. "Where would that be located?"

"It's off of North Harvest Road. A dirt road. Not clearly marked since it's mostly for the locals."

"Ah," he said. "That sounds like a good start." He started to thank her but a woman pushed him aside. He waved a good-bye and backed away, hoping to catch her gaze once more but she was busy serving the next person who had come along.

For a long moment, he stood back and watched her interact with the customer. Patiently, Sylvia listened to the woman, helped her select the products, and put them into a plain brown bag. They exchanged money and the lady moved on, opening up space for another eager tourist to request a sample before making a purchase. Each time, Sylvia maintained her composure, shyly greeting them but serving their needs as quickly and pleasantly as she could.

He imagined she was eighteen, maybe nineteen. She looked young with pretty skin and a soft demeanor. Her eyes were dark and her hair even darker. He wondered about her future. Certainly she would be married soon, have children, and tend to her family. It was a simple life, he knew that much. But, as he watched her, he knew that there was something deeper to this young woman.

He remembered her from the field. She had seemed so at peace, standing alone among the field of growing wheat that surrounded her. Her face had radiated happiness and joy. Not like here, at the market. Clearly, she was uncomfortable interacting with the strangers, especially the men. He wondered if anyone knew or even cared that she disliked being in the market. From what little he knew about the Amish, he sincerely doubted it. Obedience was part of their lifestyle.

"May I take your photo, young lady?"

Jake had been just about to leave when he overheard the question coming from the next customer, a larger woman wearing a faded T-shirt and shorts with old sneakers. Clearly one of the dreaded "tourists" Sylvia had been referencing less than a minute ago, he thought. Unabashedly, the woman had removed a camera from her purse, despite the signs posted on the walls around the market.

He watched Sylvia shake her head and start to turn away, packaging up the goods for the customer. But the woman was adamant. "It's just a picture. I don't see why you won't pose," the woman said, waving the camera in the air. Sylvia kept her back to the customer. But the woman persisted to the point of actually taking pictures of Sylvia's back.

"Excuse me," Jake said, moving swiftly between the woman and the counter, blocking Sylvia from the invasive technology. "I believe the young lady said no."

"It's just a picture!" the woman said.

A large man walked up, eyeing Jake as he spoke to the woman. "What's going on, Lorraine?"

"This man is blocking my view of the Amish girl."

The large man stared at Jake, a scowl crossing his face. "You bothering my wife?"

Jake smiled, his white teeth bright and his face friendly. "No sir. But I do believe that your wife is bothering my friend here." He took a small step forward which forced the woman to back up. He began to put distance between the couple and Sylvia. "Amish people don't like their photos taken but your wife is persisting. Perhaps you were unaware of that? I'm sure you meant no harm but, as you can see, my friend is most distressed. So, perhaps you could take your package," he turned slightly and reached for the brown bag on the counter. Handing it to the man, Jake nodded away from the area. "And explain it to your wife. I'm sure that it's nothing more than a simple misunderstanding."

"I didn't pay the Amish girl," the woman said.

Jake met her gaze. "It's my treat today, ma'am. You have yourself a great afternoon." He stood between the couple and

18

the counter, blocking their view of Sylvia. His smile was warm but firm, reinforcing his protective stance and encouraging them to leave. They had no choice. Reluctantly, the couple left, shaking their heads as they moved along the aisle, most likely to harass another Amish vendor.

He waited until they had left before he turned back to Sylvia, "You alright?"

She hadn't turned around and her back was facing him, her shoulders trembling. It only took him a moment to realize that she was crying. Jake looked around. There was no one else to help. The other vendors were busy. He wasn't certain what to do. Comforting women was not one of his strengths, especially women he didn't know and certainly not an Amish woman.

"Sylvia?" he said, his voice low as he leaned forward. "Is there someone I can ask to come over here?"

She waved her hand over her shoulder, shaking her head. For a long moment, she stayed that way, her back straight but her shoulders trembling. It was shameful to cry and certainly much worse to do so in public.

Jake glanced around again and, taking a deep breath, he walked around the counter and stood next to her. He hesitated as he reached out to touch her arm. "Sylvia?" he repeated softly.

She turned around but didn't meet his eyes. "I'm sorry. It doesn't usually bother me." There were tears in her eyes and her face was blotchy.

"But it did today," he said quietly.

She glanced up at him, looking at him through her tears. "Yes. It did today."

He took a step backward, giving her some space. "It's understandable."

"I don't like being here," she whispered. The color rose to her cheeks. The words had slipped out, surprising both her and Jake. She glanced up again, a newfound strength in her expression. She had thought the words so many times before but never before had she felt the courage to actually speak them. "I want to be at the farm, not here with these people." She glanced around to make certain no one could hear her. "I know I should care about Susie Zook and her cancer but I don't. Not if it means I have to be here with these Englischers."

Jake didn't understand what she was saying but he could see something in her eyes that stopped him from asking questions. He knew enough about women to know when to keep silent. This was one of those moments. "Perhaps you should call it a day." he suggested. "The market is closing in an hour anyway."

The brazen glow left her and her shoulders slumped. "My ride..." She was back to the quiet Sylvia with her eyes downcast and her voice soft, barely audible.

"Well," he began slowly, taking a moment to run his fingers through his curls. "I suppose I could find myself lost near your parents' farm again." He waited until she looked up. "That is if you'd like a ride back there. I'm headed that way anyway...to look for the North Harvest Road market. It was highly recommended by a friend." This time, he smiled and was glad to see a hint of a smile on her lips. Yet, as quickly as it was there, it was gone.

She shook her head. "I don't know you. It wouldn't be proper," she whispered.

"Neither is subjecting yourself to harassment by complete strangers." He started to walk back around the counter. "Get your things, Sylvia. You don't belong here. I'll take you back to your farm." It was clear that he was making the decision for her.

There was just a moment's hesitation. But in that moment, she knew. She looked into the future for the briefest of seconds. She knew that there are times in everyone's life that are turning points. In her insulated world, she wasn't given exposure to many of them. In fact, that was a key objective of her parents. They wanted to insulate her from life changing moments. Yet, they had failed and this was that moment.

The decision that she would make in the next second would change everything. The image of the large woman with the camera flashed before her eyes, along with the image of the dozens of others who had stolen her photos over the past few weeks. When the image faded, she looked up at the man waiting for her and, without knowing why, she nodded her head and whispered a soft *"Danke."* And she left the market with Jake Edwards.

Chapter Three

Except for market day, Sylvia spent her time helping her mother prepare meals and *redding* the house. There was always something to do...wash the floor, wash laundry, change the beds, dust the furniture. It was quiet work for the most part, except for when her sister-in-law, Lillian, stopped into the house with her children. She lived in the house next door, the *grossdaadihaus*.

Many years ago, Sylvia's grandparents had lived there, the small house attached to the main one that Jonas had built just for his aging parents. After they had passed, Jonas Jr. took his new bride to live there. One day, Jonas and Katie would move into the *grossdaadihaus*, after their children were married. At that time, Jonas Jr. would move his family into the bigger section of the house. It was the way that it was done among the People. Roots were the people, not the things, that surrounded them.

Some times, Sylvia would hear the children's laughter from next door or see them run by the window, chasing a kitten or playing with the dog. She loved the sound of their childish voices and, often, she would stop to watch them play. She had heard that Englischers lived only with their immediate family, rarely with their extended families. She couldn't imagine such an unhappy life. She wondered if it was lonely. She knew for sure and certain that she wouldn't like that since living with her family kept her life full of fellowship and joy.

In the afternoons, Sylvia was able to work alongside her father in the fields or in the barn with the cows. With so many cows, it took a long time to clean the manure and the evening milking required as many hands as possible. Sylvia didn't mind the work, even thought it was hard and draining. When she lay down on her bed at the end of the day, in those restful moments before sleep overtook her, she knew that she had a full day, despite the aches and weariness in her body. In truth, her parents knew that her brothers' help was sufficient. But, everyone was also well aware of the fact that the time Sylvia spent outdoors was her favorite. And they all loved to see her face glowing with such happiness.

Sylvia was the last of the Lapp daughters and, in many ways, the favored. She was quiet and shy yet always alert and, when asked, ready to give her opinion...but only if asked. She was a pretty young woman with dark chestnut hair and rich brown eyes. And when she worked outside, her eyes sparkled and her face lit up in unspoken delight. So letting her skip indoor chores to help outside was the one indulgence that her parents gave to her. They would disguise their gift under the auspice of labor. She loved when it was time to help her father and brothers plow the fields or cut the grass. The smell of the fresh cut grass and the feel of the dry dirt beneath her bare feet made her happy. It reminded her of the closeness she felt to God.

Dinner and supper were always happy times in the Lapp house, despite the shrinking number of people surrounding the kitchen table. Sylvia missed her older sisters and brothers sitting around the trestle table for the noon meal. Most of her siblings had married and moved to their own farms, with the exception of Jonas, Jr. and his small family.

Sylvia loved listening to her brothers, Steve and Daniel, talk about their work in the fields that morning or her younger brothers, David and Samuel, talk about their day apprenticing at Junior's carpentry shop in the mornings. Her father might ask her a question or two about how things had gone at the market the day before but, for the most part, dinner conversation centered around the crops and farm. Sylvia preferred it that way. She didn't like speaking about the market and didn't like being the center of attention anyway. She preferred to hear about what had happened on the farm or with their neighbors.

So, Sylvia was surprised when, one day, her father looked up and announced, "We have a new neighbor."

It was unusual for someone new to move into a neighboring farm. Typically, farms passed down from generation to generation. Worst-case scenario, they tended to be sold among each other. Farms were in short order. So, for a new neighbor, an unknown person, to move in without advanced notice was newsworthy, indeed! Certainly the tongues were wagging amongst the entire community.

Katie looked up and raised an eyebrow. "Which place?"

"Took over that small parcel that hasn't been tended for so long," her father replied.

"The one next to Smucker's place, then?"

"Ja, that be the one. Can hardly see it from the road." Jonas bent back to his plate, wiping the sides with a piece of homemade bread. "I didn't even know it was for sale. Wonder if it was passed down." Jonas shoved the piece of bread into his mouth. "Heard about him from Whitey. Says the new owner is a gentleman farmer, I s'pose."

"An Englischer?" Daniel asked.

Their father nodded. "Ja, Englischer. Looking for some help with the house during the week. Mondays and Fridays."

24

Katie nodded, chewing her food carefully as if in deep thought. "If he's looking for help with the house, he's not married, then?"

"A widower, I heard."

Sylvia saw her mother take a deep breath. Death was never discussed in much detail in the house. She knew that her own mother had buried two babies before Sylvia was born. And, it was only two years back when her sister-in-law, Shana, had a stillborn baby. But no one talked about it. Death was final. But it was also a time to return to God. So, while the earthly family mourned, the heavenly family rejoiced. Sylvia didn't always understand it but, thankfully, hadn't been exposed to it very often.

"No wife? He'll be needing some help for sure and certain, ja," Katie said, shaking her head and clucking her tongue.

Jonas leaned back in his chair, nodding to Sylvia. He was finished and it was her job to clear the table. Quickly, she jumped to the task and began clearing the empty plates. "Ja, for certain." He paused, tugging at his beard. That was always a sign that he was up to something. "I was thinking of Sylvia." A silence fell over the table. Sylvia hesitated before setting the dirty plates in the sink and, quietly, returning to the table to retrieve more dishes. Her brothers looked at her, which made her feel terribly uncomfortable "It would be just the mornings, *redd* up the place. She could be back for helping me with the afternoon chores and the evening milking. And the pay is right *gut.*"

Katie glanced at Sylvia, too aware of the question in her eyes. "Lest we not forget, she's helping Jacob Zook on

Wednesdays and Fridays, Jonas," she gently reminded her husband.

Jonas nodded once. He seemed deep in thought again. No one spoke. The silence was broken only by the soft clanging of the dishes as Sylvia began to wash them. She worked as quietly as she could, listening and waiting for her father's next words. It would be the final decision.

Truth be told, she didn't know how she felt about cleaning a strange man's house. She imagined a widower, older with grey hair and set in his ways. He'd be particular, especially if his wife had passed recently. She had enough experience with widowers to know that the older the man is when the wife passes, the more fastidious they became. Yet, if cleaning his house meant that she didn't have to go to the market anymore, she'd be happy to accept the job. Plus, it would allow her to work around the farm in the afternoon and evening. She held her breath, waiting.

"Ja, that she is." He glanced at Sylvia. "If she was willing to help the neighbor, Whitey's granddaughter could work for Jacob Zook on those days. Whitey has some goods he could sell, too. Jacob is willing to share the stand with him." He smiled at Sylvia and, to her surprise, added, "And I get the impression that Sylvia is more comfortable closer to home."

With a deep breath, Katie nodded her head. "It wouldn't hurt Sylvia to learn more about caring for the house, I suppose. And to help someone like a widower, *ach vell...*" There was a hesitation in her voice. "But an *Englischer*, Jonas?"

Jonas took a deep breath. "Can't say I like that idea much, our girl working for a fancy man, but Whitey vouched for his character and, like you said, he is a widower."

"Daed, when would I start?" Sylvia asked.

Jonas stood up to leave the table. The other two boys followed his lead. It was time for the evening milking. "Suppose I can take you over there in the next day or so to meet the widower, see what he needs, and make proper introductions. Now, it's time for afternoon chores. You finish helping your Mamm, Sylvia, then come to the barn for the cows." And with that, the conversation was over and the afternoon routine had begun.

Chapter Four

By the time that Jonas mentioned the widower again, it was Thursday. Sylvia had all but forgotten about this new arrangement. She had been busy helping her mother with the spring house cleaning and getting the laundry washed. Laundry was an all day affair in the Lapp household, especially if her sister-in-law, Lillian came over from the *grossdaadihaus* with the children's dirty clothes. While Sylvia always thought that the fellowship was *wunderbaar gut,* she didn't like that her arms ached and her fingers got puckered from wringing out the heavy, wet clothes in the machine, then hanging them outside on the clothesline.

But, on Thursday, at the noon meal, Jonas reminded her about the new arrangement. Since the man wanted Sylvia's help on Fridays, Jonas had said, they should go over to meet him later that day.

Sylvia was surprised to find that she was experiencing mixed feelings. Part of her dreaded the meeting. She didn't like meeting new people, especially older ones. She had never worked for a complete stranger, either. Yet, part of her was excited for something new and different. She knew that her mother was concerned with how often Sylvia tried to rush through house chores in order to help her father and brothers outdoors. That wasn't a fine quality for an Amish wife. But Sylvia didn't care.

Unlike some of her friends, she was not in a hurry to get married. She liked being at home and enjoyed helping her family. She didn't look forward to the responsibility of caring for her own house and, hopefully, farm. At nineteen, she was becoming a concern for the family. She had not experienced her share of beaus yet, nor did she like to go to the singings on the weekend. Even when Steve tried to persuade her to go, Sylvia shook her head shyly and would disappear into the barn or fields.

She looked forward to when Steve finally made his own announcement with Emma Weaver. The family expected a fall wedding. It would be a happy time with the entire family coming together to celebrate with the community. Then Steve would move away with Emma. While he didn't talk about it, Steve had hinted about buying a small 20-acre farm near brother Emanuel's place. Farms were not easy to come by since they often were passed down through the family. Those that did come onto the market were often too expensive or too small to live off of the acreage. But, when a reasonable one came along, even if small, it didn't usually take too long for some young Amish man to venture out on his own.

In this case, being near Emanuel and Shana would be an extra special blessing. Steve would help work his brother's farm until he could expand his own. Sylvia had her own reasons to be extra happy: her father would really need her help on the farm when Steve left. There wouldn't be any talk of going to Farmers Market or cleaning widowers' houses then, she thought to herself. And, at least for a while, she wouldn't have to worry about their unspoken concerns that she might remain a *maedal* and never get married. She knew it would happen in time but she wasn't ready yet to think about such things and certainly not with any *buwe* that she had met.

The ride to the new neighbor's farm was quiet. It was closer to walk through the fields since the road went up the hill before cutting left along the top of Daed's farm. The fields along the road were all plowed with the hint of new growth in each row. Some of the growing crops were taller than others. She knew those would be the wheat fields. The horse and buggy sang across the macadam, with the wheels humming behind the rhythmic clip-clop, two beat, of the horse's hooves. No one else was on the road. For the moment, it was theirs alone. Her father didn't speak and Sylvia didn't initiate any conversation. The silence was reflective and she shut her eyes, letting the gentle rolling of the buggy soothe her nerves.

Whenever she had to meet new people, her stomach was in a turmoil. Going to Farmers Market was starting to look like it wasn't such a bad deal, she thought. At least she knew what to expect from the tourists. And to have to work in a stranger's house? She began to wonder why she had agreed to this. Yet, she knew that the decision rested with her parents. Between the church and her parents, her freedom was limited. Arguing was never an option so, as usual, Sylvia accepted her fate and tried to be agreeable with the decisions that were made on her behalf.

When her father turned the horse into a narrow lane, Sylvia sighed. It wasn't far from her father's farm but it would take her a good fifteen minutes to walk there if she cut through the fields. She knew her father wouldn't drive her during the week. He was too busy with other things. While she didn't mind the walking, she did mind being left alone in the company of a stranger. She hoped he wasn't too unorganized or critical. She knew plenty of older men that became cantankerous in their old age. While her supply of patience was rather plentiful, it was not endless.

The farm was larger than she thought. When her father had mentioned it, she envisioned one that sat on a few acres.

He had called the widower a "gentleman farmer" so she was surprised to see rolling acres of green pastures and a large white barn. It was surrounded on two sides by trees, which separated the rear and far side of the farm from neighbors. She imagined there were a good thirty acres or more; small compared to her Daed's place but certainly not a gentleman's farm.

The house was small, an old farmhouse with a crooked porch. It was two stories and looked like a box. There was moss growing on the roof. Since it sat under the shade of two large oak trees, it was likely to be cooler in the summer as well as the winter, the sun not being able to penetrate the full coverage of leaves to warm it. There were electrical wires running to the barn, which surprised her, but also a windmill by the house. Unlike most houses in the area, it hadn't been added onto for the typical Amish family expansion. It would be easy to maintain, she realized.

"I've never been here before," she said quietly to her father.

"Ja, me neither." He stopped the horse and buggy in front of the house. They looked around for a moment before he reached to open the door. "I didn't even know it was back down that lane. Farm was abandoned, Whitey said. No one lived here for years. House looks it, ja?"

Sylvia didn't respond but accepted her father's help getting out of the buggy. She looked around. The gardens by the house were jumbles of weeds. The house needed a fresh coat of paint and some repairs. But the barn looked wonderful. It was large and new. It was obvious that the widower had done quite a bit of work on it since he had moved to the farm. For all that the house was neglected, the barn was magnificently well tended. For an older man, Sylvia thought, he certainly must have been busy...no wonder he needed help with the house. For a lone man with no sons to help, the barn would keep him busy from sunup to sundown and beyond.

"Hullo?" her father called out.

They heard a faint reply from the barn. Jonas nodded to Sylvia and they walked over toward the side door. Sylvia let her father enter the building first but she stayed close behind him. Her heart pounded in her chest and she felt her palms sweat. They saw the man's back as he bent over a large piece of equipment. Sylvia recognized it as a dairy cooling system, but it was old and rusty. It hadn't been used in years. The barn itself was unused and, from the looks of it, had needed a lot of work. She could see some of the widower's efforts in new boards on the walls and swept floors but there was still need for more attention and repair.

"Alright then! I give up!" the man said good-naturedly. He stood up and turned around to greet his guests, wiping his hands on his jeans. "Well, hello! You must be Jonas!" When he turned to look at her, Sylvia felt her heart skip a beat and her eyes widened. She saw him start to say something but she gave a quick shake of her head. He hesitated then, understanding the hidden meaning, he quickly regained his smile and said, "And you must be his daughter. Jake Edwards, nice to meet both of you." He extended his hand to Jonas and smiled at Sylvia, his eyes twinkling with unasked questions.

"You trying to get that started, eh?" Jonas said, suppressing a smile as he shook Jake's hand. "Think that has seen better days."

Jake laughed and ran his hands through his sweaty

curls. "I think you're right."

"You looking to raise cows, then?" Jonas asked. "My Sylvia can help you with that. She knows a lot about the dairy farm." He put his strong hand on her shoulder, pride apparent in this gesture, if not in his words.

Jake eyes locked onto hers for just a moment. "Good to know." His voice was low and soft. It soothed her nerves. She wanted to look away but his gaze was too steady. She felt a flutter inside her chest, especially when he smiled softly at her. "I'm sure she's quite resourceful. But I'm not certain about getting into cows yet. Horses, definitely. Cows...well, we'll see."

"Whitey said you needed a woman's hand around this place, Mr. Edwards," Jonas said.

"Please, just call me Jake. We're neighbors after all," he said. He gestured toward the house. "Whitey said you'd be bringing your daughter so we could talk."

"Ja, Sylvia would be right *gut* helpful if she can help you," Jonas said.

Jake smiled, his eyes briefly meeting hers. "Well, that would be much appreciated. Come on inside the house and I'll show you the place."

The tour was brief. As Sylvia suspected, the house was small. There were two rooms on the first floor and three small bedrooms upstairs. The smallest bedroom didn't have much furniture but there were boxes stacked inside. The master bedroom was larger and was at the top of the staircase. Still, it was sparsely furnished. It wouldn't take long to clean the upstairs.

There was only one bathroom on the first floor. It looked as though it had been added years ago as an afterthought. On the first floor, the kitchen was smaller than Katie's and the appliances were old. But the room adjacent was a nice size. There was a sofa and two chairs plus a television that, clearly, didn't work. Sylvia noticed a piano against the far wall. That, too, needed repair.

"It's not much," Jake said. "But I have my hands full trying to get the barn ready. I don't have time to cook and clean." He sounded apologetic, perhaps a bit embarrassed.

"Know much about farming, Jake?" her father asked.

He cleared his throat. He knew it was the question that everyone was asking. All of the locals that he had met in the past few weeks seemed to want to ask the question. Their expression gave it way. But none of them had ventured forward to ask. They all knew too well that privacy was of the upmost importance in Lancaster County, Pennsylvania.

"I know about horses, Jonas. But not much about farming." There was a brief silence. Sylvia stole a glance at his face. His jovial expression was gone and a look of deep pain covered his face like a shadow. "I suppose you're wondering..." Jake started.

Jonas held up his hand. "No explanations to questions that aren't asked," he said good-naturedly. Her father was not one to pry. "But, if you need help, we are neighbors, ja?"

"That sounds fair," Jake said. The shadow vanished and he looked back at Sylvia. She felt small in his house, standing next to her father. It was surreal, almost as if it wasn't happening. He held her eyes in his stare and added, "If your daughter could help out two...maybe three times a week, clean up the place, maybe prepare some food, I'd be quite thankful for that. I'm not much of a cook and getting tired of eating out every night."

Sylvia frowned. She had thought it was just two mornings a week, not three. And now he wanted her to prepare meals? She wasn't certain how she felt about this arrangement anymore. She had expected an older man, not a young handsome one, and clearly not one that she knew. But to tell her father this would be to admit what had happened at the market and that she had rode home in this stranger's car. She had never kept a secret before and realized that the weight of it was heavy on her shoulders. And the secret became heavier when she heard her father commit that she would start working for Jake Edwards in the morning.

They rode home in silence, Jonas thinking about his afternoon chores and Sylvia wondering what she had just gotten herself into.

Chapter Five

Sylvia walked down the lane toward the house. When she had arisen that morning, she had felt butterflies in her stomach. Leaving her parents farm always caused her anxiety. This time, she was nervous about working so closely with an Englischer. After morning chores, she sat down with her family for breakfast. Unlike other mornings, when she had finished her eating, she didn't help her mother clean the dishes. Instead, she had left immediately, carrying a small-bagged lunch with her, as she made her way to Jake Edwards' house.

The walk was long but the morning was cool so she didn't mind. She waved to the few buggies that passed her along the way. No one stopped to ask if she wanted a ride. She was glad. She needed the time to think and to sort her mind. Each step brought her closer to Jake's farm. Each step took her further from her parents' farm. She could feel something in the air, an invisible hand guiding her down the road despite her desire to run the other way.

When she arrived at the house, it was quiet. She set her bag onto the table and gave a quick assessment of the room. There was electricity in the house, which surprised her. She hadn't seen wires leading to the house the day before, only to the barn. She had thought that it had been an Amish farm in the past. There were hints of Amish in the house, from the color of the paint on the walls to the simple layout. Nothing was complicated, just as if an Amish family had lived here. Apparently not.

The kitchen wasn't necessarily untidy but it was clearly dirty. It would never have passed her mother's inspection.

From the dusty baseboards to the dirty windows, it was a neglected room; yet, Sylvia knew that the heart of every house resided in the kitchen. The kitchen was the source of nourishment and fellowship, the place of good smells and happy laughter. It was a place to be cherished and maintained. Instead, at Jake's place, there were dishes in the sink and a pot of coffee on the stove. It was still warm but not hot.

Jake must have gone off to the barn already. She didn't know whether she should find him or get started. She contemplated the choices and, quickly, decided to immediately set to work on the kitchen. He was paying her to tend his house, not to keep tabs on his whereabouts.

Thirty minutes later, she had finished the dishes and stood drying them by the sink. It was quiet in the kitchen. She liked the quiet. At her mother's house, Junior's children were always running around, playing with kittens, and making noise in the yard. When Sylvia washed the dishes at home, she could look up from the sink and peer through the window, watching them as they played in the yard.

Unlike her mother's house, there was no window over the counter at Jake Edwards' house. On the other side of the wall was the next room. There were, however, cabinets over the counter. She was stacking the dishes when she heard his footsteps on the front porch. She waited but there was only silence. She turned around, not really surprised to see him leaning against the doorframe.

"Hey you," he said quietly.

He was smiling at her, his tall frame filling the doorway. He wore faded blue jeans with a plaid shirt, unbuttoned at the neck and not tucked in at the waist. Sylvia averted her eyes, uncertain how to respond to such a familiar greeting.

"Full of surprises, aren't you?" Again, she didn't respond. The silence was broken only by the gentle tick-tock of the old fashioned clock on the wall. Jake cleared his throat, uncomfortable in the awkward silence. "You're probably wondering..."

When he hesitated, she quickly looked up and frowned. "I'm not wondering anything, sir."

"Sir? We can't start off like that. It's Jake, please," he insisted. "Sir sounds so...old."

"I'm not wondering anything, Jake." She lowered her eyes again.

He walked toward her. "You mean you aren't wondering why I didn't tell you that I lived down the lane? You aren't wondering why I moved here? You aren't wondering about this farm?"

She looked up and met his gaze. Her heart fluttered again, hating how close he stood to her. She wasn't used to people invading her personal space. She wasn't used to engaging in conversation with men. But she forced herself to stay calm as she replied, "No, I'm not wondering anything."

Inside, she fought the urge to say otherwise, knowing full well that she was curious about everything. However, she didn't want to get involved. She didn't want to know anything about this man. He was leaning against the counter, his arms crossed over his broad chest. With his curly dark hair and bright blue eyes, she could almost imagine him as Amish, even though he was taller and more muscular than most men she knew. But, she warned herself, he's not Amish and I am. It was dangerous and she knew it. The way he smiled at her on the hill when he asked for directions. The way he had rescued her from the market and those horrid tourists. The way her heart fluttered when he looked at her just now.

She had seen movies during her *rumspringa*, the only time in an Amish youths life when they were allowed to experience Englische ways without ramifications from the church. It was a time when the community and family looked the other way, didn't asked questions, and prayed that their offspring would return to the community, eager to take their vows.

Most Amish youths tested their limits, going to restaurants or traveling to other states. Sometimes an Amish youth might approach the world of the Englische with more curiosity than was appropriate. They might drink or date. But, typically it was short lived. For the most part, the Amish youth emerged from their *rumspringa*, eager to take the kneeling vow and settle down within the church.

Sylvia's time had not been spent experimenting with particularly risky behavior. She had avoided the Englische and their modern ways but she had favored the theatre. The fancy world that she experienced in the dark movie theatre thrilled her. She couldn't imagine the world that was outside of her family, her farm, and her county. The beautiful scenery, the fancy houses, the beautiful clothing. Even how the characters spoke to each other.

Each movie had fascinated her. The lifestyle of the characters and plot of the movies intrigued her, especially when the stories centered on a romance or adventure. And always the main characters were so beautiful with chiseled features and blazing eyes. Yes, Jake Edwards looked the part. Unfortunately, while he may have been one of the characters in a movie, she knew that she most certainly was not.

While her mind had wandered, he seemed to be studying her. His own expression seemed reflective and she wondered what he had been thinking. Wherever he had traveled, he quickly came back and, with a shake of his head and a deep breath, he exhaled. It was a loud sigh that hinted of disappointment.

"Ok then, no questions." He scratched his cheek and looked around the room. "Just work. I get it and that's fine, Sylvia." He forced a smile. "You finding everything OK here? The place really needs some fixing up...a woman's touch."

A woman's touch. The words floating inside her head. To her parents, she was still a *maedel*...a girl. She would remain a girl until she married. She would change hands, being the responsibility of her parents until she became the responsibility of her husband. There was no middle ground. It dawned on her that no one had ever called her a woman. In fact, Sylvia had to think about the word, letting it roll around her head for a few minutes. Did she even think of herself as a woman?

"I've found everything I need," she replied, her voice soft and barely audible.

"Great!" He clapped his hands once, the noise startling her. He gave her a quick grin as he moved toward the door. "I look forward to having you around, Sylvia. It's too quiet here. Nice to have someone else on the property." He hesitated before adding, "I'll break through that shy shell of yours yet." To her shock, he gave her a friendly wink before disappearing out the door.

Jake's departure left an empty presence in the kitchen.

For a moment, she stood there, staring at the place where he had just stood. No one had ever talked to her like that. No one had ever been so bold. So exciting. Winking was too close to outright flirting and she realized that she had been holding her breath. In fact, she had tensed all of her muscles. Now that he was gone, she took a few deep breaths and tried to relax, to shake the feeling from her core. But it was hard.

He left an impression on her that no one else had ever done. From the day in the field to the afternoon at the Farmers Market, she had realized that she was not herself around this man. But, it hadn't mattered at that time. After all, she hadn't thought that she'd ever see him again.

Now, she was thrown into his life...or was he thrown into hers? She would see him every Monday, Wednesday, and Friday. How would she be able to protect her heart, to stop it from fluttering when he was near? She couldn't work for him and avoid him at the same time. It just wasn't possible. Nor could she fool herself into thinking that any of this was a good idea.

She spent the rest of the morning buried in her work. She was relieved that he didn't come into the house again. He would have distracted her from her duties. And, regardless of the inappropriateness of his behavior with her, she took her job seriously. If she was being paid to clean this house, then clean it she would. It was interesting to work in a quiet house with no interruptions and without her mother to direct her. Sylvia found herself enjoying herself, even when she washed the windows, the one task she dreaded at her mother's house.

The kitchen table was pressed against the wall, directly under the window. She had to move the table in order to clean the windowpanes. Standing by the windows, she used soapy water with vinegar to wipe the dirty sills. That was the only time she saw him during the morning. He was walking outside near the barn, carrying lumber and wearing a tool belt. But he didn't glance at the house, at least not that she saw. She left the window open to get a fresh breeze in the room. Occasionally, she could hear noises from outside. Once, she heard him hammering at something. She couldn't tell if he was in the barn or in the fields. The noise was a reminder that he was there and that she wasn't alone.

The house was old and hadn't been kept well. Sylvia didn't know anything about the previous owners. In fact, she hadn't even noticed this little farm during all of her years living nearby. Farms began to look alike after years of living on one, she thought. This one had obviously been neglected, unattended, and unloved for years.

Despite the "no questions" pact, she was, indeed, curious. She wondered why a man of such big city caliber would move to this unkempt house in such a small country town in the middle of Lancaster County, Pennsylvania. It wasn't uncommon for people to visit or even to rent a home or farm but those people never lasted. Life was too hard for those who had not been born into it. Besides, it was an area of generational residents, most of them Amish or Mennonite. Outsiders didn't belong and rarely lasted...at least not for a long time.

Before lunchtime, she tackled the small bathroom. It had a faded cream cast-iron bathtub with a matching toilet and sink. The cabinet under the sink was dark wood. It hadn't been cleaned in years. She did the best that she could to scrub the rings from the bathtub and toilet. But the sink was definitely stained. The floor was linoleum and in desperate need of being replaced. Still, when she finished, it definitely looked and smelled better. The cobwebs were gone and the floorboards were clean. She took satisfaction in that she had completed a job and done it well, even if it was hard work.

There was a clock hanging onto the wall next to the window. It chimed once and Sylvia looked up. It was half-past eleven. She wondered if Jake would be expecting a proper dinner at noon. She hadn't even started cooking anything. Uncertain what to do, she glanced through the cabinets and refrigerator. There wasn't a lot of food and he hadn't said anything about cooking.

To be truthful, Sylvia had to admit that she wasn't the finest cook. At her own home, it was mostly her mother who cooked all of the meals and that had been fine with Sylvia. When she had been younger, sister Sarah, Ana, and Susie often helped their mamm while Sylvia entertained the two little brothers. Once her sisters married and left the farm, there were plenty of times that Sylvia might help her mamm but, clearly cooking wasn't Sylvia's favorite chore. She certainly wouldn't know where to begin with the limited supplies in his kitchen. Yet, she knew that women prepared the food and Jake needed something to eat. She didn't want to disappoint him and lose her job on the first day, especially if it meant going back to the market and possibly never seeing him again.

Her heart fluttered in her chest at the realization that she wanted to impress him. She knew that the line she walked was dangerous and childish. Foolish, in fact, for he was a grown man and she knew nothing about him except for one very important fact: he wasn't Amish. And, she chided herself, that was the only fact that she had to remember.

It was twelve-thirty when he walked back into the

kitchen. He greeted her with a smile, one that lit up his face. When he smiled, his eyes sparkled and there was an energy that filled the room. "Looks like you've been busy, Sylvia." He strode to the sink, quickly washing his hands. There was dirt on his clothing and his boots were muddy. "I can't tell you how much I appreciate your help. I'd never be able to take care of all this without someone to tend to the house."

She didn't respond. To do so would sound prideful. Instead, she kept herself busy, bringing his lunch to the table. She set the plate of reheated ham and a baked potato in front of the chair, pausing to straighten the fork and knife that she had set by his plate. When she turned around, he was behind her and she couldn't help but press against him.

"Oh." She caught her breath and, quickly, took a step backward, lowering her eyes, embarrassed and flustered. "I'm sorry," she whispered and moved over to the refrigerator. She thought she heard him laugh softly, more of a chuckle under his breath, but he said nothing as he sat down. She set down a bowl of applesauce next to his plate then retreated to the sink.

There was a moment of silence and then she heard him ask, "You are not joining me?" His voice was sincere and honest and when she looked at him, she saw that he was frowning, wondering why she was not having the midday meal with him.

"I..." She didn't know what to say. It had never dawned on her to sit at the table with him. She had never sat with a man before, unless it was one of her brothers or her father. "I have my own lunch." She paused. "It wouldn't be proper," she finally added.

There was an awkward silence. He didn't say anything in response. So, Sylvia quickly busied herself with washing the frying pan while she listened to the gentle scraping of the metal fork and knife against his plate. It filled the room with a deafening noise that made the silence even more apparent. She hated the silence, wishing she was more interesting and had something to say. But that wasn't her way, even if she wished she could be more outspoken.

"I'll take you home after dinner," he said, breaking the stillness of the moment.

She shook her head, even though his back was facing her. "Thank you but I can walk."

He turned around and looked at her, a twinkle in his blue eyes. "I know you can walk. I see God gave you two legs," he teased. "But I'm headed out anyway. I'll drop you off. It's not out of my way and will get you home quicker to help your folks with the afternoon chores."

She knew better than to argue. He was her employer, after all. No one liked an argumentative person. Besides, she had already accepted a ride from him before when she didn't even know much more about him than his name. Now, she was working for him.

"Perhaps Monday I can do the laundry," she said. "If you have laundry facilities..."

He nodded. "Believe it or not, I do! They are out in the barn. Guess there wasn't much room in the house to add on a laundry room and they probably couldn't run plumbing down the basement." He paused. "Maybe I'll build on a room behind the bathroom one of these days. But I have enough on my plate for now. I suppose that can wait."

Another silence. Several birds flew by the window, landing on a tree limb just outside. It was spring, after all. It was time for the birds to enjoy the warmer weather and contribute to future generations. Sylvia watched them for a moment. Robins. They were her favorites. The harbinger of spring...the season of outdoor work and new life. From new calves to baby kittens, spring seemed to renew the world around her. It was also the season when courtships began. Many of the Amish youths would start pairing up, get to know one another, and, if all went well, publish their intent to marry in the fall if they were both baptized members of the church.

She could sense him standing up and, before she knew it, he was next to her. She could feel him staring at her and she turned away from the window, busying herself with drying the last of the pans that she had used to cook his dinner meal. Had he been watching her? He didn't move and she looked at him. Their eyes met again and, as before, she felt herself swept into a whole new world of emotion. Did he know what she was thinking? She felt the color rise to her cheeks and she looked away. It was so pleasantly uncomfortable, yet she knew that she was behaving foolishly. He was a man, an Englischer man. He was a widower. And she was just a plain Amish girl.

He set the plate on the counter and cleared his throat. "That was fine, Sylvia. Thank you kindly," he mustered as he started to walk toward the door. "I'll wait for you outside. I'm sure you have plenty to do at your parents' farm."

For a moment, she merely stood there, trying to gather her thoughts. She was ashamed of herself and her thoughts. She knew better than to get any silly ideas. After all, Englischer men only meant trouble for Amish women. She had heard of Amish girls who snuck off with Englischers, usually during their *rumspringa* and before they took their baptism. She had heard stories of girls with unwanted babies, banned from the community...sent away from their families. She knew the turmoil that had happened in her own family when her brother Emanuel had married an Englischer. Yes, she admitted, that turned around when his wife took the baptism. But it rarely worked out that way.

Besides, she scolded herself, he was a widower. What interest could he possibly have in someone like her? She had been foolish, indeed. Yet, there was something so warm about his presence, so strong about his gaze. Had she truly only imagined it?

Her heart continued to beat fiercely inside her chest. She knew that she should go home and never return but that was something that she wasn't able to do, at least not without a lot of questions from her parents and even community. She wasn't willing to tell them about how she had accepted a ride home from a complete stranger. Plus, she admitted, she didn't want to go home and never return. For sure and for certain, she wasn't able to put her finger on what it was but she knew that there was something that intrigued her about this farm and that man.

With a deep breath, she quickly cleaned up the rest of the kitchen before collecting her few belongings and going outside to where Jake stood by the truck. He was leaning against the hood, his arms crossed over his chest and his eyes shut. The sun warmed his face as he waited.

For a brief moment, she paused and stared at him. With the sun shining down on his face, his skin almost appeared bronze. His shirtsleeves were rolled up and his arms were tanned and muscular. He seemed to sense her presence and looked up. Seeing her standing on the porch, he smiled and opened the truck door for her, waiting patiently for her to situate herself before he shut it and walked around to the driver side. They rode in silence, neither speaking as they mulled through their own thoughts.

The ride was only a short mile and a half but he drove slowly. When they approached the farm, Sylvia glanced over at Jake. "Perhaps you could drop me off here?" she asked.

He frowned, his one hand resting on the steering wheel and the other resting on the open window. "Whatever for, Sylvia?"

She stumbled over her words. How could she explain it to him? Why would he even question her? "I...it would just be easier, I suppose."

The muscle in his jaw tightened but he did not respond. Instead, he continued driving the truck until her father's farm came into view. No one was outside which helped Sylvia to breathe easier. He slowed down and put on his blinker, coming to a complete stop in front of the driveway.

"A compromise," he stated.

She started to get out of the truck but he reached out to touch her arm. She jumped, startled by the feeling of his hand on her skin. It was warm and soft, a feeling that she had never felt before. No man had ever touched her. She lifted her eyes and saw his own searching her face.

"Sylvia, you don't have anything to fear from me. I came here to find myself." She started to protest but he held up his hand to stop her. "I know you said you aren't wondering, that you don't have any questions. But, it's important that you know that all I'm looking for is...myself." He hesitated. "You might not be able to understand."

She was bewildered. She didn't understand his words or

why he spoke them. "I have to go," she murmured and quickly jumped out of the car.

Her heart pounded inside of her chest as she hurried down the driveway. She stopped once to glance over her shoulder. He was watching her and, when he saw that she turned, he waved before slowly driving down the road. Sylvia hurried past the barn and into the house. She felt as though her world was turning upside down, that her day had been completely surreal. These things didn't happen to people, she told herself. No, she quickly corrected herself. These things don't happen to me.

Her mother greeted her with a warm smile, unaware of the turmoil in her daughter's head. "How was the widower, Sylvia?"

She set her things down on the bench by the door and hurried to the kitchen to wash her hands. She could smell the remnant of her mother's cooking. She must have made fried chicken and mashed potatoes. The house smelled familiar and comforting. Yet, at the same time, as she dried her hands, she realized that everything was different. In just one day, it had all changed.

"Fine, Mamm," she heard herself reply. She looked up and smiled softly at her mother. "Everything was fine."

Chapter Six

The following Monday, Sylvia walked slowly to Jake's farm. His farm was only a mile from her father's if she cut through the fields. She didn't mind the walk. April was one of her favorite times of year. The day was early, the sun barely cresting over the hill. Birds chirped from the trees, greeting the morning with a song of spring and a gentle breeze cooled her face. As she crossed through the field behind her father's farm, she heard the neighbor's rooster crowing. A dog barked in response. The day was awakening. It was her favorite time of the day. She felt alone with her thoughts, listening to the sounds and smelling the damp earth. Her shoes were wet from the morning dew that clung to the grass. She tightened her shawl around her shoulders, knowing that the coolness would disappear once the sun shone over the horizon.

He was sitting at the kitchen table when she knocked softly at the door before entering. There was a newspaper before him and he was drinking coffee. When he looked up, he greeted her with a broad but sleepy smile. His hair was tousled and his shirt unbuttoned at the neck. Sylvia averted her eyes but felt the familiar rush through her veins when he spoke,

"Good morning, Sylvia!" He gestured toward the stove. "Help yourself to some coffee. I'm afraid I'm not very good at making it but..."

"That's alright," she said. "I can make a fresh pot for you, if you'd like."

"That would be most kind, Sylvia." He leaned back in his chair, staring at her thoughtfully. "I haven't had a good cup in ages, it seems. I never mastered that skill, I'm afraid." He continued watching her. She could feel his eyes on her back. But when she glanced at him, his eyes were glazed over. He was miles away, somewhere else. He shook his head, caught her look, and smiled. "Suppose I better get to planning my day, eh? Looks like it's going to rain later this week. Need to get my outside work done."

She felt emboldened by his attention. Unlike at her parents' farm, she was not in the shadows here. In fact, Jake seemed to want to engage her in discussion. "What are you working on, if I may ask?"

"You may," he said, his tone light and teasing. "I have an idea in my mind to do more than just breed horses. I wanted to try my hand at some crops...I was thinking wheat."

"Corn," she said.

"No, wheat."

She laughed. "I meant you should plant corn. Your soil is good for it and it is easier to tend. Less equipment to harvest, too."

He raised an eyebrow. "Huh."

"For your first crop, anyway," she added. "And the time to plant is coming up. Knee high by the fourth of July. Besides, wheat should be planted in September or October. The season is underway. You'd be too late and the wheat would miss the market. But when you harvest the corn, you can plant the wheat for next season." The expression on his face stopped her in mid-sentence. Was he angry that she had contradicted him? She chewed on her lower lip. "I'm sorry. Did I say too much?"

"No," he said, leaning forward. The chair legs hit the floor and, as he pushed the chair back in order to stand up, it squeaked against the wood flooring. Carrying his coffee mug, he walked toward her. "Not at all, Sylvia. In fact, there's a sparkle in your eye and animation in your voice. I rather like it." He leaned against the counter next to her, watching her through his deep, thoughtful eyes. "You like working outside, don't you?"

She wanted to answer but she couldn't. He was standing close to her, his presence filling the space between them. She caught her breath, fighting the urge to stare at him. His nearness overwhelmed her with his faded jeans and halfway opened shirt. She could see the golden brown color of his skin and the hint of muscles. It made her too aware of how plain she must look to him. Her dark brown hair was pulled back in a tight bun at her neck. Her dress was a simple green with a black apron covering her waist. For the first time in her life, she felt awkward with her appearance.

"Sylvia?"

"I'm sorry. Did you ask me something?"

He laughed at her. "I said you like working outside, yes? That's the most animated that I've seen you yet."

"Oh," she flustered. She didn't know how to respond. A flush covered her cheeks. Had she been animated? Overly enthusiastic? Lowering her eyes, she backed away. "I need to get started upstairs today," she finally said. "The coffee should be ready in a few minutes."

Without waiting for his response, she hurried to the staircase and quickly retreated upstairs. She stood at the top of the stairs, catching her breath and waiting...for what, she didn't know. When she heard the door shut, she exhaled loudly and leaned against the wall, her heart pounding inside her chest.

For a moment, she felt the sting of tears in her eyes. The

confusion that she felt was a new feeling to her and she didn't like it one bit. There was something about him, something strong and powerful that made her realize that life was much greater than the four walls of her parents' house. She was standing in a man's house, outside of his bedroom door, thinking thoughts that had never occurred to her. Yes, life was calling to her and she was torn between feeling frightened and feeling exhilarated.

Gathering herself, she took a deep breath and moved toward the master bedroom. She had only glanced inside when Jake had shown the upstairs to her and her father last week. Now, she took the time to look around and see the room with curious eyes.

It was a simple room with a dresser, bed, and nightstand. The furniture matched and was clearly not homemade. The bed was a dark oak sleigh bed. It was fancier than beds that the Amish used. Most Amish made their own furniture and Sylvia's house was no different. Their beds were simple and light in color. She had never seen a store-bought bed before and this one looked rather elegant to her. She ran her hand along the headboard. It was smooth and cool to her fingers. She could tell that it was new by the way the wood shone. A new bed for an old house, she thought.

She looked at the dresser and saw a picture frame. While she had seen pictures in the calendars that her father hung in the kitchen and out in the barn, she had never seen a real photograph of a person. Curiosity got the best of her and she went over to it, picking it up gently to see who was in the photo. It was a couple. Jake and a young blond woman. She had long hair, pulled back from her face in a simple ponytail. They were standing on a beach but Sylvia could tell that it wasn't warm by the way they were dressed. The picture was sun bleached. It was hard to make out the woman's features but, clearly, she was pretty. Sylvia sighed. It was apparent that they had been happy.

She set the picture back on the dresser, next to a bottle of cologne. She reached for it, hesitating for just a moment before she sniffed at it. It was musky and strong. She couldn't imagine wearing something so pungent and strong. Yet, it wasn't unpleasant. She shut her eyes and tried to imagine her brothers wearing cologne. The idea was completely foreign to her and she smiled to herself.

On the light blue walls were the typical hooks used in the Amish houses. Amish didn't use closets and hung most of their clothing on hangers from simple pegs or hooks in the wall. Sylvia frowned, not quite able to understand. The house had electricity and appliances but the bedrooms lacked closets, using Amish hooks instead? Yet, Amish had never lived here.

For the next hour, she tidied the upstairs. She found a spare set of sheets, changed his bed, and carried the dirty sheets downstairs so that she could wash them. She had found a hamper in one of the other bedrooms and brought that downstairs, too. She was glad to be downstairs. She was uncomfortable being so near the place where Jake slept. It felt awkward and inappropriate to touch his clothing and his sheets. Besides, the upstairs had a sad feeling to it, more so than the kitchen. The rooms were bare and empty, except for the master bedroom. But even that was sparsely furnished and plain. Too plain for an Englischer. The house had been unloved for so long that Sylvia wondered if it missed the former families that had lived there. She wondered if it knew that someone was trying to make it feel loved once again.

It was almost ten o'clock when she finally ventured outside, carrying the basket of dirty clothing toward the barn. She didn't know where the laundry facility was but she remembered Jake said it was in the barn. The sun was shining and it was warm. Springtime. She noticed an overgrown plot of land near the side of the house. The ghost of a garden. Sylvia could imagine tomato plants, cucumbers and lettuce thriving in the sunny patch of land. At one point in time, it had been well tended and the food that was harvested must have fed the family. But now it only grew weeds.

Inside the barn, she was overcome with the emptiness. The floors were clean, the stalls were empty. Even the air was still. A few sparrows darted in and out of the barn's rafters but, other than that, it was deserted. At her father's farm, the barn was either full of cows, waiting to be milked, or empty with rows of manure to be cleaned. There was always noise, whether from within the barn or from the paddocks. Sylvia could tell that this had once been a dairy farm, small in comparison to her father's. There were only two rows for the cows whereas her father's barn had six. But, unlike her father's barn, this one had stalls for horses. She counted at least five along the back wall. Her father had a separate building for the horses.

"I thought I saw you walking toward the barn." His voice startled her and she spun around, almost dropping the basket of laundry. "Sorry," he said, but his eyes glittered and she could tell that he wasn't.

"I..." She tried to catch her breath. "I was looking for the washing equipment."

He took the basket from her and motioned her toward the back of the barn. "I was fixing the fencing in the fields. Saw you walking from the house. Come along, I'll take you to the laundry area."

"Fencing?" she asked as she followed him.

"Horses arrive in a few weeks. Coming in from Connecticut." He glanced at her as he stopped in front of a door. "Standardbreds." She didn't comment but acknowledged what he said with a simple nod of her head. "Thought I'd try breeding them here...break them and sell them. But I need to build more stalls for all of them and must have good fencing so they don't wander over to your father's and eat all of his crops," he teased.

Without realizing it, she frowned and chewed on her lower lip. "How many acres do you have?"

"Fifty acres."

She was surprised. It didn't look quite so large. She had guessed thirty acres. How could she not have noticed this farm before? True, it was nestled between two other farms with the driveway being the only public announcement that it existed. But fifty acres was a nice sized farm for a county that had high demand for farmland with shrinking availability. Land was so hard to come by that many Amish families were relocating outside of Lancaster County in order to acquire farmland in order to continue growing crops and raising dairy cows. She knew that her father's cousin had moved to Ohio many years ago for that very reason.

So fifty acres was a generous sized farm. Sylvia realized that some of the pastures that she thought were Jake's neighbors must be part of his farm. It was a shame for such a nice parcel of land to be used for breeding and not farming, she thought to herself. Then, immediately ashamed of herself for such a selfish thought, she lowered her eyes.

"That's a good size farm for horses," she said quietly.

When he swung the door open, she looked into the tiny room. The walls were painted white and in the center was an older washing machine. To her relief, it was a wringer washer powered by a small diesel machine. It was similar to the one that her mother used, although a bit older, and in good shape. "You know how to use that?" he asked.

She couldn't help but laugh. "Of course!"

A sheepish expression crossed his face. "It's a little different than what I'm used to," he explained.

She didn't reply. There was nothing more to say. It was just one more reminder that they were two very different people with different pasts and beliefs. Despite herself, she couldn't help but wonder why he was here after all.

The silence was awkward. Neither knew what to say. Thankfully, Jake ended it by clearing his throat as he took a step backward toward the door. "Well, I'll let you take care of this. You let me know if you need anything, yes?" He didn't wait for a response and quickly disappeared out of the room. The air seemed to leave the room with him and Sylvia found herself staring after him. His presence brought so much energy that, when he left, the room felt empty and heavy.

It was close to noon when she had hung up the last of his freshly washed clothing on the line that stretched from the corner of the house to the corner of the barn. There was something satisfying about seeing the clothing wave gently in the spring breeze. The farm looked lived in. Now, she thought, to make it look loved. She glanced around the outside of the house and wondered if Jake would let her plant some flowers or tackle the garden. At home, she always worked in her mother's garden but it was always under her mother's firm guidance.

Sylvia longed for the day when she could plant her own garden. But that day was a long way off and she knew better than to approach Jake. He hired her to help in the house, not the garden or fields. But in her mind, she could envision the garden with climbing bean plants and bushy tomato trees.

She turned around, scanning the horizon. The fields were lush and green, tall grass waving. He had said that the horses would arrive in a few weeks. The fields would be grazed down in no time. By fall, many of the fields would have dirt patches where grass currently grew. The farm would transform into a living entity once the animals were there. New sounds, new smells, new life. She shut her eyes and listened. It was quiet now. But the quiet was peaceful and happy. With the sun shining down on her face, she felt relaxed and carefree. This is my time, she thought to herself.

Chapter Seven

For the next few weeks, Sylvia's days began to fall into a welcomed routine. The flow of the days became very rhythmic. During the week, she'd walk to Jake Edwards farm every other morning. She would alternate which floor she cleaned before cooking him a nice midday meal. He was often busy in the barn, fixing and cleaning in preparation for his horses.

When he came in for his dinner, she tried to find a way to excuse herself, purposefully saving a last minute task that kept her out of the kitchen. He quickly caught on and tried to ask her to do something in the kitchen while he ate. It was an unspoken battle of wits that she didn't always win.

Fortunately, she had been blessed with good weather, using that as an excuse to walk home. Every day that she worked at his farm, he insisted on driving her back to her father's farm but Sylvia was always quick to point out that she enjoyed the warm spring air. That argument she tended to win.

During the days that she did not work at Jake Edwards' home, she'd was happy to help her mother in the house during the mornings and work outside during the afternoons. She didn't even mind helping her father spread fertilizer in the fields or mow the front yard. By Sunday, she was ready for the day of worship, rest, or visiting.

For the first time in a long time, Sylvia was happy. She liked being near home and liked not having to interact with the Englischers at the Farmers Market. She didn't even mind caring for Jake Edwards' house, despite being alone for most of the time. For the most part, it was quiet at his farm and gave her time to think and reflect.

"You seem relaxed today," he said to her when he came inside for his meal.

It was Monday. Sylvia had been working at his farm for three weeks now. It was clear that he seemed to enjoy her company, trying to engage her in conversation by asking her questions or telling her stories. At times, Sylvia wasn't always certain how to respond to his friendly overtures. After all, she wasn't used to such attention from men.

"Ja, I am," she finally replied since he seemed to be waiting for a response.

"Suppose I am too," he commented. He stood at the sink, washing his hands. When he was finished, he leaned against the counter and dried his hands on a towel that Sylvia handed to him. "I'm learning to like it here."

If she was a forward girl, she would have asked him why he had moved to Lancaster County. She would want to know why he would leave everything to move to a strange place where he didn't know anyone or have any roots. To say that she wasn't curious would be a lie. In fact, every morning when she made his bed, she would pause and stare at that photograph on his dresser. She had made up stories in her head about the woman. What had happened to her? How had it affected him? Where was his sorrow? Or had he already healed? But her curiosity remained hidden and she knew much better than to ask such forward questions.

"That's right *gut*," she managed to say, reaching for the now damp towel. When he handed it to her, she noticed that he didn't release it right away. She lifted her eyes to look up at him. "Being that it's your home now, you should be relaxed and enjoying it, ja?"

He laughed. "I suppose you are right, Sylvia. Home should be where your heart is." He sat down at the table and waited until she placed his plate on the table before him. "I will say that I'm learning to like your cooking, too!" He smiled at her. "You don't know what it's like to miss home-cooked food."

A compliment. No one had ever complimented her over such simple things. Compliments were empty plates and full bellies, not words. "*Danke*," she whispered and hurried over to the sink to clean up the dishes so that she could leave after he finished.

"You know," he continued between mouthfuls of mashed potatoes and ham. "I wanted to ask your opinion about a garden. I suspect I should be growing some of my own food...vegetables. But I don't have any idea how to go about that." He looked at her. "I was thinking that you could help me with that. It would be best to plant it now before the horses come, yes?"

Her heart skipped a beat. In the past, she always loved tending her mother's garden. There was nothing like working outside, feeling the dirt on her fingers and the sun on her back. She loved to watch the vegetables and herbs grow, the young shoots of a tomato plant or head of lettuce poking through the ground. Even better, she loved when her mother cooked with food that came from their very own garden. Was Jake asking her to grow a garden for him? To plan it, plant it, and tend it for him?

"I suppose that would be a *wunderbaar gut* idea," she began slowly. It was an exciting idea but she didn't want to seem too eager. After all, he had hired her to tend to his house, not spend time gardening. "But it might be hard to get started with all of the housework. That garden plot needs a lot of preparation since it is overgrown for sure and certain."

"We could work on it together until the horses arrive," he suggested.

The thought of spending time with Jake Edwards unnerved her. She had worked so hard at keeping her distance from him. It was safer that way, she had convinced herself. Working for Jake Edwards kept her away from the market, something she greatly appreciated. But working for Jake Edwards caused too many thoughts to float through her mind. His smile and laughter caused her heart to flutter. When he was in the kitchen, she felt the power of his presence. While she found herself looking forward to interacting with him, she dreaded it at the same time. She wasn't used to the dangerous feelings she had when he was near.

"I...I suppose that would work," she said when she realized that he was looking at her.

After dinner, he insisted on her walking out to the garden with him. It was very weedy and overgrown with grass. She took a deep breath, kneeling down to dig into the soil with her bare hand. It was dry and crumbly on the top but, deeper under the topsoil, it was rich. He watched her while she paced the perimeter. She could see the finished garden in her mind. But the reality was that the garden had basically turned into a patch of spotty grass and weeds.

"We're going to need to plow it," she said when she stood back at his side. She rubbed her hands together to free them from the dirt. "And you should think about spreading some manure. Makes *wunderbaar gut* fertilizer."

"Do you think I could buy some from your father?" he asked.

Sylvia almost laughed. "Buy manure?"

"What's so funny about that?" he retorted, a smile on his face.

"With all of his cows, there's plenty of manure to give away, ja?"

It was a nice moment, the two of them standing in the future garden, laughing together. She had a pretty laugh, light and soft. It was genuine because she didn't share it with him too often. So, when she did share it, that delightful noise, he appreciated the special gift of her sharing such happiness and joy.

On Wednesday, when she arrived, she noticed Jake was already at work on the small plot of ground, shoveling at the overgrowth. It was warm, despite it being early. He wasn't wearing his shirt; she could see the shirt was tossed on the ground next to him. Stopping on the driveway, Sylvia found herself staring at Jake, her eyes unable to look away as he worked. His bare skin, already golden brown, glistened with sweat and there were streaks of dirt on his shoulders. He was muscular and toned in a way that was unfamiliar to her. After all, she had never before seen the naked chest of a strange man. Watching Jake brought the color to her cheeks and she felt ashamed of her own thoughts.

"Hey there," he called out and leaned against the shovel. "Almost finished here."

Quickly, Sylvia averted her eyes. "Ja, I see that."

Jake frowned. "Sylvia, are you OK?" She glanced at him but, once again, looked away. It only took him a second to register the source of her discomfort and shyness. He chuckled to himself. "Ah," he said. "My apologies."

Out of the corner of her eye, she saw him reach for the almost forgotten shirt that he had tossed over the side of the fence. To her relief, he turned his back to her while he pulled it over his head. "It's hard work," he explained sheepishly.

She didn't respond, her cheeks still pink from her embarrassment.

He cleared his throat, trying to figure out how to defeat her modesty. "Come here, Sylvia, and let's plan out the rows, yes? Then I can buy the plants for Friday." She didn't move right away so, setting the shovel on the ground, he walked toward her. "Sylvia?" He stood before her and reached out, tilting her chin up so that she was forced to look him in the eyes. "I'm sorry. I didn't realize the time." She glanced away. "It won't happen again, I promise," he said softly.

With the hint of a nod, she stepped back and collected herself. She realized that she wasn't necessarily offended but, to her shame, she realized that she was intrigued. Her interest in Jake Edwards alarmed her more than anything else. She felt guilty of her own thoughts. Where did they come from? In all of her life, she had never felt interest in anyone outside of her family. She had no inclination to the ways of the world. Even when her brother Emanuel had begun courting the Englischer, Shana, Sylvia's interest was more in the beauty of their romance, not in any exposure to the outside world.

She felt foolish, knowing that such a worldly man, a widower at that, would never think twice about a young Amish girl. After all, she was but nineteen and, from what she could gather, he was at least thirty. But when he was near her, even when he worked outside while she was tending to the housework, she felt a warm feeling grow inside her chest that frightened her. She had done what she could to avoid being alone with him, too intimidated by his unspoken power over her thoughts and the intensity of his presence. Yet, his attention made her feel special in a way that no one had ever done. It was as if a wall inside of her was crumbling down and, unbeknownst to her, on the other side was a magnificent and fertile valley that she hadn't even known existed.

"So, about those plants?" he asked, breaking her train of thought.

"Being that it's almost May, we're getting a late start," she finally managed to say, breaking the silence that had befallen them. "I'd start with green beans, tomatoes, cucumbers, and peppers. They can be used for chow-chow and canned for the winter."

"Wonderful!" he said cheerfully. "Then that's what we will plant!"

True to his word, on Friday, when she arrived, there were dozens of plants waiting by the garden plot that they had cleared earlier in the week. She stopped and stared at it, wondering at the quantity as well as where he had purchased them. She was used to planting seeds, nursing the seedlings throughout the season. With the plants already started, he would have a bountiful garden indeed. Tending to it would take most of her time, a realization that sent a wave of panic through her. What if she couldn't do both? Would he send her away?

They spent the day planting neat clusters of the vegetables. They didn't speak while they worked, but the silence was comforting. A few times, Sylvia kneeled back on her heels, wiping the sweat away from her brow only to find him nearby and watching her. He'd smile, say nothing, and continue working. It was as if he was waiting for her to notice him watching her. Inside of her chest, her heart would flutter and she could feel the color rise to her cheeks.

Once again, she found herself wondering about his interest in her. She was concerned that she was imagining it as it befuddled her to think that such a worldly man could find her to be anything more than hired help. But, as the day wore on, she began to consider that there was that possibility as an explanation for his attention and kindness. The only thing she could not understand was why.

She glanced at the sky, noticing that the sun was overhead. "Oh," she exclaimed. "I forgot about your meal." She started to stand, wiping her hands together to shake the dry dirt from her skin.

"Sylvia," he said softly. "I have the meal covered."

"Covered?" She turned around to look at him. "I don't understand."

He stood up, wiping his hands on his jeans. There was a mischievous and boyish twinkle in his eyes, one that made her want to smile but, instead, she felt a wave of panic. "Wait here," he commanded with a hint of a smile. He disappeared into the house but was not gone for long.

The warmness crept back into her chest, radiating throughout her body. What was he up to, she wondered, partially afraid and partially excited to discover this secret that had bought such a twinkle to his eyes.

When he emerged from the house, he was carrying a picnic basket and an old blue blanket. He motioned toward the shade of a tree near the barn. The pounding of her heart increased and she wondered if he could hear it as she approached him. She stood back, watching as he spread the blanket on the grass and set down the basket.

"Today," he announced. "I will wait on you." He paused, waiting for her to meet his gaze. "To thank you for all of your help."

She stood there, feeling quite awkward and uncertain about what to do. It dawned on her that, indeed, he might be flirting with her. If she had convinced herself that she had only imagined the emotion behind his words and actions before, she knew now that she had only been fooling herself. "Jake, I..."

He waved his hand at her. "Sit, Sylvia. I won't take no for an answer. You work hard for everyone else, don't you? But when do you ever get treated and pampered? When does anyone ever thank you for what you do?"

For a moment, she felt tears at the corners of her eyes. She fought the urge to cry while trying to understand why she had the urge at all. Was it fear of where this might go or was it simply because he spoke the truth? Dare she take this first step beyond an employee relationship?

She looked into the sky at the sun, blinking back those dreaded tears. What would he think if she cried, she wondered. And why on earth did she care? But she knew that she did care. It dawned on her that she had made the first step over a month ago when she had accepted the ride home from him, letting him rescue her from the dreaded marketplace and those intrusive tourists. If he had rescued her from that, from what else did he intend to rescue her?

True to his word, he waited on her, pulling wrapped sandwiches from the basket and store-bought bags of chips. He made no apologies for the informality of the meal but served her with great aplomb, bowing down before her with a smile on his face. She couldn't hide her own smile, joining him in his jovial mood. He was so alive and so different from anyone she had ever met before. His attention to her needs challenged her senses.

The few Amish boys that she had interacted with at singings or other social gatherings were just that...boys. They were awkward and quiet. They didn't know how to take command of a situation. They weren't confident when they spoke to her. Sylvia found herself enjoying herself, despite the growing pit of apprehension in her stomach.

He talked during the lunch break. He told her about his plans for the farm, his hopes for the horses he would breed and sell. He mentioned that he was curious about the dairy business but not certain if he wanted to embark down that path. It was outside his realm of knowledge, his zone of comfort, he explained. When they had finished eating, he laid back on the blanket, his hand tucked behind his head as he stared into the sky. After a few minutes, he shut his eyes and his breathing slowed down.

She took advantage of the quiet to watch him. He was handsome, she couldn't argue that. There was a rugged look to him, mostly because his skin was bronzed and his features chiseled. He was refined looking with dark hair that fell in large curly swoops over his forehead. Most of the Amish men she knew were short and stocky or tall and lean. There weren't many that were tall and muscular.

She looked away and gazed around the farm. He had worked hard on it over the past month. The fields were no longer overgrown, the fencing was fixed, and it was looking lived in. They had accomplished a lot even just that day. The garden was planted and ready for an evening watering. She wondered if he knew not to water them under the midday sun. But he was sleeping. The warmth of the spring air mixed with the gentle breeze had lulled him into a peaceful nap.

It was time for her to leave, to return to her father's farm but she didn't want to disturb him. As quiet as she could, she stood up and gathered the remnants from his picnic surprise. She didn't want to leave him with things to clean up, especially after he had gone to so much trouble to do something so special for her.

It was almost one o'clock by the time that she finished tidying up the kitchen. The dishes were put away, the basket was set on the floor of the pantry, and she even had set the table for his supper meal. By the backside of the house, a small patch of daffodils had started to sprout. She clipped a few and put them on the table, arranging them in the center so that he'd be certain to notice.   Glancing out the window, she was surprised to see that Jake was gone from the blanket under the tree.

"You left," his voice said from behind her.

Startled, she jumped and spun around. "Jake!" A soft laugh escaped her lips. "You scared me."

His hair was tousled and he looked more tired than he had before his brief interlude with sleep. There was something endearing about his just awoken look. He looked boyish and even more charming. "You were gone when I woke. How long did I nap?" He looked around the kitchen. "Ah, I see. Long enough for you to tidy the place, eh?" He smiled and leaned against the counter. "Lucky for me, I suppose."

"I must get going," she replied. "I'm later than usual."

"Let me drive you home."

She shook her head. "*Danke,* Jake, but I can walk."

"Sylvia, I know you can walk. But I'd like to drive you. It's faster…"

Against her best judgment, she relented, if only to avoid unwanted questions from her mother or father about why she was returning later than usual. "But you will drop me at the lane, ja?"

He rolled his eyes and sighed. "I can drop you at the lane, yes," he said, the defeat apparent in his voice. "That seems a bit silly but…"

"It's just not proper," she said softly and turned around so that he couldn't see her face. "It makes it easier, Jake," she added but she wasn't certain if he heard her.

True to his word, he stopped before her driveway. "I want to thank you," he said before she got out of the truck. "We did a lot today…perhaps more than you bargained for when you signed up for this gig." His eyes tried to catch hers but she was adept at looking away from him. "You are helping me in many more ways than you can imagine, Sylvia. And it's not just the help around the house that I'm talking about."

She reached for the door handle and started to open it. But she felt his hand on her arm. Looking over her shoulder, she couldn't help but get caught in his gaze. "Jake, please…" she pleaded, despite wishing she could shout just the opposite.

"I know, I know," he said and released her arm. "No questions, no curiosity. Maybe one day you will have those questions and I'll be ready to answer them, Sylvia." He paused before he added, "Friends are allowed to ask questions of each other, you know."

Friends. The word lingered between them and the confusion struck her once again. Had she misjudged his attention? Had she almost made a fool of herself with this man? How could she have let her imagination run so wild as to think that there was a possibility that he could have been interested in her?

"I have to go," she replied, her voice trembling from embarrassment at her presumptions. How could she have made such a mistake?

Friends, he had said. It was an unusual concept in her world. Men and women were not friends. Not like that. A man and his wife shared many things, friendship being one of them. But that was the only friendship that existed among the sexes, that between man and wife. Other men might be family or neighbors but they were never friends. Even courting couples were not true friends. That was something that would take years to develop...years that involved hard work, children, good times and bad.

Sylvia hung her head down as she hurried down the driveway and into her parents' house, more confused than ever. It was a feeling she wasn't used to and one that she didn't like very much at all.

Chapter Eight

The weekend went by too quickly. She knew the routine of a typical Saturday at her parents' farm. She'd help in the yard as much as she could before working inside with her mother. Cooking and cleaning never seemed to end and, when it did, it was time to catch up on mending and sewing. Sometimes her mother would talk, sharing stories of her own childhood. Other times, they worked in silence, deep in their own thoughts.

This Saturday was one of those quiet days. Sylvia glanced up at her mother, watching her with her head bent over a tear in her father's pants. She wondered what her mother thought about, what she reflected on when she was so absorbed at times like these. In many ways, she wished that she could talk to her mother. She had questions that needed answers but few resources to turn for assistance.

Sunday was a worship day. Sylvia always enjoyed worship Sundays. It was time to gather with friends, family, and neighbors. Since she had finished school four years back, she rarely saw her good friends, Leah and Millie. Worship Sundays were always a good time for catching up with them during the fellowship meals that followed the three-hour service.

However, on this Sunday, she was particularly pleased to see her brother Emanuel and his wife Shana arrive with their two children, Noah and Hannah. Despite being with her friends, Sylvia quickly excused herself and made her way over to Shana's side. With a third baby due in early September, Shana was always most appreciative for any help with her young children. She had always welcomed Sylvia's help at their farm, especially after Noah had been born three years ago. Yet, now it was Sylvia who sought Shana's help, hoping that her brother's wife could provide her with answers to the many questions floating in her head and heart.

They were sitting at a table alone, a delightful rarity after Sunday worship. Everyone else had eaten and the other women were busy cleaning up the dishes while the men gathered outside and the children played. Usually there were always people around, talking and laughing. But today, they sat at the table under the shade of a tree without anyone else. Sylvia held young Noah while he slept in her arms. Hannah nursed at Shana's breast. No one disturbed them and it gave Sylvia the opening that she sought.

"I have a question, Shana, about your past life," Sylvia began slowly, making certain that no one could overhear her.

Shana looked up from her nursing baby and frowned. "You mean when I was an Englischer? You've never asked me anything about that before."

Sylvia took a deep breath. "Was it hard to leave it behind for Emanuel?"

At that question, Shana smiled. "Ah, I see what you want to know." Her eyes skimmed the crowds of Amish people until she spotted her husband. With the exception of the beard that he had grown, he looked exactly the same as when she had met him so long ago. As if he knew, he looked up and noticed Shana watching him. He smiled back, his eyes bright and shining at her before he quickly looked away so that no one else would notice. That one simple moment, missed by all except Shana and Sylvia, said words about the relationship he shared with his wife.

"No, it wasn't, Sylvia. I wouldn't do anything different in the world. I am very happy to be your brother's wife." She looked at Sylvia. "He was my friend before my husband, you know. And that is very important, Sylvia."

Friend. There was that word again. The same word that Jake had said. "What does that mean, this 'friendship'?" Sylvia forced herself to ask. She wanted to know what it meant to the Englischers to be friends amongst the sexes.

But Shana had caught the undercurrent of Sylvia's question. "What do you mean by 'this' friendship?" She frowned, looking around to make certain no one could overhear them.

Sylvia stammered. "I...well, I was just curious, I reckon."

Shana wasn't fooled. She started at her young sister-in-law, trying to get a solid reading on the young woman sitting before her. "Does your question have to do with that widower? The Englischer?"

Sylvia started to protest but her words failed her. Instead, the tears came to her eyes and she fought hard to blink them away. "Oh Shana," she began, her voice sounding desperate and sad. "I just don't understand."

Shana held up her hand and quieted her gently, her eyes quickly darting around the room to make certain no one was approaching them. It would do no good for anyone to overhear such a conversation. "This is not the time nor place, my dear Sylvia." She spoke quietly, rocking her baby Hannah as she stopped nursing and began to sleep. "Be careful, however. It sounds like you are courting more than danger. A young Amish woman's reputation, once torn, is not easily mended. Your situation is quite different than mine," she whispered.

There were too many people nearby so Sylvia couldn't answer. But, if she could, she would have yelled "Yes! It is very different and I don't know why it is happening to me!" Instead, she maintained her silence, rocking the sleeping Noah and keeping her eyes on the floor so that no one could see the expression of distress that she wore.

The following day, Sylvia trudged across the field, not caring that her shoes were wet from the morning dew or that the hem of her skirt became soaked. Her mind was in too many places, trying to juggle this concept of Englischer friendship among sexes with Shana's admission about how important it was that she was a friend with Emanuel before they wed. In the Amish world, true friendship developed afterwards. But it seemed that the Englischers' developed it before committing to life together. If the latter were true, Jake's admission about their "friendship" meant more than met the eye.

He wasn't in the house when she arrived, for which she was grateful. She wanted to be alone, to not deal with the conflicts inside of her. If she focused on tending to his house and garden, she wouldn't need to consider the other issues that knocked her off balance. She made certain to water the garden before the sun rose too high in the sky. She was surprised at the number of weeds that had sprung up in just three short days.

The house was in near perfect shape; it didn't appear as though Jake spent much time in the house. But she found herself lingering, yet again, in his bedroom. After making the bed, she had paused by that photograph, staring at the blank face of a woman long gone. It was eerie to see the photograph every time she was there. Even worse, it tore at Sylvia's heart to know that, at one point, Jake had loved that woman and now, despite youth, she was gone and he had moved on.

It was shortly after twelve-thirty when he came into the kitchen to eat his noon meal. Sylvia tried to pretend that he wasn't there. He ate quietly at the table while she silently cleaned up the few dishes and pots that she had used to prepare his meal. She followed her mother's pattern of cooking, making larger meals for noon than what they typically ate at suppertime. It felt odd working while he ate. She was used to groups of people at the table, talking and sharing with each other.

It dawned on her that, indeed, Jake was probably lonely. He had told her as much a few weeks prior. She wished that she could be more social with him but, as she had already pointed out, it just wasn't proper. She set the towel down on the counter and stared into the clean sink. Perhaps she had more in common with Jake than she had realized, she thought. After all, in many ways, she was lonely, too.

"Penny for your thoughts," he said quietly.

She turned around, startled to realize that he had been watching her. His blue eyes stared at her as she stood at the counter. Color flooded her cheeks and she looked away. "It's quiet here," she managed to reply.

"Ah," he said as he stood, carrying his plates over to where she stood. "Yes, it is quiet. But it's nice, isn't it?"

"I..." She couldn't finish the thought out loud. She wanted to say that she didn't like the quiet. She was used to noises and people, even if it was a dog barking from the barnyard or cows mooing from the fields.

"You what, Sylvia?" He stood close to her, too close. The

invasion of her personal space made her uncomfortable and she leaned back, away from him. "You have a lot to say, don't you?" His voice was low and soft. "But you are afraid to speak. I wonder why?"

"It's not..."

He shook his head and stopped her in midsentence. "I know. It's not proper." He smiled but there was a sadness about it. "I don't know why everything is not proper with you, Sylvia. You are a woman and women have a right to speak their mind. Maybe not on your father's farm but you can speak your mind here."

In a moment of brazen clarity, she lifted her chin and met his gaze. Before she knew it, the words formed on her lips and she could hear herself speak but didn't recognize her own voice. "You make me nervous." As soon as she said it, she wished that she could take the words back.

"I make you nervous?" he asked incredulously. He leaned closer to her. "Is that because I frighten you? Have I threatened you in anyway?" There was a teasing tone to his voice and his blue eyes seemed to dance at her.

"It's not that," she stammered.

"It's what then?"

"I..." She hesitated. "I don't want to presume anything..."

He raised an eyebrow but didn't move away from her. "By all means. Go ahead, Sylvia." He lowered his voice and bent down toward her. His breath felt warm on her face. "What exactly do you think that you presume...if anything at all?"

She paused, the hesitation giving rise to her courage. "You're not Amish, Jake," she whispered, her voice barely audible as she stated the obvious. The color continued to flood her cheeks and she felt her heart throbbing from inside of her chest. She wished she could take the words back as soon as she said them. He would think her forward for certain now.

"Ah," he said again. This time, he did back away. "I see." But his eyes never left hers. "I'm not Amish. This is true. And that makes you uncomfortable because...?"

He waited for her to explain but she didn't. She wanted to tell him how she felt...how he made her suffer with such conflicting emotion. She didn't understand how she could feel so excited and uncomfortable at the same time. She wanted to ask him to tell her if she was imaging these things, if she had a right to feel so exhilarated in his presence. Certainly he would know if these things were natural and he could enlighten her on what, exactly, she was feeling. But such things were not to be spoken and the silence lingered between them.

He reached out and touched her cheek. It was as if an electric shock ran through her. "You weren't uncomfortable last Friday, were you? I saw the flowers. You left them on purpose. In fact, I see your touch everywhere. You aren't that uncomfortable, are you?" He took a deep breath and continued to caress her cheek with his thumb. "Would it make you more comfortable if I was Amish?" he finally said.

His question bewildered her. This wasn't how it happened for Amish couples. There was never a discussion; it just happened. Only it had never happened for her. She wasn't certain how to respond. "It's not my place to say something," she managed. "You can't change what you are. That isn't how it works."

"Let's pretend for a moment, yes? If I were Amish, would it be my place to make the first move then? Is that how it works?"

He didn't wait for her to answer before he leaned down and gently brushed his lips against hers. The kiss was soft and light, non-threatening but full of promise. For a moment, the tension between them lifted and he pulled back, just briefly. He stared into her eyes, seeing the conflicting emotions that she felt.

"I don't know you," she whispered.

He put her hand on the back of her neck and pulled her closer. "We can fix that, Sylvia. I want to fix that indeed..."

This time when he kissed her, there was a passion between them. She had never kissed a man before and had never imagined that this was how it would feel. She closed her eyes, his lips pressed gently but firmly against hers. The kiss was stronger than the first one and she could feel the closeness of his body against hers as he held her close. His arms wrapped around her and she relaxed in his embrace, feeling alive and on fire. A warm feeling spread throughout her body and she felt tears spring to her eyes. She wasn't certain why. Was it joy or fear?

When he pulled back, he noticed the tears and, with his thumb, gently brushed them away. "You have nothing to be afraid of, Sylvia."

She shut her eyes, fighting the tears that threatened to flow down her cheeks. "I have everything to be afraid of, Jake."

"You feel something. I know you do," he murmured. The softness in his voice made her feel weak and she was glad that he was holding her for fear that her knees would give way beneath her. "I know that I feel something, Sylvia. I have for weeks...perhaps from the moment that I saw you in the field."

His lips pressed against her forehead, soft and warm with a tenderness that she had never even imagined. "It's meant to be..." he mumbled.

Those words triggered a spark inside of her and, for just a moment, she felt as though she were awaking from a dream. Nothing that had just happened seemed real. And, his words echoed in her mind. Meant to be? Amish girls didn't kiss Englische men. There was certainly no good that could come out of this and a wave of shame washed over her.

"This isn't happening," she whispered and backed away, despite wanting to do the opposite.

It was surreal, sinful and shameful. It would destroy her parents, her family, her future. She opened her eyes and found her voice. "This can't happen." She pushed him away. How could he take her purity away? How could she have let him? His sweet words, his gentle voice, his overbearing presence had forced her to take leave of her senses. "This simply cannot happen," she repeated.

Without waiting for Jake to respond, she grabbed her basket and ran for the door. She heard him calling for her but she ran as fast as she could. The tears blinded her as her feet carried her through the pastures and far away from the lingering memory of his kiss.

When she was a safe distance and was certain that he had not followed her, she sank to her knees and covered her face with her hands. The tears flowed freely now and she cried, her back aching with each heavy sob. She knew that she had no choice but to confess to her parents and explain why she could never return to Jake Edwards' farm.

Chapter Nine

On Tuesday, she complained of a headache and spent the day in bed, miserable in the knowledge that she had to tell her parents but too aware that she couldn't. Too much time had passed and too much information would be sought by the eventual confession. The previous day, she had returned home but her mother was visiting one of her sisters and her father was nowhere to be found. Sylvia was alone in the house and, with her heart still pounding and her head completely befuddled, she took to her bed.

When her mother finally returned home, Sylvia was sleeping, finding it the only safe haven from the guilt that overwhelmed her. Later that night, her parents had been in such a good mood, her mother sharing the news from her sister, Ana's farm and Jonas eager to talk about the auction in New Holland. She couldn't bring herself to divulge the upsetting news that the Englischer widower had taken advantage of the family when he had kissed her in his kitchen.

By Tuesday afternoon, having spent so much time upstairs, she was hesitant to emerge downstairs. Sylvia's nerve had further vanished. She didn't know what to say to her parents. How could she tell them that Jake had kissed her? What would they think of her for having waited so long to tell them? Surely they would think she had encouraged it. Tomorrow was Wednesday and she was supposed to return to Jake Edwards' farm. She knew that she couldn't be alone with him again. To show up at the farm would be to encourage his behavior, to acknowledge that, indeed, she felt something. To refuse to go to work would be to raise unwanted questions from her parents. There was no graceful way out of the situation.

By late afternoon, she knew that she had to get up and move around. To linger in bed any longer would only prolong the inevitable. She needed fresh air to help clear her head and find answers. Laying in bed only made it worse. Her mind wandered and her heart pounded. When she closed her eyes, she felt his lips on hers. She could feel his arm around her, the strength of his embrace. It was too much to think about and she had to escape the memory of such an intimate moment. She understood now why such intimacy was reserved for after marriage.

"Sylvia, are you feeling better now?" her mother asked when she walked down the stairs. "I can fix you a nice cold lemonade."

"No Mamm," she said. "But *danke*."

"I wonder if you are being touched by allergies," her mother said.

Sylvia shook her head. "Just a headache, t'is all."

"Mayhaps too much time at that widower's place," her mother said. "Tuckering you out some."

Just as quickly as her mother said it, Sylvia felt the need to defend herself and Jake. "Oh no, Mamm," she gushed. "It's not that at all."

Her own words shocked her. Why had she jumped to his defense? Why had she automatically protected him? Why hadn't she taken advantage of the opportunity to tell her mamm the truth? And Sylvia knew, at that moment, that her spiritual existence was on the line. She was too far into the situation to escape and the realization alarmed her. *Nothing good can come out of this*, she scolded herself, wishing desperately that she had used her mamm's opening to stop working at Jake's.

Her mother gave her a sideways glance but said no more. Instead, she busied herself with preparing the evening meal. It wasn't as heavy as the noon meal but she knew that the men would be hungry after working outside all day. "Well then, you might as well go help your daed in the barn."

Sylvia was thankful to be released from inside chores. Working outside was exactly what she needed. It would give her the time to think, to sort through the mass of confusion that was clouding her mind. She didn't wait for instruction from her father before she began picking through the cow manure, cleaning up any droppings. The cows would come in for the evening milking just before supper. She made certain their troughs were filled with water and fresh hay was spread. The smell of the hay tickled her nose and twice she sneezed. When she was finished in the main barn, she went to the horse shed to muck their stalls and fill their water. Steve and Daniel would feed the horses grain and hay later, usually after supper.

The noise in the driveway startled her. She lifted her head. A car. It wasn't often that cars pulled into their driveway. Usually it was a lost tourist, seeking directions or a rare glimpse of a real Amish farm. She listened and heard only one door open and shut. But she couldn't see anything from where she stood. With a shrug of her shoulders, she went back to work. Her father or mother would take care of the stranger. She had enough on her mind to worry about without taking on a new issue. Besides, she didn't like strangers. They usually meant trouble.

A few minutes later, she heard her father call out for

Steve. Low voices were talking and the car engine started once more. Within minutes, the car slowly pulled out of the driveway and the noise faded away. Sylvia exhaled loudly. It always made her feel uncomfortable to have strangers at the farm. They invaded her private life, her sanctuary. If only the Amish could surround themselves with their own people, she thought. But she knew that the tourists helped the Amish in many ways. They bought Amish food, furniture, horses, carriages, and quilts. It was a necessary evil, her father would say.

Later, when she helped with the milking, Sylvia noticed that Steve was missing. She wondered why he wasn't helping but, rather than ask her daed, she kept her head bent down as she worked through the line of cows, alongside her younger brothers. It was a systematized routine. No need for words or talking. Just dealing with the cows and getting the job done.

Sylvia liked milking the cows because it was quiet. She felt closer to God when she was working in the barnyard or fields. The cows didn't ask questions or judge. But, when they looked at her with their big brown eyes, she knew that she was appreciated, even if only because she fed them or relieved their swelling udders. It was a beautiful relationship, one that was pure and good. For a moment, she forgot about her encounter with Jake Edwards and found happiness in the moment.

The lapse was only momentary, however. She finished the chores and went inside to help her mother with setting the table for the men. As she laid the last plate down, she heard them stomping into the porch. The men always stomped their feet, kicking the mud off before they walked into the house. She recognized the stomping but not the voices. It was only when the door opened and her father walked in that she heard the

84

too familiar voice of Jake Edwards.

"I can't thank you enough for lending Steve to help me," she heard him say to her father. "I'd never have gotten all that feed and hay stacked."

Sylvia turned around, the color draining from her face. She could barely believe that he was standing in front of her in her parents' kitchen. He was much taller than her brothers and father. He filled the room with his presence. For a second, she had to lean against the counter to steady herself, her knees feeling weak. No one seemed to notice. In fact, they acted as if it was the most natural thing, to have an Englischer in their home. In all of her years, she had never seen a non-Amish person in their home. The surreal feeling returned and she had a hard time understanding how this was happening.

"That's what neighbors are for, ja?" Jonas clapped him good-naturedly on the back. "Katie, meet Jake Edwards. He's dropping Steve off."

"Good evening, Mrs. Lapp," he said.

Sylvia glanced at her mother. Something was wrong in Katie's expression. Sylvia saw her mother staring at Jake Edwards, her mother's eyes seeing more than she wanted. There was a dark shadow that fell across Katie's face, if only for a moment. Sylvia had only seen that look one time before when Emanuel was courting Shana. Sylvia caught her breath and waited, knowing that her mother was putting together the pieces. The look on her face was clear enough to Sylvia. But, just as quickly as the look was there, it vanished and Katie was back to herself.

"Mr. Edwards, it's nice to meet you," she said, her voice soft but clear. "We are getting ready for the evening meal." Her mother hesitated but knew that she had no choice when she asked, "Perhaps you would care to join us, Mr. Edwards?"

"Call me Jake, please," he insisted. "We're neighbors after all." His eyes flickered to Sylvia. She hadn't moved from where she stood, frozen in place as she tried to understand what was happening. "It sure is lonely dining by yourself every night. That would be quite appreciated."

Sylvia watched as her father gestured toward the table and Jake sat down to the right of her father. The boys found their spots while Katie began putting the pots and plates of food on the table. Baked chicken and beans and fresh, warm bread covered the table. Slowly, Sylvia moved toward the table, realizing that the only open chair was next to Jake. She saw him start to stand as she approached. He held her chair for her and, when her cheeks reddened, her brothers chuckled. She was glad that her mother hadn't seen that one small gesture and her reaction.

After the silent prayer over the meal, Steve and Jonas began talking with Jake about the horses that were to arrive the following morning. They asked questions about the horses, surprised to learn that Jake had raised horses in Connecticut prior to moving to Lancaster. Sylvia sat stiffly beside Jake, barely touching her food. No one seemed to notice her lack of an appetite since the focus of the conversation centered on their guest.

"That's a great property you have there, Jake," Steve commented to Sylvia's surprise. Steve was usually shy around strangers. They all were shy among Englischers. It was part of their defense mechanism against the outside world. Less said, better protection from intrusions. Clearly, the two men had connected during their time together. "Some of the outbuildings need work but it's in decent shape considering. I didn't even know it was for sale! I'd have bought it myself."

Jonas chuckled. "Thinking about buying your own farm now, ja?" He laughed as Steve flushed, realizing that he had made an admission about his upcoming desire to wed his girlfriend. It wasn't really news to the family; the autumn announcement was anticipated. He was at the right age and had taken his baptism just recently. Marriage was the obvious next step.

"You wouldn't have known because it never was for sale," Jake said flatly. The unspoken question lingered around the table. He looked up from his plate, surprised to see all eyes upon him. All eyes except Sylvia's. He cleared his throat as he continued. "It's been in the family for several generations, you see. It was my grandfather's farm, passed down to me from my mother."

Sylvia looked at him for the first time since sitting down at the table. "But surely it was an Amish farm at one time!"

He looked at her and met her eyes, his own sparkling once again as he laughed at her sudden contribution to the conversation. "Yes it was Amish, if you can call a farm such a thing. Usually people are Amish but you're quite observant," he teased. The color rose to her cheeks and he smiled at her before turning his attention back to Jonas. "My grandfather's family was Amish," he admitted. "Somewhere along the way, my grandfather left the faith...or merely never joined the church. But he was the only son and inherited the farm when his father died." His voice trailed off as though he was thinking of something else. "My grandfather tried his hand at farming, tried to modernize the place. But it was too much for him. He took the family to Connecticut but refused to sell the property."

Jonas took advantage of Jake's pause. "I never knew that," he said. "Been here for thirty years and never knew about that place."

"It's a flag lot," Jake explained. "The bulk of the property is between two farms with only the driveway entrance on the main road. Easy to miss since you can't see it from the road and it is rather overgrown along the property line."

"Well, I'm sure that it is nice to have new life in such an old place," Jonas finally said.

Steve agreed. "That land's been fallow for years. Could sure get some rich crops out of it."

"So I've been told," Jake said, the hint of teasing in his voice with his head inclined toward Sylvia. She hoped that no one else noticed. "In fact, I was thinking about some corn. Heard from a reliable source that it would be a good first-time crop for a gentleman farmer like myself." He looked at Steve, a twinkle in his eyes as he added, "It's a shame that I couldn't learn from someone willing to put in the labor and share in the profit."

Jonas scratched at his beard and leaned his elbow on the table. "You looking for some help, then? Mayhaps Steve might be interested." He glanced at his son. "I understand that he might be having some need for some extra money come October," he said, the hint of a smile on his face as he insinuated again about Steve's intention to marry in the fall.

The rest of the table laughed, aware of Steve's discomfort. But it was all in good fun, no harm was meant. Sylvia, however, sank in her chair. Now she'd never be able to tell her parents that she couldn't go back to Jake's farm. They'd ask questions and the answers would hurt more than herself.

Now it would impact the entire family, especially Steve if he was going to plant corn in Jake's field.

Yet, part of her was glad that the decision had been made for her. Even though she didn't want to admit it, she was relieved. Being around Jake was exciting and just a bit dangerous. Even now, sitting next to Jake, she felt her heart pounding and that familiar warmth spreading throughout her body. Every once in a while, she could feel his leg brush against hers. Accidental or on purpose, she wasn't certain. It sent a chill down her spine and color to her cheeks.

"You feeling poorly again, Sylvia?" her mother asked. The rest of the table turned their attention to her, which made her want to squirm in her seat. "You look flushed." Katie looked at Jonas.

"I'm fine, Mamm," she replied softly. She could feel Jake's eyes on her and she refused to look anywhere but at her plate, still full of food.

"You've barely eaten and you were in bed most of the day," Katie chided. "I think you must be coming down with something."

Jake cleared his throat. "You looked pale when you left my farm yesterday. I would have been happy to drive you home, Sylvia. It's a long walk and as the weather gets warm, well..." He looked up at Jonas. "If your father wouldn't object, of course."

She saw it coming and cringed. Her father leaned back in his seat, wiping his mouth with his napkin as he said, "That would be most kind, Jake. Would get her home quicker for helping her mother. If it's not bother, of course."

Jake held up his hand. "Not at all. My pleasure."

And with that, the decision was made. There would be no further excuses from Sylvia. She felt a sense of dread inside of her chest as she watched her father push back from the table and stood up, waiting for the other men to follow. "Now, let's go discuss the details on your corn proposition, Jake. I'm sure Steve will be anxious to make his plans to get started." Jonas winked at the younger boys as he added, "Seeing that wedding season is just round the corner."

The room was quiet after the men left. Jake paused to thank Katie, mentioning again how nice it was to share a family meal. Sylvia noticed that her mother didn't extend future invitations. Katie was uncomfortable with strangers in the house. She was more comfortable with her own family surrounding her. But she did notice that Katie watched as Jake gave Sylvia a warm smile and said good night as he left.

Sylvia tried to avoid her mother's eyes but, as she helped clear the table, she knew her mother was watching her. No questions were asked out loud but Sylvia knew that plenty were being thought about this tall, handsome stranger who had moved into their neighborhood and was quick to become an important part of the family's life.

Chapter Ten

The following day, she forced herself to walk across the fields of growing corn and through the hill of wheat toward Jake's farm. She hadn't slept well the night before and had awoken at five to help her father and brothers with the milking. By eight o'clock, she had already put in a full morning. But her mind was on the events of the past 48 hours.

She wished her older sisters were still living at the farm, although she probably wouldn't have confided in them. It didn't matter, she thought to herself. Susie and Ana were both married now with their own families to concern themselves. And Sarah was much older. Sylvia had never been very close with her. Besides, none of them would understand Sylvia's attraction to the Englischer anymore than Sylvia understood it.

When she arrived at the farm, she quickly threw herself into the task at hand. She felt as thought she was getting into a routine. She started upstairs, making Jake's bed and straightening up his room. There wasn't a lot to straighten up...a pair of pants tossed over the back of a chair, a shirt dangling from the foot of the bed.

She took the time to fold the shirt and lay it in a drawer, smoothing out the wrinkles. She glanced at that photo as she had every day that she had worked at Jake's house. The questions continued to flood her mind but never crossed her lips. Before she left the room, she turned and glanced back to make certain that everything was in order. Her eyes lingered on the bed, just long enough for a blush to cover her cheeks. Quickly, she retreated back downstairs.

She spent more time than usual cleaning the kitchen

and sitting room. She made certain to get on her hands and knees to wash the baseboards. She even rid the ceiling corners of any lingering cobwebs. Every farm had spiders and with spiders came cobwebs. But Sylvia knew that cobwebs belonged in the barn, not the house. Finally, she washed the windows until they sparkled and even took the musty curtains outside to shake off the years of dust.

Now that she knew that Jake's family had lived in the farmhouse, she felt a new sense of purpose. The older items in the house were clearly antiques from his great-grandparents. The newer items were obviously more recent acquisitions. A blending of the past with the future. There was a story here in this old house, she thought to herself, and she was increasingly aware of her curiosity to learn more.

There was some activity in the barnyard. Sylvia hurried to the kitchen window and peered outside. Two large horse trailers were pulling down the long driveway. For the first time that day, she saw Jake outside by the barn. It dawned on her that he had avoided the house all day and she wondered why. Was he giving her space or was he merely busy?

Despite her determination to focus on work instead of the fluttering in her heart, she felt a wave of disappointment at the realization that he would be occupied for the rest of the day with the horses. It's better that way, she told herself. She would prepare his meal, leave it covered in the oven, and retreat back home without any interaction with Jake Edwards. Yes, indeed, it was much safer to just leave, she admitted to herself. There was no harm in putting distance between them after that unsettling kiss from earlier in the week.

So it surprised her when she heard him enter the kitchen, an eagerness in his footsteps. She was just getting ready to dry the dishes from cooking when he walked up to her, his face shining with excitement.

"Sylvia! You must come to see the horses!" He took the dishtowel from her hand and laid it on the counter. Instead of releasing her hand, he held it, just long enough to lead her out of the kitchen. "I just got them settled in. I'm surprised you didn't come out when they arrived."

She wasn't certain how to respond. It had never dawned on her to go out to the barn when the trailers pulled in. She was his housekeeper, after all. What happened in the barn didn't necessarily concern her. "I didn't realize that I should," she finally said, withdrawing her hand from his. It made her feel weak, this attention that he gave to her. Truth was that she had been avoiding him, more for self-preservation rather than to distance herself.

Ignoring her comment, he hurried her into the barn. "They're gorgeous, all of them. I had forgotten how beautiful and graceful they are."

The barn was different. There was noise and life from the stalls. The dairy aisles were still empty but she could feel the energy. Everything was clean, almost too clean. Jake must have spent hours, if not days, cleaning and sweeping the barn. There were new boards nailed to the wall in random places. When she looked up, she noticed that there were also new boards on the ceiling above. Jake had been busy, indeed. She was impressed with the amount of work that he had invested in repairing the old barn.

He led her to the back of the barn, to the place where the horse stalls were kept. It was darker there, the windows tucked back and small, allowing only a little bit of light. The barn had minimal electricity, a few random light bulbs hanging from the ceiling. The further into the barn, the cooler it was. The horses would thrive in this barn, she realized, especially in the heat of summer.

Jake took the time to show her each one. They were large horses, each one a deep chestnut color with dark mane. Their faces were narrow and elegant with attentive ears and intuitive eyes. Some of them seemed to recognize Jake. He would pause at a few of the stalls, spending a moment to caress the horse's neck or tug gently at its ear. He smiled at Sylvia when he came to the end of the stalls. "What do you think of them?"

Her opinion was not something that many people sought. She chewed on her lower lip for a moment, trying to formulate a response. She didn't know too much about horses, not like she knew about crops and cows. But she knew that they were beautiful and she knew that he was proud of them. "God makes lovely creatures, doesn't He?" she finally said.

For a moment, Jake didn't respond. He was silent as though pondering her words. Yet the silence was not uncomfortable. There was a sense of reflection, perhaps on both of their parts. She tried to avoid watching him, but his expression was so honest and pure as he stared at the horse before him, rubbing its neck. The horse nickered and nuzzled at his hand. Jake smiled softly, still thinking about something else as he rubbed the horse's nose. "Yes, lovely creatures indeed," he finally said quietly. He looked up and met Sylvia's gaze.

She felt flustered again. "I really should be going."

"Is it noon already?" he asked. He sounded genuinely

surprised and a little disappointed.

"I've finished my work and your meal is warm in the oven," she responded, trying to focus on the one subject that was safe: her work. "I was planning on leaving to help Daed," she explained.

He moved closer to her and touched her arm. "Not yet, Sylvia. Don't leave yet."

"Jake," she pleaded softly, backing away from his looming presence in the darkness. She felt the barn wall at her back and, for the briefest of moments, she felt trapped. He was too close and she had no escape. Yet, while escape was on her mind, it wasn't what she really wanted. Her heart pounded inside of her chest as he stood over her. She flashed back to those movies that she had seen, thinking about the heroines and heroes who, in the throes of passion, fought their feelings for each other. Surely this was how they felt.

"I had hoped you would help me with the horses today, Sylvia."

She frowned. It had appeared that he had everything under control. "You don't really need my help," she chided gently.

Even in the darkness, she could sense his smile. It was soft, warm, and just for her. "OK, perhaps I just want you to spend more time here," he said, closing in on her. His hand was still on her arm. It felt warm and sent tingles throughout her body. "Spend more time here with me," he added, his fingers resting on the naked skin of her arm.

"That's impossible," she replied flatly. Her voice sounded stronger than she felt. For a moment, she wondered who had actually spoken those words. Had they truly come from her mouth?

"Why is that?"

"You're not Amish," she reminded him, her voice a stern whisper.

"Are you?" he retorted too quickly.

She realized the trap that she had stepped into and she faltered. Had Steve told him or had he merely guessed that she had not yet taken her baptism? Until she did, she wasn't truly Amish. Most Amish took their baptism before marriage or after their *rumspringa*, the years of running free from Amish rules. While Sylvia wasn't close to being married, she certainly had no interest in running free.

"You said I have nothing to fear from you," she whispered.

"You don't."

"I have everything to fear from you. This isn't...."

He finished her sentence with a simple "proper." She heard him sigh. "No, I suppose it isn't."

"You don't understand," she said softly, suddenly feeling more like herself. "This...whatever this is...could ruin me with the community, the church, with my family. There is no return if tongues start wagging, even if I have yet to take the kneeling vow."

"I'm not so sure of that," he countered.

"Jake," she whispered.

"No, Sylvia. There is something different about you. I haven't been able to stop thinking about you. You haunt my every thought. In my life, dear Sylvia, I have never felt so overwhelmed with anyone. You have a peace about you. I want to find that peace. I think you can help me and I can help you. You are special, Sylvia. I sensed it then."

"You don't know me," she said, her voice barely audible.

"Ah, perhaps that is what intrigues me...wanting to get to know you." He reached out and brushed his fingers across her cheek. His touch stung her skin, leaving a warm trail where his fingers had been. "I want to spend some time with you...away from here, away from farms and Amish."

She recoiled as if his words physically hurt her. "I couldn't do that!"

"A dinner out? Has anyone ever taken you out?" Her silence confirmed his suspicion. "Or even a walk through a park, a place to talk." His hand lingered near her neck, his touch sending a burning sensation throughout her body. "Anything to be near you, Sylvia." He leaned down again, his lips pressed against hers, holding her captive in the barn, but not exactly against her will. She felt his chest pressed against hers and it warmed her. But she knew that it was wrong and leading her to a place she wasn't prepared to travel.

"Please Jake," she managed to say, her cheek pressed against his and her hand gently against his chest. "I simply cannot..."

He backed away, just enough to give her some space. One hand rested above her head on the wall and the other gently touched her shoulder, her arm...her hand. He sighed but smiled in the dim light. "I understand, Sylvia...and I will wait." Reluctantly, he backed away and, with a final touch of his hand to hers, he stood at a respectful distance. "I won't bother you anymore. Perhaps there will come a day when you will understand better. Perhaps you will ask me to continue." He lifted her hand and brushed his lips against the back of it. "The intention is honorable, I assure you."

"You are not Amish," she repeated softly, her eyes downcast so that he could not see the tears that formed on her eyelashes. "It will never be honorable, I assure you."

He took a deep breath and exhaled, still staring down at her. There was sadness in his expression, a look of disappointment that was unmistakable. But she couldn't help wonder what had he expected from her? "Then I suppose I should be taking you home. After all, I promised your father, didn't it?"

They rode in silence on the drive home and, when he pulled into the driveway, she felt beads of sweat on her forehead and palms. She had never arrived at the house in a car. The few times she had ridden in a car, she had always been with her mother or a neighbor. Mennonite neighbors often drove them places for a few dollars to cover gas. But her exposure to traveling by automobile was limited and always shared with the company of others. Of course, she reminded herself, the exception was the three previous car trips with Jake. But he had dropped her at the lane, a clandestine drive that hid more than could be revealed in the open.

"Friday then?" he asked before she jumped out of his truck. "You will come back on Friday, yes?"

She answered with a slight nod and averted eyes. Then, before she knew it, he was gone and she was left alone with the racing questions that flooded through her mind. He had seemed more reserved today. On the one hand, she was grateful. Perhaps he was as remorseful as she was about the indiscretion. On the other hand, she was embarrassed to admit that she felt alive in his presence. She would be lying to think that she hadn't enjoyed the kiss, if only there was no guilt associated with it. If it was right, she told herself, there would be no guilt. That realization made her feel even worse.

Her sister-in-law, Lillian, was in the house with her children when Sylvia entered. She was cleaning up from the noon meal. Her family had obviously shared it with Katie, Jonas, and the boys. Sylvia felt a pang of envy that she had missed such a joyous gathering with her family.

The difference between her daed's house and Jake's was tremendous. Sylvia loved having the little ones around the house. She loved their laughter and jokes, their silly observations and comments. In fact, when the little ones were underfoot, that was the only time she didn't mind being inside. She loved visiting with her other sister-in-law, Shana, when she gave birth, first to Noah and then to Hannah. She had helped Shana during those first few weeks, taking care of chores as well as the babies.

"Gut day, Sylvia," Lillian said. She was always cheerful, always smiling. Sylvia felt the weight of the world lift from her shoulders when she was in Lillian's presence. "Haven't seen much of you these days. Been keeping busy with that widower, ja?"

"I've been working there, if that's what you mean," Sylvia said softly as she leaned down to pick up little Abram. He was just starting to crawl now, chasing after his two older sisters and one brother. His soft gurgling and gentle cooing made Sylvia laugh. "Such a big boy, ja?"

"Mamm mentioned the widower was here for supper last night," Lillian said innocently. "She was surprised at how young he is."

"I suppose," Sylvia replied.

She wasn't surprised that her mother had commented on Jake's youth to Lillian. Certainly Mamm had also pointed it out to Daed, too. Sylvia had seen the look in her mother's eyes. Her mother had wisdom that ran deep when it came to her children. Nothing could escape her. Thankfully, Sylvia realized that her mother was not in the house, although she wondered where she might be. It was unusual for her mother to not be in the kitchen, helping to clean and sharing in the fellowship. But Sylvia didn't mind. It was always much nicer to clean up after the meal with Lillian was around.

"When I first heard about you working for a widower, I thought he'd be old and pining for his wife," Lillian confided. She set the last plate on the drying rack before she turned around. "But I understand Steve will be helping him with the farm, too. Seems Jake Edwards is terribly eager to farm that land, ja?" She laughed. "What takes us centuries to figure out, Englischers want to learn in one season."

"I wonder what happened to his wife," Sylvia said out loud, immediately wishing that she hadn't. She didn't want to call attention to the fact that she had been thinking about him and asking questions about his past. Lillian didn't seem to notice as she reached out for Abram. The baby stretched his chubby arms out toward Sylvia and both women laughed as he wiggled in his mother's arms, trying to return to Sylvia's.

"*Ach vell*," Lillian said. "I'm sure he's bound to miss her."

The conversation was interrupted when Katie walked through the kitchen door. She greeted Lillian and Sylvia before turning her attention to the grandchildren. They spent the rest of the afternoon in the kitchen, crowded around the kitchen table, mending clothes and talking. It wasn't unusual for Sylvia to not contribute much to the conversation. Instead, she just enjoyed listening to Lillian's light voice tell stories or her mother share the latest news from her afternoon visit to a neighboring farm, which explained her absence when Sylvia returned earlier.

"Seems like Ida Ebersol is having a quilting this weekend," she said.

Lillian responded with a cheerful, "Oh, I'm ever so glad. Now that spring is here in full bloom, it seems no one gets together anymore. I miss visiting folks."

Katie looked up from the shirt she was mending and looked at Sylvia. "There's a singing on Sunday evening, too. Millie asked if you'd be going."

"Where at, Mamm?" she replied, her voice barely hiding her lack of interest. She'd much prefer to stay at home than stand around singing all night, especially since the singing was a cover up for the real purpose: finding a future husband.

"The Smucker's farm," she replied. "I'm sure Steve or Daniel would take you."

Everyone seemed to be staring at her, waiting for her answer. Truth be told, Sylvia had no desire to go to a singing but she knew it would do her some good to be away from the farm, away from Jake Edwards, and away from the crazy thoughts that were lingering in her mind. If she didn't go, they would wonder why. If she did go, she'd be one step away from Jake Edwards and perhaps closer to getting back on track.

"Yes, I think that sounds like a fine idea, especially if Steve or Daniel would take me," she finally said before bowing her head to concentrate on the mending and fighting the lingering memory of Jake Edwards' lips on hers.

Chapter Eleven

It was raining on Friday, torrential rain that created big swelling puddles in the fields and large muddy pits in the paddocks. The cows were drenched and dirty. It took longer than usual to round them into the barn and tackle the morning milking. Everything was wet and cold. It was a rain that chilled to the bone.

Sylvia shivered as she ran from the barn to the house. The hem of her dress was caked with mud mixed with manure. Days like this were exhausting and gloomy. The grey skies and wet weather seemed to drain everyone of joy. Once inside, Sylvia quickly changed her clothes so that she wasn't wet or dirty. Despite being inside, she couldn't get warm. The cold had taken ownership of her and refused to leave.

The rain increased her dread of having to walk over to Jake's. She'd have to take the roads and that would double the amount of time to get there. With the horrible weather, she'd be drenched in no time. And it didn't help that she'd had too many sleepless nights, nights spent tossing and turning with her mind in a whirlwind. Frankly, she was beyond tired. But she knew that to not go would create a situation where questions would be raised. While part of her wanted to stay home and to avoid the entire situation, the other part of her was longing to be there, near him, even if just for a few hours.

"You take a change of clothes with you, ja? No use getting sick, daughter," her mother reminded her as she began her own morning chores.

With her bag of clothes under one arm and a plain black umbrella in her free hand, she set off down the lane. The rain would help the crops grow so she knew there was no use in complaining. And, despite her mother's warning about getting sick, water didn't get people ill. So she kept her head down, tucked under the umbrella for as much protection as she could get from the driving force of the raindrops.

She heard, rather than saw, the truck pull up next to her. She was walking on the right hand of the road and, for a few seconds, the truck seemed to drive alongside of her. Finally, it slowed down then stopped. The passenger window rolled down and she heard him calling her name. "For God's sake, Sylvia! Get in the truck!"

It took her a moment to realize that it was Jake calling for her. She looked up, peering out from under the umbrella. "Jake?"

He leaned over and opened the door. "Get in, Sylvia!"

There was no hesitation in her step as she moved over to his truck and slid inside, shaking her umbrella twice before closing it and putting it on the floor at her feet. She shut the door and shivered, thankful to be out of the rain but wondering what she was doing sitting inside Jake's truck. He fiddled with a dial on the dashboard and she suddenly felt a blast of warm air.

"Let's get you into some dry clothes before you get sick," he said. There was an edge to his voice. Gone was the cheerful, jovial tone that she was used to hearing. Instead, he seemed annoyed and irritated.

"I suppose I should thank you," she said.

"I suppose I should be upset with you," he replied.

His words shocked her. She couldn't think of anything that she had done that could offend him. "Upset with me? Whatever for?"

104

"Sylvia, did you honestly think that I would let you walk to my farm in this weather?" He frowned but didn't take his eyes from the road. "I'm surprised that your father or brother didn't drive you. I'm even more surprised they let you walk!"

She couldn't help but laugh. "It's only rain, Jake!"

"'It's only rain', she says." He rolled his eyes when he said it. "All it takes is one car to come over the hill to hit you, Sylvia. It's hard to see in this weather and cars can hydroplane." He hesitated, immediately aware of the expression on her face. "Hydroplane means slid out of control," he explained. "Plus, you're soaking wet and shivering. You'll get sick, Sylvia."

"You sound like Mamm," she said, her tone teasing.

"I'm serious," he snapped. "Promise me that you will never do that again. I will come to get you if the weather is inclement. If I don't, stay home. Don't risk the walk. " His voice was strong and agitated. "Promise me!" he demanded.

No one had ever before spoken to her in such a sharp tone. She shrank back into the truck seat and looked straight ahead. She nodded her head and mumbled a quick, "Promise." But she couldn't look at him. She felt ashamed that she had done something wrong but confused because she wasn't certain what. She didn't want to have Jake Edwards upset with her but she wanted to understand what she done to upset him. If her job was to be at his farm to clean on Friday, why would he be upset that she had tried to walk there?

Once at the farm, she hurried into the house. She wanted to change out of her wet clothes and get started on her tasks. She could hear Jake in the kitchen while she retreated to one of the unused bedrooms upstairs. He was moving around downstairs and she could hear him running water and clanging dishes. She double-checked that the bedroom door was shut and latched before she quickly stripped off the wet clothes that clung to her skin. She pulled the dry clothes from the bag that she had carried and promptly slipped a fresh dress over her head. There was a mirror over the dresser. She paused to push any stray hairs back from her face. There was a rosy color to her cheeks but the rest of her face was pale, completely drained of color. She pressed her hand to her face. Her skin was cool and damp.

Back downstairs, she smelled fresh coffee brewing. She stood on the bottom step, hesitating before she came further into the room. Jake was standing at the counter, pouring two cups of coffee. After he had set the coffee pot back on the stove, he stood still, staring at nothing for a few long seconds. He seemed deep in thought. Sylvia contemplated retreating back to the second floor, ashamed at disturbing him. Was he talking to God, she wondered. She had heard that Englischers did that...talked directly to God. Finally, she softly cleared her throat to alert him to her presence.

"Ah," he said, turning to face her. He reached for the two cups of coffee and walked to the table. "That's better, eh?" He motioned to the one empty seat as he sat down. "Drink some coffee to warm up, Sylvia."

Obediently, she did as she was told. She sat down at the corner of the table, directly to his right. She didn't normally drink coffee but it smelled right *gut* and the cup warmed her hands.

"*Danke,*" she said shyly.

She had never sat at a table next to a man before, at

least not one that wasn't part of her family. During Sunday fellowship, the men ate their meals first, then the women. The girls were usually the last to eat and always together. They would sit at the wooden tables or even on hay bales during the summer months to talk and laugh over news that they had heard amongst the community. But now, sitting alone in his kitchen, she felt a new sensation, one of intimacy with the man next to her.

"I suppose we should talk, Sylvia," he started.

"About what?" she asked innocently.

The chair creaked as he leaned back. He ran his fingers through his hair and his eyes looked upward, as though searching for the right words. "I suppose I should apologize for speaking to you that way." He rubbed his eyes. "I know we agreed on no questions but I think you should know that she was killed in a bad...accident." He paused, trying to think about how much to share. His next words seemed strained. "Yes, an accident. I saw it happening but I couldn't get to her in time. " Lifting his eyes, he looked at her. "When I realized that no one was bringing you, I knew you'd start walking. I worried that I wouldn't get to you in time. I panicked."

"You panicked...?" she repeated.

"I worried," he explained. "I was worried that you'd get hurt...or worse. I had a vision of..." Words failed him and he stopped. He shook his head. "No, I don't want to have visions of that. It was a long time ago anyway." He tried to push away the memory.

"I'm very sorry, Jake," she said. She could feel his pain and it touched her. Clearly he was thinking about his wife. Part of her wished she could comfort him. To love someone and to lose her so tragically? There were accidents among the Amish, accidents on the roads or the fields, even tragedy in a one-room schoolhouse when two worlds collided, resulting in so much senseless death. But she had never personally known someone who lost a loved one in such a manner. "I wish I could take away the pain," she whispered.

He forced a small smile. "It's alright but thank you for that. Remember I told you that I'm here looking to find myself. Now you know why. I'm looking for forgiveness and I'm looking for answers. But instead," he glanced down at his coffee cup. "I found something else."

Forgiveness? Answers? Sylvia wanted to ask questions but she didn't want to intrude. She could feel his pain and sorrow. It was still fresh. And fresh wounds needed to heal. "It will come in time, Jake," she managed to say. "Hard work can repair the soul and the spirit."

He took a deep breath and gave her a genuine smile, breaking the melancholy of the moment. "If that is true, I'm well on the way to repair. Fixing up old farms is full of hard work!" He pushed back from the table, the legs of his chair screeching against the floor, as he stood up. "And I have plenty of it ahead of me, especially since your brother wants to start on the fields as soon as the rain breaks." He glanced at the window as he carried his empty coffee cup to the sink. The sky was dark and the splatters of rain on the windowpanes told the story. "Which does not appear to be happening anytime soon."

"It'll let up by afternoon," she said.

"Well, in the meantime, I'm going to run a few errands. I'll be back in time to take you home, rain or shine. No sneaking out of here, Miss Sylvia," he said, shaking a finger at her teasingly.

There was a special feeling about the house that day. The rooms were dark and there was a steady patter of rain against the windows. A few times, she heard the rumble of thunder in the distance. She liked the darkness as it made the rooms look different, smaller, and more welcoming under the mysterious cloak of grey shadows. The old piano seemed to speak about its past. She wondered who use to play it and how often. Why had it been left there? The old television reflected some of the light from the kitchen doorway. She wondered when it was last used and why it was still here. Clearly it didn't work. She liked the smell of the rain and how the house began to take on its own damp scent. But the dampness was also of spring, of new beginnings and fresh growth. She could sense the importance of the storm. It would set the scene for the upcoming season of growth.

It was getting close to eleven when she found herself feeling drained. Her eyes felt heavy and she knew that she was completely without energy. She needed a few moments, even if it was to just sit. Sit, she thought, and just rest my eyes. The past few nights of sleeplessness, of the constant barrage of thoughts and questions, had taken its toll on her.

As she sat on the sofa, she leaned her head back and closed her eyes while she thought about what Jake had told her about his wife, that she had been killed in a bad accident. Sylvia wondered how he had happened to be there. Why would he have mentioned forgiveness and peace? Why would an accident warrant asking for forgiveness? These were questions that she knew she could not answer but they were there, on the tip of her tongue and the front of her mind.

The rain continued to hit against the windowpanes and

it lulled her into a very soft, light sleep. She dreamed of the upcoming crops and how nice it would be to help her father with the first harvest. She felt the warmth of summer heat on her body, the moist humidity in the air. In her dream, she was barefoot, running through the fields, helping with the wheat chafes. It was only Sylvia and her father; the boys were nowhere to be found. But then, when she turned around, there was a figure, a tall silhouette against the sunlight. She raised her hand to her eyes and squinted. From the height and build of the man, she knew immediately that it was Jake Edwards. He approached her and brushed his finger against her cheek. She smiled at him but turned back to the harvest. When she glanced over her shoulder to the place where he had stood, he was gone.

She woke up with a start and looked around the room. It took her a minute to place herself. And then she remembered. Her head was on the arm of the sofa and there was soft blanket over her shoulders. How long had she been sleeping and when had Jake returned? What on earth must he have thought about her, sleeping when she should be working? Quickly, she stood up, folded the blanket, and, after setting it on the sofa, hurried back into the kitchen.

He was sitting at the kitchen table, drinking coffee and reading the newspaper. He was facing the window with his back to the doorway of the living room. She wasn't certain what to say or do. So, after a few long seconds, she cleared her throat, "I'm terribly sorry, Jake."

The sound of her voice startled him. He hadn't been aware that she was standing there. Setting the paper down, he turned around and stared at her. She was in the doorway, her arms crossed in front of her chest and the expression on her face was a bit sheepish.

"I didn't mean to sleep while working."

"It's a perfect day for a mid-morning nap," he replied, his words soft and reassuring. "You looked very peaceful. What were you dreaming?"

No one had ever asked her about that. Dreaming? She tried to think back to her dream. She could remember the peaceful and reflective feeling in her dream. But it took her a moment to recall the details. "About the spring planting." she finally answered. "It's just a few weeks away. The fields will need to be plowed for the corn planting."

"And you enjoy that?"

She smiled and leaned against the doorframe. "Oh yes. But not as much as the wheat harvest," she answered. "That doesn't happen until late June. We all work in the fields behind the binder. The mules pull it and we stack the bundles in shocks. At the end of the day, it's quite beautiful...rows and rows of wheat shocks. The neighbors often come to help and we have a great fellowship meal afterwards."

He nodded thoughtfully. "It does sound nice, Sylvia."

"I suppose..." she began slowly but hesitated. She didn't want to sound too forward and the words had slipped out before she knew what she had started to say. But he knew.

"What do you suppose?" he asked, a slight smile on his lips. It was as if he knew what she was going to say.

She looked down at the floor, refusing to meet his gaze. "I suppose you might be invited to help this year." She glanced up. He was smiling at her and she flushed. "Seeing that we're neighbors and all."

"Well, that would be something," he replied. "Seeing that

we're neighbors and all."

"I suppose I should get your meal ready," she said softly and began to hurry toward the counter. By napping, she had completely forgotten to do her last chore before leaving.

He stood up and walked over to her. "It's OK, Sylvia. I grabbed a sandwich while I was out. I can take you home anytime you'd like. The rain is still coming down hard."

"But I didn't finish my chores," she stated.

He glanced around the room. "Seems to me that everything is in order. And your father will probably need extra help today with the rain. Must not be easy to care for the dairy farm when it's so miserable out."

She nodded. "Ja, takes a lot more time to feed, water, and clean. We have a busy weekend for sure. Fields will be a mess from the storm and this is a church Sunday. " She hesitated. Dare she plunge ahead? Should she cross that line? She immediately realized that she already had, back on the day when she had accepted an escape from the market in his car...a stranger...and from an *Englischer* man at that! She had, indeed crossed the line of no return and, with the longest of hesitations, she began to close the door behind herself. "Plus, you see, there's a singing that night so I have to be ready early for Steve to take me."

He raised an eyebrow. "A singing?"

Her heart pounded inside of her chest. She felt as if she was floating above herself, watching the scene unfold. It was like one of the movies she had watched during her *rumspringa*. While she knew that she had disclosed too much, she was surprised that he had picked up on it. Would he care if she was at a singing? Perhaps it wasn't of any interest to him. "Ja, at the

112

Smucker's."

"The next farm past?"

She nodded.

"What happens at a singing?" he asked, leaning against the counter, watching her thoughtfully.

She laughed. "We sing!"

He joined her laughter. "I see! I suppose that would make sense. Do you go with your parents?"

She shook her head and, as she did, she felt a stray hair against her forehead. "It's for the youths," she explained. She was surprised when he reached out to brush back a stray hair that had fallen from beneath her white organza prayer *kapp*. His touch was gentle and warm, caring. For the briefest of moments, she almost had to catch her breath. Waves of electricity seemed to flow throughout her body and, in the boldest of moves, she raised her eyes to search his face. "Usually a young man will escort a woman home." Her words were soft and low. She didn't know why she was explaining this to him but the words just flowed from her mouth. "It's the beginning of courtship."

"Ah," he said. "So that's how it begins?" He kept staring at her, watching as she nodded. "And how does it end, Sylvia?"

She hesitated. Why was he asking her this? She wondered at his motives. But his expression seemed honest and open. "They meet secretly for a while," she replied, her words slow and quiet. "That's the courtship time. If they get along well and find admirable qualities..." she didn't finish the sentence. The words simply would not escape her lips. She had been so bold and so brazen. It felt awkward and sinful. She almost felt ashamed of herself. Where was this coming from, she wondered? Had the months of *rumspringa* and watching so many movies ruined her? She looked away, chewing on her lower lip. Had the exposure to the outside world done exactly what the People didn't want...captured her soul?

He honored her silence, waiting to see if she'd continue. When she didn't, he nodded his head and pursed his lips. "Well, let's hope a nice young man asks to take you home then, yes?" He glanced at the clock on the wall. Almost one o'clock. He took a deep breath. "It's getting late so I suspect it's that time. Gather your things, dear Sylvia, and I shall be the one escorting you home now," he said, bowing down before her teasingly. "Your chariot will await you outside."

It took her a moment to catch her breath when he left the kitchen to "warm up the truck". This is too much, she thought. Her sister-in-law, Shana, had been correct when she said she was courting more than danger. She had to regain her strength and focus. She stood there, alone in the kitchen, staring at nothing in particular. But her mind reeled.

Yes, she thought, I must stop it now before something much worse happens. Her heart sank inside of her chest but she knew what she had to do. She had to tell her parents that she could not continue working for Jake Edwards. She would accept a ride home from a young man at the singing, start the courting process, and she would get back into the fold of the Plain way.

Chapter Twelve

The barn was full of kerosene lights that glowed in the increasing darkness. The barn smelled of fresh hay and animals with the faintest hint of manure. It wasn't unpleasant and certainly not something that offended any of the Amish youths that crowded around the few homemade tables set up with bowls of popcorn and pretzels. There was a warmth among the group, with the boys on one side of the barn and the girls clustered together on the other side. The separation created an interesting flow of color with black and white on the male side and bright blues, greens, and purples on the other.

Sylvia stood with her friends, Millie and Leah. She felt awkward, knowing that she was being watched by both the young men and the young women. She hadn't attended many singings in the past few years since she was old enough to join them. In fact, she avoided them, knowing that there was so much pressure for pairing up with a young man. With that pressure came the eventual and inevitable joining of the church.

Of course, during *rumspringa*, Amish youth were supposed to explore the outside world. Their parents looked the other way while their children tested the ways of the Englische. It was a true testament to the family that most of the children came back, disheartened by the blackness that they saw. Their exposure to the non-Amish way of life usually confirmed their loyalties and ties to the Amish community. Sylvia hadn't met many youth who did not take the baptism but she did know quite a few who had run wild, both the men and the women. Some of the men drank and did drugs. It wasn't unheard of for one or two to be arrested. For the women, their reputations were often ruined and they usually had to seek a partner from another Amish district. And if there was a baby involved, well...that created its own set of problems.

For Sylvia, she had used her time wisely, to reflect and to explore but from a safe distance. She wasn't interested in the Englischer way of life, she knew that already. But she wasn't ready to commit to a life of obedience and childbearing. She wanted to enjoy life for a while longer. Of that she was certain.

Leah touched her arm. "We haven't seen much of you, Sylvia. You been working at the market still?"

Sylvia shook her head. "Daed has me cleaning for a widower in the mornings. Then helping at the farm."

Millie peered around over Sylvia's head. Her eyes were scanning the anxious faces of the young Amish men standing on the other side. "A widower? The market seems more promising for meeting a young man," she said.

Leah jumped to Sylvia's defense. "You don't know what you are saying, Millie. That market is no place for Sylvia. You know she likes the farming more." She smiled at Sylvia. "Ain't that so, Sylvia?"

"Ja," she agreed. "Too many Englischers at the market and too many busy bodies."

Millie turned her attention back to her friends. "Well, you're here now," she said lightly. "Seems someone might have her eyes set on joining the church and settling down now, ain't so?"

Sylvia flustered under Millie's direct question. "Just wanted to be social, that's all."

Leah sighed and nudged at Millie's arm. "Leave her be,

Millie. You'll scare our dear Sylvia away and we'll only see her at church for the next few months!"

Dear Sylvia. The words rang in her ears. Wasn't that was Jake had called her? At the thought of Jake, she felt the familiar flutter in her chest and the color rose to her cheeks. She hadn't told her parents yet. Her father had been busy the day before, helping out at a neighbor's farm. She already knew that she would tell her mother that she didn't feel well tomorrow. She'd blame the singing and being out late. It was a mistruth...but not quite a lie. She didn't feel well...not about being alone with Jake Edwards anymore.

Even God would forgive such a small white lie, she reasoned with herself. After all, that would give her time to talk to her father. She wouldn't tell him about the kiss or her feelings. No, that would only jeopardize Steve's great opportunity to plant his own crop of corn before he was to get married in the fall. Instead, she'd tell her daed that she felt uncomfortable working for an unmarried Englischer and she wanted to just work at home. Certainly he'd understand that.

Yes, she thought, that was exactly how she would handle this and she'd be free from Jake Edwards and his powerful presence that simply overwhelmed her. Just thinking about him made the color rise to her cheeks, especially when she thought back to his kisses.

"It's warm in here, isn't it?" she asked.

She felt hot and wanted to get some fresh air. It was also getting late. The singing had started at 8 o'clock and by now, at least two hours had passed. She noticed some of the men and women leaving together. Those that were known to be courting were usually the first to leave. The time that they spent together was part of their courting. He would drive her home in his buggy, taking the longest route possible so that they could enjoy time together. The unattached girls that were left behind began to mingle in smaller groups. Occasionally, a young man might join the group, bringing his intended a cup of punch to break the ice and begin talking. Sylvia knew that she wasn't ready for that and, instead, just wanted to slip out of the door so she could walk home by herself.

"I'll be back," she said and did just that...slipped away so that no one would notice. They'd think she was asked home by a young man and that suited Sylvia just fine. She wanted to be alone, away from the speculation and questions of her peer group.

The night air was cooler than usual and she shivered as she escaped the activity and warmth of the barn. Darkness surrounded her and she felt a bit safer. She wouldn't have to worry about anyone bothering her now. No Adam Knoeffer or Samuel Zook to try to talk her into riding home with them. No, she realized. That wasn't what she wanted tonight. Not a reminder of what was expected of her when she wasn't ready yet to commit to that.

"Chilly?"

The voice startled her and she spun around. "Jake?"

He emerged from the shadows. "I wasn't certain that was you," he said as he approached. His hands were in his jacket pockets and he wore a wide brimmed hat on his head. "Headed home? No lucky Amish man escorting you to your father's farm tonight?" His words were slightly teasing.

She was astonished to see him standing before her. Just when she was trying to forget about him, here he was...at an

Amish singing no less! "Whatever are you doing here?" Desperate, she looked around, hoping that no one else was standing outside. If anyone saw the Englische widower standing by the barn, talking to her with no chaperone, the bishop would certainly hear about it and she'd get the what-for from Daed.

She saw him shrugged his shoulders as he walked closer to her. "Well, truth be told, Sylvia, I thought I'd see about walking you home, especially since you don't seem to have an escort now, do you? I don't have a buggy but it's a fine night for walking." He unzipped his jacket and, without asking for her permission, laid it across her shoulders. It felt heavy against her back but she could smell the sweet scent of his cologne. "That's where you were headed, yes? Then let's go, Sylvia." He didn't wait for a response but started leading her down the lane and toward the road.

ndaded her as her thoughts ran wild. What was the meaning of this? What would people think when they drove by on their way home? With his jacket over her shoulders and the night being so dark, they wouldn't recognize her. And, to be fair, with the dark wide brim hat on, Jake could pass for an Amish man in the darkness. She felt the too familiar pounding in her chest and the chill of the night vanished as the blood pulsated through her veins. Somehow her feet carried her down the lane next to Jake Edwards.

"So," he began. "Now that we are headed home, what are we supposed to talk about?" He looked at her. "In an Amish courtship, that is."

Courtship? "Jake," she said, her tone a simple reprimand.

"That is what this is the beginning of, Sylvia, isn't it?"

"I can't work for you anymore," she blurted out. The words surprised her more than they did Jake. "I just can't, Jake."

Silence. But only for a moment. "Ok, I can see that. It wouldn't be proper for a courting couple to be alone in the house, right?"

She couldn't believe what she heard. Courting couple? Was he serious? She actually started to laugh. "I'm not courting you, Jake Edwards!"

He looked at her, his eyebrows raised as he said, "I do believe you are. You are walking home with me from a singing, aren't you? That's how it all begins. You said so yourself. And here we are."

She shook her head in disbelief. He was the most peculiar man and persistent. "What on earth would you want with an Amish girl?"

"Woman," he corrected.

"You are very forward," she scolded, but good-naturedly.

"Ah, yes." He walked closer to her, his arm brushing against hers. "Now we are starting to get to know each other. That's part of the ritual, isn't it?"

She was starting to relax, despite herself. "You didn't answer my question, Jake."

"I thought we weren't going to ask questions…" He nudged her with his shoulder.

For a moment, neither spoke. The silence was comforting, however. It gave them both time to catch their breath and sort their thoughts. She was relieved when, finally, he sighed and broke the silence.

"That's a fair enough question, I suppose. Look Sylvia, I can't profess that I'll ever be Amish. But I am here to find my roots. You know my grandfather moved away from the community and I never knew much about it at all. In fact, no one really talked about our background. But after what happened..." He paused, his own mind racing. "Well, I don't need to go into details right now but it was powerful enough that I decided I needed to return to my roots. That's where my family should have stayed, you see. And then, you were there, on that hill...you gave me directions to my house but I'm suspecting you will give me more and far greater direction than that."

She gasped at his words. She had never heard anyone speak so poetically. And to think that he was saying that about her? "Why me?"

He shrugged again. "You were there when I needed you. I was lost. You helped me find my way. And let's not forget that it couldn't have been a coincidence that when you needed help, God put me in your path. "

"At the market..." The words came out like a soundless breath.

He nodded. "At the market." He reached down and took her hand in his. He was pleased that she didn't fight him. "Look Sylvia, I wouldn't ask you to come to my world. It's an ugly world and I don't ever want to return. But, let's put that aside and get to know each other. I told you that you have nothing to fear from me. My intentions are honorable."

"But..."

He stopped her by gently squeezing her hand. "I know. I'm not Amish. Let's worry about that later. I trust in faith and in the good Lord that things will have a way of working out for the best. Isn't that what you believe, too?" He didn't wait for her answer but brought her hand up to his lips and gently kissed the back of it.

She pulled her hand away from his. That wasn't something that she was used to, a man touching her. If anyone drove by, they would see a man and woman alone, walking closely together in a more than casual way. She couldn't chance wagging tongues, even if they couldn't recognize her in the dark. If word of Jake's behavior traveled back to her father or, heaven forbid, the bishop, she'd have a lot of questions to answer.

"I do believe in faith, Jake. But it seems you are asking me to believe in fate, too."

"Yes," he said slowly, thinking as he answered. "I believe I am asking you to believe in fate."

Silence. They walked side-by-side, the gravel of the loose macadam cracking under their shoes. Did she believe in fate? She wasn't certain. "What if fate doesn't exist? Then what is the point of this?"

He took a step ahead of her so that, when he stopped, she had no choice but to do the same. She stood in his shadow, looking up at his handsome face. She felt her heart flutter so she averted her eyes. "Sylvia," he said softly. "What is the purpose of courtship to Amish youth?"

"You're not Amish."

"Neither are you," he reminded her.

She couldn't hide the smile and was thankful for the

darkness when she said, "But I intend to be."

"You didn't answer the question," he prompted her.

Their teasing banter had broken the ice and, despite not wanting to, Sylvia found herself relaxing. She wasn't used to speaking her mind or engaging in any type of conversation like this. She found it exciting and challenging, refreshing even though she was quite sure that it would be frowned upon on many different levels by the bishop of the church district. "Mayhaps I forgot the question, Jake," she said softly.

He laughed and his laughter rang through the night. She found herself smiling and, once again, wondering why he was interested in her. Certainly there were plenty of women in his world that would find him even more exciting and handsome than she did. Why was he pursuing her? She could sense that he was determined but she didn't understand for what.

If he were Amish, she realized, she would have avoided him. He was too forward and bold, too persistent and demanding. Yet, because it was Jake and because he wasn't Amish, she found it endearing and exciting at the same time. Not for the first time, she felt as though she was one of the characters in those forbidden movies that she had watched. Not for the first time, she realized that he made her feel different and special. And, not for the first time, she recognized that she was starting to like feeling that way.

Chapter Thirteen

The following morning, she did not tell her mother that she was not feeling well nor did she tell her father that Jake Edwards did not need her help anymore. Instead, she acted as if nothing had happened. Upon completion of her indoor and outdoor chores, she packed a small lunch bag and set off across the meadow toward Jake Edwards' farm.

The sky seemed brighter and the birds louder. She smiled to herself as she remembered the long walk home, hand-in-hand with Jake. She couldn't believe what was happening to her, Sylvia Lapp, of all people. She was the most favored of the group, the quiet dear Sylvia to her parents, to her friends, and now to Jake. And, as long as he kept it honorable, she would believe in God to guide her. If this was the path that He had chosen for her, she would follow it.

He was waiting for her in the kitchen, a broad smile on his face when she walked through the kitchen door. "There you are! I was wondering if you'd show up." He took a few steps toward her. "I said to myself, 'Jake, she either is or she isn't, not a darn thing you can do about it but wait and see.' Yet, here you are." He winked at her. "If I was a betting man, I would have lost."

If she had ever felt shy in his presence before, she felt even more shy now. She wasn't certain what she was supposed to do or how to act. After all, he was more than her employer now. He was her beau. "I thought it was best," she said. "Didn't want any questions asked that I didn't want to answer."

He laughed and, with both hands, reached out for hers. "That I can agree with." He leaned forward and planted a soft, harmless kiss on her forehead. "Now, today we should have a new arrangement, yes? I want you to help me...outside in the barn."

"With the horses?"

"The horses, of course. But I have a surprise for you." He turned her around and, with his hands on her shoulders, guided her toward the door.

"A surprise? What kind of surprise?"

He made a gentle clicking noise with his tongue. "Now, now. Isn't patience a virtue? I seem to recall having heard that a few dozen times in my life. So, if I told you, it wouldn't be a surprise now, would it?"

"I reckon not," she conceded.

"I reckon so!" he teased.

They walked together to the barn, innocent in their closeness to each other. To an outsider, it would appear to be a young couple enjoying themselves on a beautiful spring day. That was how Sylvia felt and she could tell that Jake felt the same way. And, in that moment, as the birds chirped and the sun shone, she decided that she was doing the right thing, throwing caution to the wind to be with this amazing man...a man that made her laugh and smile and feel more special than she had ever felt before in her life.

He had made it clear that he needed her. She was convinced now, that she, too, needed him. It was a moment of release and rebirth for Sylvia and she relaxed, enjoying his teasing and gentle caresses. True to his word, he did not cross any lines of impropriety. He remained honorable, if perhaps just a little too forward at times. But she knew that there was no turning back and, at this moment, she no longer cared.

They were entering the barn and he placed his warm hands over her eyes. "Close those pretty brown eyes of yours," he said softly, his breath grazing her ear. "And no peeking." A shiver ran down her spine at his last words, spoken low and deep, his chin gently brushing against her neck. He guided her to the barn, telling her when to step up and when to duck so that she didn't hit the low doorframe. The entire time, his hands covered her eyes. But then, he didn't need to cover them anymore. She could hear what awaited her.

"Cows?"

He released her. "My surprise is ruined! How did you know?"

She couldn't stop herself from laughing at the disappointed look in his face. "I could hear them!" True to her observation, there were twelve cows lined up in the barn. They weren't the typical black and white Holsteins but the creamy tan Jersey cows with giant brown eyes and white chins. "You bought cows?" She looked at him, her face shining and her eyes bright. "Whatever for?"

He scratched as his chin and shrugged his shoulders. "Seem to recall someone telling me that dairy was a good business out here. "

"You need more than twelve cows to turn a profit!" she remarked with humor in her voice.

"But it's a start, right? And since it's only just me working the barn, I figured twelve is a good start. However, I do have one problem..."

"And that is...?"

"I don't know anything about cows."

She burst out laughing and covered her mouth with her

hands. "Poor cows!"

"Yes, poor cows."

"You're different, Jake Edwards," she remarked, her eyes still shining and bright. "Quite different." She walked along the two aisles of cows, running her hands across the cows necks and backs. Indeed, tending to the cows was one of her favorite outdoor activities. She loved listening to them chew their food and call out to each other. Each cow had their own personality, much like people. "When did you decide to do this?"

"Few weeks ago, I suppose. Remember I said I had that errand on Friday?"

"During the storm?" she asked, looking at him over the hind end of one of the cows.

"During the storm," he confirmed. "I went over to the farmer who was selling them to finalize the deal. The truck brought them over late Saturday afternoon after it cleared up some."

Saturday afternoon? She did a quick calculation in her head. That was almost 36 hours ago. "Have you milked them yet?"

He look at her with a blank expression on his face. "Was I supposed to?"

"Oh," she gasped. "We best get to work! I hope it's not too late."

Without another word, she hurried about the task at hand, explaining everything that she was doing. She asked him for certain things, a bucket, a stool, warm soapy water, and a clean rag to wash the teats. The cows watched her curiously and Jake obliged her every request. As she began milking the first cow, Sylvia talked him through the entire process, her voice soft and gentle as she pressed her cheek against the cow's flank. The cows were patient and she continued to talk to each one. The milk was hard to flow and it took Sylvia at least three cows to fill one bucket. She presumed that was because they hadn't been milked since their arrival. After the first bucket was filled, she stood up to carry it to the storage unit.

Jake guided her over to the back room where the old dairy equipment had been. She was surprised to see new equipment there, some with the tags still on it. She didn't ask any questions, just hurried to pour the milk into the container. But when she opened it, Sylvia was surprised to see milk already in it. It took a second to register and then she started to laugh. What a sight she must have been, rushing around and explaining to him about the milking! To think that he wouldn't have known that the cows needed to be milked twice a day!

She shook her head and tried to hide her smile. "No wonder they didn't produce much milk," she said. She gave him a sideways glance. "You tricked me."

"It was in good fun, dear Sylvia." He reached for the bucket and poured the contents into the storage unit. "I wanted to make certain you really knew your stuff about cows."

"Did I pass?"

"With flying colors!" He smiled at her as he handed her the bucket. "Now if you'd be so kind to wash that, I have a few things to do then I'm going into town. I'll let you alone...you can do your own thing, yes? I won't be back for lunch but I'll see you on Wednesday then, alright?" If he noticed the disappointed expression on her face, he didn't give any indication. "You'll be OK walking home. Preferably not on the road but through the field. It's dried out from the rain already. Promise?"

She nodded and, reluctantly, retreated from the milk storage room, torn between the disappointment of knowing that he would not be at the farm during the day and confusion as to why he would leave her alone. Wasn't this the time that he should want to be near her? To get to know her?

Experience told her so. Second-hand experience from watching her sisters and brothers. She knew from her older sister Ana's courtship days that she could hardly wait to sneak off to see Isaac. They tried to be so secretive but everyone knew what was happening. They looked the other way, their silence the unspoken blessing on the eventual union.

With Steve, it was different. He courted his girl, Emma, for almost a year before anyone knew about their relationship. He made up errands, drove off late at night, or simply didn't come home after church. No one knew which girl had captured his attention. After all, he had courted more than his share of girls before he seemed to settle down with his intended.

As for Emanuel, well...Sylvia smiled. Everyone saw that coming a mile away and it didn't please her parents whatsoever. There was a lot of turmoil in the house during those weeks after his announcement. After all, Shana was an Englischer and, when they first married, Emanuel didn't take the kneeling vow. But they did eventually. And it worked itself out.

So, too, would this, she told herself, retreating to the quiet of the house to get started with her day. She knew that God would take care of her. If this was the path that He intended for Sylvia, it would work itself out. She just had to have faith.

Once in the house, she went upstairs to begin cleaning the second floor, as she usually did. The narrow stairs creaked under her weight as she walked upward, holding onto the railing. She glanced into the two unused bedrooms, careful to note that nothing had been touched. She had gotten into the habit of only cleaning them once a week, seeing that no one went in there.

When she opened the door to Jake's bedroom, she noticed immediately that the room was unusually orderly. Clothes were carefully draped over the foot of the bed, the sheets were not as jumbled as usual, and the top of the gentleman's chest was not scattered with money and pieces of paper. Her eyes traveled to the place where the photo had been. To her astonishment, it was gone. In its place was a clear glass vase, small and delicate with a single white flower in it.

Without realizing it, she smiled. She walked over to the chest and reached out to touch the flower. A simple carnation. Nothing too fancy, in fact, perhaps just a little plain. But it was beautiful standing on its own.

She started at it, stroking the soft petals that had opened, each one layered behind another. It was not threatening, the perfect touch to allay her fears. That was Jake, she realized,

But as she stood there, her eyes lifted to the mirror over the dresser and she stared at her reflection. It wasn't something that she did very often, perhaps just a quick peek in the small square mirror at home when she was fixing her hair each morning.

Looking into the mirror over Jake's dresser, she saw

herself in a different light. Her hair was pulled back from her forehead in a tight bun that was pinned at the nape of her neck, a few stray strands hanging near her ears. The white prayer covering was heart shaped, a bit less conservative than some Amish folk preferred but it was acceptable in her own district. Standing between her and the reflection was the carnation, so pretty in its simplicity, so alone in that vase.

The next thing she knew, she put her head into her hands and wept. That carnation, she realized, is me.

Chapter Fourteen

For the rest of that week, Jake was hardly around the farm when she was there. She found herself both relieved and disappointed. He was always there to greet her in the morning, sometimes with two nice cups of black coffee in his hand. But, after sharing a short moment or two together, he'd excuse himself and leave. She never mentioned the flower to him but always, when she arrived, it was there. The water had been changed and it had not wilted. A reminder, she thought.

The fluttering in her chest became less frequent or, she wondered, maybe she was just getting used to it. To be truthful, she began to like the routine. He often left the farm after finishing his outdoor chores with the horses and animals. She began to realize that he was giving her much needed space. If he had crowded her, she might have wilted like a carnation will do if crowded with too many other flowers.

On both Wednesday and Friday, she walked home through the fields. She didn't mind. The sun was warm on her face and she loved the feeling of the dirt under her feet. Often, she'd take her shoes off so that she could walk barefoot through the fields. She noticed that her tracks had cut a small and narrow track through the plowed lines. She was always careful not to step on anything that was growing.

The next Sunday was another singing, this one a little further away. Sylvia was reluctant to go but, after some prodding from her brother, she consented. This time, she waited until she knew no one was watching and she slipped out of the barn door. She didn't want to risk someone asking her to ride home in his buggy. She wondered if he would be there. Perhaps he had forgotten. But, despite her trepidation, he emerged from the shadows and greeted her with a warm "Good evening. May I escort you home, dear Sylvia?"

The following week, Steve began to walk along with her to Jake's farm as he was eager to get started with the plowing of the two acres that would be designated for corn. Again, Sylvia didn't see Jake at all, except for when she brought out a fresh pitcher of tea at ten o'clock and a basket full of dinner at noon. He was dirty and sweaty, his brow getting a typical Amish farmer's tan line from where the hat had rested on his head. She tried not to smile when he took off the straw hat that he had bought in town and wiped the sweat from his face. He noticed her stifling an innocent laugh, trying to mask her pleasure and he knew exactly why. With an exaggerated effort, he fanned himself with the hat and then, ever so delicately slid it back onto his head with a carefully discreet wink in her direction.

But always, no matter what happened or who was there, she saw a fresh white carnation on the dresser. It welcomed her to his room and to his life. It symbolized his growing feelings for her as well as Sylvia's feelings for what was happening in her life.

She began to feel more comfortable, recognizing his efforts to conform as best as he could. He developed an honest friendship with Steve. They worked well together, laughing as Steve taught him how to break the field using mules and a special mule-pulled plow. That first day, Jake had borrowed Jonas' mules but, when she returned on Wednesday, she was surprised to find that he had his own pair of mules in an extension of the barn, munching on their morning hay when she arrived.

Sylvia didn't interrupt to ask about them and she tried to hide her smile when he stood between the two giant mules, one hand on each, talking gently into their rabbit-like ears. He didn't know she was behind him and she couldn't hear what he said. But the moment was tender and she backed away quietly, not wanting to break the spell.

At her own home, the talk at the dinner table was often focused on Jake's latest exploits in the field. Sylvia would listen to Steve tell grandiose stories about Jake's inexperience as a farmer. Jonas, Daniel and the two younger boys would laugh, good-naturedly but Katie often kept her eyes on Sylvia as though monitoring her daughter's reaction to any mention of their Englischer neighbor.

Too aware of her mother's keen watch, Sylvia never contributed to the discussion but sat quietly, poking at her food. While Sylvia's silence was not unusual for she had always been rather quiet, her determination to not laugh at the stories clearly concerned her mother. It disturbed Katie enough that, one Wednesday evening about midway through May, she raised the subject under the guise of the upcoming crops.

"Seems like it might be time for Sylvia to stay home, Jonas. With our own crops needing tending to and all," Katie put forth. Daniel and Steve frowned and looked at their mother. It wasn't like their mamm to voice an opinion like that at the table. Most of those discussions were kept for behind closed doors.

Jonas tugged at his beard and pursed his lips. "Well now, you must have some reason to think she should stay home, Katie."

Katie sat primly at the table, her hands folded on her

lap. "Can use all the hands that we can get. And with Steve working that corn at Mr. Edwards, there's an awful lot of work here for just you, Daniel, and the younger boys, t'is all." She looked up at her husband. "And I could sure use an extra pair of hands, too. Not begrudging Mr. Edwards the help of our dear Sylvia but he's hired two of our five remaining children. We need the help here, ja? Especially with Samuel still in school."

"Reckon you do have a point there," he said, still pulling at his beard. "Suppose I could have a talk with Edwards to see if he could make do without Sylvia during plowing and planting season. Would make it go faster for us."

Silence. Sylvia kept her eyes down but she felt her heart racing. It would be all right, she told herself. Everything would be all right. But her mother was not quite finished. "And seems like Shana will be needing an extra pair of hands soon. Sylvia's always been quite helpful with the young'ns." At that, the decision was made. Sylvia knew that her days helping Jake were over. Her father would not argue with Katie on that point. And Sylvia would be sent away for at least two months to help Shana, perhaps longer.

For the first time in almost two months, Sylvia stayed home on that Friday and helped her mother around the house. For the next two weeks, she would help her father prepare the fields for planting corn. After that, Sylvia knew there would be a long couple of days cutting, binding, and gathering the wheat shocks. She never heard about the exchange between her father and Jake. She only knew that it had taken place. Nothing further was said; there was no need for a discussion.

It was a long Saturday and even longer Sunday, sitting through a three-hour church meeting, two hour long fellowship, and helping with the evening milking. She didn't know if Jake knew where to find the singing that night. There was no way to get a message to him. By eight o'clock, she was fidgeting and anxious for Daniel to hitch up his buggy to take her to the Sunday night singing, despite his own reluctance to go.

Even at the singing, she was quiet, glancing around, forgetting the words to the songs. Leah noticed and asked if everything was all right. Sylvia shrugged and tried to smile but she was waiting for a moment to break free and leave the gathering. It was hard to do, however. There was an extra large group of Amish youths at this particular singing, probably because it was the last lull before different crops began to need harvesting and new crops needed planting. Many of the young men would be busy or helping out family members. They might be too far away to attend the local singings for a while.

"Heard you going to your brother's after the harvest," Millie said between songs.

"Who told you that?" she asked, surprised that anyone knew.

"Oh, someone," she replied casually. But her eyes gave her away when she glanced over at a group of young men standing nearby, one of whom was Sylvia's brother, Daniel. Sylvia wasn't necessarily surprised. She suspected that Daniel had fancied Millie just a little but, like Sylvia's other brothers, seemed determine to select a girl later in life. The Lapp boys were shyer than most Amish young men. Steve was the only one that had courted more than one girl for an extended period of time. Sylvia was certain that if Millie was riding home with Daniel after the singings, he, too, beginning to think about the future.

136

It dawned on Sylvia that, without Steve and without Daniel, there would only be three children left at the house. The thought sent a chill down her spine. While she now suspected that her mother was aware of the brewing situation with Jake Edwards, Sylvia also understood the intensity. When Sylvia married, her parents and the two younger boys would soon move into the *grossdaadihaus* and Jonas Jr. and Lillian would move their growing family into the larger section of the house.

For her parents, Sylvia realized, it would be the bittersweet beginning of a new stage in their life. And who would help Daed then? Certainly he couldn't plow and harvest so many acres of wheat and corn with just David and Samuel. And who would help with the daily milking? Jonas Jr. was busy with his own business, the carpentry shop at the back of the property. Sylvia had never considered this before and the thought troubled her.

"You look far away," Leah whispered. "Where are you?"

Millie nudged her. "Ja, where are you?"

Brought back to the moment by her friends, Sylvia tried to smile. "Just thinking," she replied.

"Thinking about whoever you been riding home with after the singings?" Millie teased. Sylvia blushed and looked away. "We can't figure out who it is," she whispered. "But you sure do disappear awful early. Left Adam Knoeffer terribly *ferhoodled* when he was looking for you."

"Millie! Now you leave her be," Leah scolded gently. "Sylvia, never you mind her. She's just frightfully fit that she doesn't know who it is but it's none of her business."

It concerned Sylvia that her two dear friends were

talking about her and her private business. But she didn't say anything. It wasn't her style to confront others so she turned the other cheek and tried to participate more in the singings, giving more appearance to having fun than she actually felt. However, Millie's comment about Adam Knoeffer certainly had her on edge and she made certain to avoid him, not wanting to have to let him down should he ask to give her a ride. Of course, she didn't know if Jake was coming or not but she sure knew she didn't want to accept a ride with any of the young Amish men at the singing.

It was only nine o'clock when she excused herself to visit the house bathroom. She had figured that she'd start making her escape around ten, the normal time that she had been sneaking out of the barn, her disappearance apparently not as unnoticed as she had hoped. But on her way back from the farmhouse, she saw him, leaning against the far corner of the barn. He didn't call for her and she didn't wave or acknowledge his presence. Instead, she quickened her pace and hurried into the shadows where he had been waiting. He said nothing, just reached for her hand and held it gently in his as they began to walk into the darkness and away from the singing that seemed to bid them farewell.

It would be a longer walk than usual since the singing was further away. Sylvia didn't mind, as long as Jake was by her side. She didn't speak, waiting for him to say something first. But for the first few minutes, the silence remained. Their shoes made crunching noises against the loose gravel of the macadam. But, other than the crickets singing their spring tune, the night was silent.

"It's been a long week, Sylvia," he said, finally breaking the ice.

"Yes," she agreed.

"We missed you," he said, giving her hand a strong squeeze.

"We?"

He laughed. "The cows. The horses. Those ornery mules." He paused. "And me. I missed you." He stopped walking and held her at arm's length. In the darkness, she could see his silhouette but not much more. The moon was tucked behind some sheer clouds, which cast a blue glow around them. He rubbed her arms with his hands. "It'll be a long summer if you aren't there."

"It'll be even longer, Jake," she whispered.

"Longer?"

She nodded, not knowing if he could see her. "My sister-in-law...she's about to have another baby. They want me to go stay with her for a few months. To help with her little ones."

"Months." The word was spoken with no emotion.

"I suppose it will go by quickly," she added, but she didn't believe what she said.

"I suppose." He was quiet. Too quiet. His mood was more somber than usual. She lifted her eyes to look at his face. At that moment, there was a break in the clouds and the light from the moon shone down on the couple. He stared back at her and pulled her closer to him. Then, with just one hand, he removed her prayer cap and, with his other hand, he worked his fingers through her bun, gently removing the pins that kept it in place.

She kept her face tilted toward him but shut her eyes. Never had anyone outside of her family touched her hair or seen her with it down. The intimacy of the moment sent soft waves throughout her body and she shivered. When her hair was down, he stroked it, amazed at how long it was, almost to her waist. It was soft and silky, virgin hair that had never been cut. He leaned forward and nuzzled his face into it, smelling the fresh clean scent. His embrace engulfed her and she pressed her cheek against his shoulder.

"Jake," she whispered.

"Come," he replied with a hoarse voice as he forced himself to release her and continue walking. "This time, I have my truck parked just up the road." He paused. "Good thing. I need to get you home."

"But..." She stopped herself. It was so early. Her parents would wonder why she was home before eleven if she was, indeed, courting someone. Plus, she had hoped to spend more time with him, especially after they had not seen each other during the week. Each hour had passed so painfully slow. There were moments when all she could do was retreat to a part of the farm where no one would be in order to have herself a good cry. She was almost willing to throw away everything, just walk away to be with him. And now...she bit her lip, fighting the tears...now that they were finally together, he wanted to take her home? It didn't make sense.

"I don't trust myself, Sylvia," he said, his voice still thick and low. "And I won't do that to you."

"I don't understand," she said, her words barely audible.

"I know you don't, Sylvia. And that's part of the beauty of you." He laid his arm across her shoulder, her hair still hanging free and entwined in his fingers. He tugged playfully at one of the strands. "I'm trying to conform to your world, you see...instead of forcing you to conform to mine."

They were at the truck and she took a deep breath. "Is there a difference anymore? Are our worlds so different now?" She reached for the door handle. "I think they have already converged, ja?"

As she tried to open the door, he put his hand out and stopped it. Shutting it behind her, he pressed against her, pushing her back until she was leaning against the truck. His one hand was still over her head, blocking an escape as he tilted her chin up with his free hand. "Let me give you a taste of where I come from and what courtship is about," he murmured, his voice soft as he lowered his mouth onto hers.

She felt the warm, moist pressure of his lips as he gave her a passionate kiss that she had only seen on the theater screen. She felt herself weaken against the truck, her body slowly melting against his as he probed and sought her own passion. Shutting her eyes, she found herself giving way to him, wishing that she didn't feel so free and liberated, her hair hanging over her shoulders, pieces of it brushing against his cheek and hers. His thumb stroked her neck as he kissed her, holding her face steady. When he finally pulled back, she was breathless and weak. Softly, he kissed the tip of her nose and then her forehead.

"To the Plain people, that is considered a sin, ja?" he asked, emphasizing the word *ja*. "To my people, that is just the beginning of the most beautiful relationship between a man and woman. Now, unless you want to see what happens after the beginning, I suggest that you get in the truck so I can take you home, dear Sylvia. Our worlds have yet to truly converge, wouldn't you agree?"

Without any further questions, she did as he commanded. Her knees were weak, her face was flushed, her pulse was rapidly pumping the burning blood that flowed through her veins. The words of her mother echoed in her mind whenever she had preached *"Best to save kissing for marriage."* She had always been taught that the lustful compromise of any type of intimacy could get in the way of a proper courtship. After all, this was a time when a couple determined how compatible they were from a practical perspective.

Sexual intimacy, even of the somewhat benign nature that they had just shared, aroused sensual thoughts that detracted from the real questions that needed to be asked during courtship. She understood that better than ever, as all she could think about was the powerful feelings that Jake Edwards had instilled in her with that one passionate kiss. Yet the romantic passion that he had introduced to her life had clearly shown her the other side of the world, the world that she had been safely shielded from experiencing. Now, she thought as she looked out the window as he drove her home, her hand entwined with Jake's, she understood why.

Chapter Fifteen

For the next few weeks, Sylvia worked alongside her father and Daniel as they finished plowing the backfield and prepared for planting the acres of corn. There were two crops, one for silage, which was planted along the outer perimeter and one for eating which would be harvested later and, therefore, was planted within the inner section. Samuel would soon be finished with schooling for the year and would join the men in the fields in time for the planting, none too soon in Sylvia's mind.

The days began at 5am and ended well into the night. There were no singings on those Sundays, not for Sylvia, anyway. She was exhausted and found herself sleeping on the sofa in her parents' reading room. Her mother gently shook her awake, telling her that it was time for her to go to bed. Sylvia didn't argue. Her muscles ached, her hands were sore, and her heart felt heavy. She hadn't seen Jake since that night after the singing. He haunted her thoughts and she woke most mornings knowing that she had spent her hours sleeping in his presence, if only in her dreams.

The only word she had about Jake came from Steve who, while finished planting the corn crop on the rented acre at Jake's farm, often went over to help him with the milking or other chores, although Sylvia suspected it was more to watch for the budding shoots of corn. She did her best to look disinterested in any news but, inside, she hung on every word. Apparently the cows were doing well and Steve commented how fastidious Jake was about keeping the barn clean.

"Who ever heard of a barn without cobwebs?" he

laughed one night.

Sylvia forced a smile but she didn't feel that humor. She waited until the end of the meal to help clear the table and wash the dishes, answering any questions that were asked of her but remaining unusually silent, even for her. A few times, her mother asked if she was feeling well and Sylvia managed a simple nod with a forced smile. But, beyond that, she remained aloof and distant, her mind traveling a mile down the road to another farm where she imagined Jake sitting alone, at the table in the kitchen, eating his own meal.

By the beginning of June, the weather was warm and the days were suddenly not as full of activities. The corn was planted and wouldn't be harvested for at least four months. The winter wheat was beginning to ripen but still needed another month until it was time to be cut. Still, there was no talk of Sylvia returning to Jake's farm to help him. Sylvia spent her days helping her mother clean, cook, and do laundry. When the sun began to set in the sky, she would weed the garden until it was time for the evening milking. Often she would stare into the horizon, wondering what Jake was doing at that exact minute...wondering if he was thinking about her. But she had no way of knowing and no way of communicating with him.

The upcoming church Sunday was to be held at their farm. Sylvia knew exactly what that meant. Since the services rotated among the members' homes, it meant that at least once, although sometimes twice, a year, the church community would gather at the Lapp farm for worship and fellowship. It also meant that Katie would be frantic cleaning the house and the barn. During the summer months, they often would gather in the barns where it was cooler. But the fellowship time meant that people would be in the house as well.

During the days leading up to the Sunday worship, Lillian came over to help both Katie and Sylvia. They scrubbed floors and baseboard, wiped the walls, and dusted every nook and cranny of the house. Even when Sylvia thought the house was clean, her mother found other areas to clean. It was a never ending process to make certain that no one would be able to fault Katie's housekeeping when they attended the Sunday service.

Sylvia and Daniel took turns cutting the grass with the push mower, making certain to sweep up the clippings and drag them to the refuse pile behind the mule shed. They cleared a large area in the barn where the hay was usually stored to make way for the church wagon, a large rectangular wagon that held all of the benches and songbooks. It would sit on their property for the next two weeks until Jonas took it over to the next member's house for hosting the service.

Then there was the cooking. Sylvia would have done anything to escape the heat of the kitchen as her mother cooked pot after pot of apples for applesauce and baked loaf after loaf of bread. There were pies to bake, beans to shuck, and beets to peel. It never seemed to stop and Sylvia just wanted to disappear to the outside, to feel the sun on her face and dirt under her feet. But her mother needed help and complaining wasn't in Sylvia's nature. So, she went about her chores without saying a word.

By the time Sunday finally came, Sylvia was so grateful that she was actually happy for the first time in weeks. It felt good to see her friends. It had been almost three weeks since she had attended the last singing. Daniel had asked her if she wanted to attend one the week before but Sylvia decided against it. She was exhausted from all of the work and from the emotional turmoil of missing Jake. Besides, she didn't want anyone to ask her for a ride home since Jake certainly wouldn't know where the singing was.

Inside the barn, the women sat on one side and the men on the other. Older and married women and men sat toward the front while the unmarried youths sat behind them. Sylvia sat at the end, being an unbaptized member of the church. She didn't mind; she was closer to the door and a cool breeze. She listened as one of the Amish men began to sing from the *Ausbund*. She shut her eyes and listened as the rest of the congregation began to sing with him. Their words were low and drawn out, creating a very simple harmony with so many variations that they almost blended into one. She waited until they finished the first song and began the second, the *Loblied*, to join them.

Sylvia watched as the church elders left the barn. They left to discuss who would preach the sermons that day. It was always decided the day of the service, a way for God to lead them. While she would never have admitted it out loud, Sylvia did enjoy the preaching by Elder Miller much more than the others. She secretly hoped that the lot fell to him that day.

There would be two sermons, a short one followed by more singing then a longer one, also followed by more singing. At the end, they would discuss any church or community business. It would take about three hours to complete the service and then the real work began. The women would serve the congregation in shifts. Sylvia wouldn't eat until almost 1:30, if she was lucky, as she'd be busy serving first the men, then the women, then the rest of the congregation. As the daughter of the host family, she would probably be the last to eat today. But she had no appetite. She hadn't for days.

As luck would have it, Elder Miller was not one of the preachers on that day. Sylvia tried to sit still during the sermons but her back began to hurt and the heat was making her sleepy. She was thankful for Leah sitting next to her who accidentally kicked her foot when she shifted her weight. It gave Sylvia enough of a jolt to waken up before she actually fell asleep. The final sermon was over and the congregation began to sing a final song from the *Ausbund*. The words flowed around the barn, so gentle and peaceful. The harmony moved throughout the people like a gentle wave at the beach. It rippled and comforted. It was one of Sylvia's favorite parts of Church Sunday.

The elders stood at the front of the congregation, announcing that there was some church news. Elder Miller requested that any visitors might retire outside of the barn for this part of the service. Sylvia glanced at Leah then looked around. It was rare that they had visitors. And Sylvia wasn't the only one wondering who was attending their service that day.

But then she saw him. Jake. He was standing at the back of the church among the unbaptized men. Daniel was next to him. Sylvia tried to maintain her composure, especially when he caught her look and smiled at her. But, just as quick as she saw him, he hurried out of the barn with Daniel at his side. Since Daniel hadn't taken the kneeling vow yet, he had to leave with the others.

Leah followed Sylvia's gaze, just as amazed. "Who's that?" she whispered.

Sylvia felt her heart pounding inside of her chest. Her eyes followed him as he walked outside. He was dressed plain enough, although clearly not Amish. He even held a black wide brimmed hat in his hand. "Our new neighbor."

"The widower?" she asked, her tone sounding more surprised than actually asking the question.

Sylvia didn't answer but just nodded her head. When Jake disappeared, she turned to face the front of the gathering but she wasn't really paying attention. She couldn't imagine what Jake was doing at the church service. How had he known? People didn't just show up at an Amish service. Who would have invited him? Perhaps Steve, she thought.

She reached up to smooth her hair back, checking to make certain that there were no stray strands. She was glad that she had worn her blue dress today. It was the newest one that she had. And she didn't think that he had ever seen her in that color before.

Outside, there were almost two hundred people mingling about, waiting as the benches were rearranged for the fellowship time. Sylvia tried to find Jake in the crowd but she was hustled into the kitchen too quickly to find him. She could only hope that he stayed for socializing. It was the only way that she would get to speak with him, if at all.

Unfortunately, once inside the kitchen, Katie seemed to have too much for her to do that required inside work. Anything that needed to be done outside, Katie directed others to do instead. Sylvia felt her own frustration begin to rise, sensing that her mother was doing this on purpose. But Sylvia had no recourse. She would never challenge her mother nor accuse her of something so sinister as deliberately keeping her daughter away from Jake. Not only would that be improper, dishonoring her mother like that, it would also confirm any suspicions that her mother apparently had.

By the time Sylvia finally managed to get outside, the

crowd had slowly begun to thin out. Many of the black buggies that had been hitched to the back fence were gone. The long tables were devoid of people but there were plenty of dirty dishes and glasses remaining. She sighed, searching the crowds for the sole non-Amish man among the Amish men. But she didn't see him. The dull ache returned to her chest and, for the briefest of moments, she almost felt like crying.

"Sylvia?" Leah asked. "What's wrong?"

Sylvia turned around, forcing a smile yet again. "Nothing at all."

Her friend smiled back. "I'll help you clean this. Many hands..."

"...make light the work," Sylvia finished what Leah had started. They both laughed and began gathering the dirty remains from the fellowship meal.

Most of the women were outside, socializing while seated in chairs under the shade of the barn. Leah and Sylvia set about washing the piles of dishes. Other young girls carried in more while they worked. Leah took advantage of the emptiness and asked, "What was the widower doing here?"

Sylvia handed Leah the plate she had just washed. "I don't know."

"Aren't you still working there?"

Sylvia shook her head. "Not for two...no, three weeks past. I've been helping around here. Planting corn, cleaning house."

"He's so young! Do you know what happened to his wife?"

Did she? Sylvia wasn't certain how to answer that. "I think he said it was an accident. I suppose a car accident. Daed said it was four or five years ago but I don't know the particulars."

Leah gasped. "How awful! He must've been awful torn up."

"I wouldn't know," she answered truthfully.

They finished the plates, stacking them neatly on the table and began tackling the glasses and silverware. It took them almost an hour to wash everything. As fast as they washed the dishes, more kept arriving from outside. Since everyone ate in shifts, the work seemed endless. After everyone had eaten, it was time to clean the serving bowls. Then there were the dessert dishes to wash. Eventually, a few of the women came inside and relieved the younger women of the duties, shooing them outside to socialize and enjoy the beautiful weather with a plate of food that someone had been thoughtful enough to set aside for them.

Leah and Sylvia walked toward the barn, where the women were still sitting in their circle, talking amongst themselves. Inside the barn, there were men gathered. Sylvia wondered if Jake was among them. However, she knew that it would be improper to join them. So, Lean and Sylvia sat behind the older women, listening to their stories about friends, family, and neighbors while they ate. By 2:30, most of the people had left. Leah said her goodbyes and Sylvia was left alone. She hadn't been able to see Jake beyond that moment in the barn. It left her feeling emptier than she realized. She was a vessel and he had filled her with the outside world, a world full of feelings than she never knew existed.

Yet, she also knew that tonight was another singing, this time at their own farm. Had he heard? Did he know? More importantly, would he come for her? She didn't need a buggy ride home, that was true. If she didn't attend this one, the bishop would surely wonder why, being that she was of courting age. So, when it was time for the youths to gather in the barn, she slipped out of the door and walked across the driveway to join them. Her heart wasn't in it and she seemed jittery, even to herself. During the *a capella* songs, she looked at the barn door, wondering if she might see a shadow pass.

"What's wrong with you tonight?" Leah asked, her voice full of genuine concern. "Feeling poorly still?"

Sylvia shook her head and tried to smile. "Just tired, tis all. Been a long week with the wheat cutting."

"Ja, understand that," Leah replied. She fanned herself with her hand. "It's hot in here. Why don't we step outside while they are between songs?"

Outside, the sky was dark and the moon was but a slight crescent. Stars twinkled down on them as they stood in the cooler night air. Out in the paddock, the cows grazed, the soft mooing breaking the cicadas' nightly song. Leah sighed and leaned against the side of the barn. "Strange that widower," she said.

Sylvia snapped her attention in Leah's direction. "The widower?"

"Been thinking about that, being so young and all, with a wife that's gone. Must be powerful lonely."

She bit her lower lip, wanting to say so much but knowing that she couldn't. She didn't want to betray her feelings, not even to her good friend, Leah. "Suppose it must be."

"I'm surprised the bishop didn't object to you working

for him."

Sylvia gasped. "Why Leah!"

Leah held up her hand. "I'm not saying people are talking but it sure could have started the story mill. Mayhaps best you aren't working there anymore, ja?"

No, Sylvia wanted to yell. No, it's not best! She hated being separated from him, hated not seeing him during the week. The time apart was agonizing, making the bond between them even stronger. In just a few short months, her life had changed. She had always known that she would take the kneeling vow when she found a good Amish man that she was to marry. But now? How could she take the kneeling vow for anyone other than Jake? She'd have to confess to the love she felt. She'd have to confess to the kisses they shared. Despite not having been baptized, the community would feel scandalized by her intimacy with this man. Yet, Sylvia couldn't stop thinking about being near him again.

"Mayhaps," she agreed reluctantly.

Chapter Sixteen

By the end of June, the winter wheat was ready to be cut, bundled, and shocked. Sylvia knew that it would be a week of long labor, harder than the weeks she had spent plowing the field with her father and Daniel when they were getting ready to plant the corn. Yet, she also knew that it would be rewarding. It was truly her favorite time of year...a time to enjoy the outdoors, family, and the beauty of God's world.

The sun was bright and the weather seemed to be working with them. Jonas had heard that rain was forecasted for the following week and he wanted the cutting done early in order to not be too late. It needed time to dry out prior to going to market.

Katie made an extra large breakfast for everyone on the Monday morning when they would begin cutting the wheat. Eggs, sausage, potatoes, biscuits, and gravy. Steve, Daniel, and the boys ate heartily, knowing that they would need the extra energy. Sylvia picked at her food, her appetite having disappeared over the past few weeks.

"Going to be a long week," Jonas said as he reached for a third biscuit. "Have to beat that rain, though."

Katie nodded. "Be glad to have the wheat cut and sold, that's for certain." She nudged Sylvia's arm. "Feeling poorly, Sylvia? You've hardly ate anything."

Sylvia looked up from her plate. She shook her head and began poking at the eggs. "Sorry Mamm," she said.

"I asked some of the neighbors to come help. Whitey will be joining us at dinner," Jonas said as he wiped his mouth and stood up, getting ready to leave the house in order to harness the mules. "Need all the hands we can get, ja?"

Sylvia helped her mother clean the breakfast dishes and set the table for dinner so that Katie had less work to do for the noon meal. Then, she hurried outside to help the men. She was glad that she'd be working in the fields all week. It was a relief to escape the house. When she was outside, she felt much more peaceful than inside. It gave her time to think and reflect.

She hadn't seen Jake in over two weeks. When she thought about him, she felt her throat start to constrict and the threat of tears peeked at the corner of her eyes. Those two weeks had seemed like two months. And, being that it had been the Sunday service, she hadn't been able to speak to him. His absence from her life created a hollow feeling inside of her chest. She had never felt so alone and miserable.

Outside, she stood on the edge of the porch for a moment. It was early enough to not be too hot but she could tell that it would be a long day. By noon, the sun would be overhead and the mixture of heat with work would make them all suffer. Her hair was covered with a blue bandana and her work dress already a bit dirty from the morning milking. She walked out to the field to help her brothers and father hook up the mules to the binder.

In the distance, she heard the engine of an automobile and the sound of tires on gravel. She looked up and caught her breath when she saw Jake's truck pull into the driveway. She glanced at her father who didn't seem to notice. What was he doing here? He was dressed in work clothes and strode across the field with a purpose in mind.

With her mouth hanging open, Sylvia watched as he

154

walked up to Jonas and shook her daed's hand. "Glad I'm able to help, Jonas. You just tell me what I need to do," he said.

The flutters were back inside of her chest. Did that mean that Jake Edwards was going to be helping them with the cutting of the wheat? If so, he'd be there every day that week. She'd be working side-by-side with Jake. She told herself to calm down and slow her breathing before anyone noticed how excited she had become. Without knowing it, she hand went to her head, smoothing back her hair under the bandana that she wore to cover her head.

"Willkumm," her father called out when he saw Jake crossing the field. "Glad you could help us, Jake! The more hands, the better."

He laughed and shook Jonas' hand. "Seems only fair since you've lent me Sylvia and Steve so often." He glanced at Sylvia. "Although I haven't seen much of Sylvia for a while. How are you doing?" She didn't answer, just smiled and hurried back to help with the mules.

A few more neighbors came over and Jonas Jr. took off work from the carpentry shop to help out. Katie watched Lillian's children so that she, too, could join in the binding of the wheat. With all hands together, it would take four days to cut, bind, and shock the ten acres of wheat. Without everyone's help, it would have taken almost two weeks. The work was hard under the late June sun but the camaraderie made it fun. Whitey was always good for a few good, clean jokes and Jake shared some of his own stories about mishaps around the farm. He told his stories with such enthusiasm and embellishment that everyone was laughing, including himself, before he got to the end of the stories.

155

For dinner, they retreated to the house where Katie had a long table set up with food to rejuvenate them for the afternoon work: fresh biscuits, fried chicken, potato salad, and coleslaw. By the time the meal was over, every plate was empty and there was limited time for catching up before the afternoon chores commenced.

Whitey enjoyed a hot cup of black coffee, leaning back in his chair as he looked across the table at Jake. "Well, son, how's life as a gentleman farmer treating you? You making out OK over there, Englische?" He winked at Sylvia and Lillian.

Jake laughed. "I think you can tell how I'm making out from my stories this morning." The rest of the table laughed with him. "It'll come back to me, though, seeing that farming is in my blood. I told the Lapps about how that farm belonged to my grandfather way back. It was only a matter of time before someone came back to give it a try."

Never one to shy away from an unasked question, Whitey gave a familiar tug at his beard and ventured forward by asking it. "And why exactly is it that you want to give it a try, Englische?"

The laughter died down and everyone seemed to stare at Jake. It was the question of the hour, the one that was on everyone's lips. No one had been brazen enough to ask yet, although tongues were certainly wagging. Of that, Sylvia was certain. She had not heard the questions or the gossip but it was clear that everyone in the community had been talking about this strange new neighbor who had appeared out of no where to take on the responsibility of rejuvenating a forgotten farm.

For the briefest of seconds, Jake hesitated. Everyone

was staring at him, waiting for his answer. He glanced at Sylvia and smiled before turning his focus back to Whitey. "I know plenty of folk have been wondering that same question, for sure. I don't mind telling the tale...I have nothing to hide."

He sipped at his own cup of coffee, the pause giving him a moment to figure out how to formulate the words. Everyone was silent, waiting to hear the story. There was a sudden aura of seriousness that fell over the group and, despite trying to act disinterested, Sylvia found herself leaning forward, eagerly anticipating Jake's next words.

He looked up from his coffee cup and sighed. "I worked in finance on Wall Street but spent the weekends at our family house in Connecticut. Had horses out there." He looked over at Jonas. "When my grandfather left Leola, that's where he went. Connecticut. He started a wonderful horse farm. There's nice land there. He bred standardbred horses. Sold many of them right back here to his former brethren." He took a deep breath. "I'm the last of the family and was torn between the country life and the finance district. When my wife was killed in an accident..." He sighed, pushing his cup forward on the table. "Well, let's just say that there's no amount of work or wealth that is worth that type of sacrifice. I couldn't go back to the city. I walked away from the job and focused on the farm but it was still surrounded by the hustle and bustle of city life, I suppose. Now that I look at it, I returned to my roots for the very reason that my grandfather left." He looked up. "To find myself."

"And have you, Englische?" Whitey asked.

Jake raised his eyebrows. "That is the question, isn't it?" He glanced around the room. Everyone was watching him. His eyes lingered briefly on Sylvia's. "I think so." He smiled and looked back at Whitey. "And if not, I'm well on my way."

Jonas cleared his throat and placed both hands on the edge of the table. "Well, Jake, if you believe in the good Lord, He'll take care of you. He'll show you the path." He paused. "And that path, right now, is leading us back into the field so that we can finish cutting and binding that wheat to feed His children." Everyone laughed, the somber moment graciously broken.

During that week, despite the hard work, Sylvia found herself looking forward to each morning. Knowing that Jake would be there made the day extra special. She took extra care with her appearance, despite wearing her old work clothes. If anyone noticed the extra spring to her step and sparkle in her eyes, no one mentioned it. She tried not to engage too much with Jake in the field. But, sure enough, when he arrived, he always had a kind word for her and, as often as possible, would help her with the task at hand.

On Wednesday, she found herself working alongside Jake when the others were further away. He spared her a smile and a wink. "You getting along alright, dear Sylvia?"

She glanced around, making certain no one could hear them. "Ja," she answered, feeling shy in his presence once again.

"I was hoping to see you later."

She shook her head. "I can't do that, Jake."

Shrugging his shoulders, he asked, "Why not?" He lowered his voice and leaned closer to her. "Let everyone go to sleep then slip out. Just for a short while, Sylvia. I need to see you." He glanced over his shoulder before he added, "Just to talk to you without worrying that anyone will hear us."

It seemed so simple to him. In truth, Sylvia knew that

158

many Amish youths would sneak out when the lights were darkened to spend time with their sweethearts. But it wasn't something she had ever thought to do. "Please don't..." she started. But then, her heart began to flutter as she remembered their kisses. She needed to see him just as badly as he needed to see her. "I can try," she relented.

Later that evening, Sylvia waited patiently for her parents to close their bedroom door for the night. When she thought she heard the gentle sound of her father snoring, she figured that it was safe. Quietly, she climbed down the stairs and left the house through the kitchen door. He had told her that he would be waiting for her, down by the mailbox. Sure enough, when she walked down the lane, feeling both scared and exhilarated at the same time, he was leaning against a tree by the end of the driveway.

Seeing him standing there, his body just a dark shadow in the night, made her uncomfortable. She wasn't certain how to greet him. The last time that they had been alone had been the night had kissed her so passionately when he brought her home from the singing. Part of her wanted to run into his arms but that wasn't something she was comfortable doing. So, when he reached out his hand for her, a simple gesture that seemed safe enough, she found herself taking it into her own.

He made the decision for her by pulling her into his arms. A startled gasp escaped from her lips but he didn't try to kiss her. Instead, he only held her tightly. There was something about being pressed against his body, her cheek against his shoulder. She relaxed, shutting her eyes and just breathing. She could smell him, the familiar scent of work mixed with cologne. It was a fresh smell that caused her pulse to quicken once again.

"Sylvia, it's not the same when you are not there," he murmured into her ear.

There was no response that she could give. It wasn't likely that she'd be returning to help him in the near future...if ever. She suspected that her mother would make certain of that.

Jake took a deep breath. "I need to know something, Sylvia." He pulled away so that he could look down into her face. "Would you answer me one question? Just one?"

The intensity of his expression caused her to reply with a solemn nod. "As long as I can, Jake, I will answer." Whatever was so important to him, she knew that she must give him that much.

"Do you have the same powerful feelings about me as I do about you?"

It was a question that she asked herself every day for weeks. What were these feelings that she had for Jake Edwards? In the beginning, she wasn't certain that he had any feelings for her, other than just being friendly. After all, he was Englische and she didn't interact with them enough to know how they behaved. But he had made it increasing apparent that his attraction was of a much more intimate nature. Despite that, she didn't know what he actually felt.

"I don't know how to answer that, Jake." When he didn't respond, she continued slowly. "How can I say I feel something like you do? You are asking me to presume to know how you feel."

He chuckled under his breath. "Clever."

She continued. "But I do know one thing and that is we both come from such different worlds."

"We know that they have collided, Sylvia."

"And what does that mean? It either means something or nothing. And if it's something, one of us has to make a big decision, ja?"

Hesitating, she realized the impact of her own words. If it was nothing, her world was ruined. Word would certainly begin circulating that Sylvia had spent too much time with an older Englische man, and a widower at that, during her final years of her *rumspringa*. If it meant something, she would have to leave the Amish or Jake would have to join. The ramifications of this relationship were indeed monumental. No, she thought. Life altering.

"Well," he said, breaking the silence. "I suppose we both have a lot to think about then, yes?" He brushed his thumb across her cheek and smiled. "Now, I suspect you should be going...as should I. We have a long day tomorrow and I don't want you too exhausted." He walked her back to the mailbox and bid her goodnight with a soft kiss. "Until tomorrow, dear Sylvia."

He watched her walk down the dark driveway and waited until he thought that he heard the house door shut before beginning the walk back to his own house. He preferred to walk, using the time to sort his thoughts and clear his head. In the meantime, she hurried upstairs and slipped into her bedroom. She lay in bed, pretending that she was walking next to him until she was certain he had reached the farm and was tucked into his own bed. Only then did she try to get some sleep. It was easier to do, knowing that Jake would be back in the morning to spend the day helping with the wheat.

By the end of the week, there were more rows of wheat

shocks standing than Sylvia cared to count. They stood majestically beneath the sun, waiting to dry out in time for the thrashing. Jake had showed up every day, offering his help, which was gladly accepted by Jonas.

On the other hand, Sylvia noticed a severe change in her mother's demeanor. Her mamm was less lively and talkative than she normally would be during the dinner hour. With her lips pressed tightly together, she would greet Jake politely but that was the end of her interactions. Jake didn't seem to notice, nor did Sylvia's brothers. Instead, Jake would share stories and make her brothers laugh. Even Jonas seemed to enjoy his company. Sylvia would try to avoid laughing at his stories but, even she couldn't keep herself from smiling. Yet, the more everyone seemed to enjoy Jake's presence, the more withdrawn and distracted Katie became.

The following morning, they began thrashing the wheat. No one was surprised to see Jake show up in the morning, walking across the field to join the work party. He found his place next to Sylvia and helped her carrying the bundled wheat toward the thrashing machine. It wasn't hard work but it was hot with the sun overhead.

The dry wheat felt splintery in their hands. Once, Sylvia cut her hand and it started to bleed. Jake hurried to her side and leaned down, taking her hand in his. The way that he handled her was gentle and caring. He dabbed at the blood with the edge of his shirt until the cut stopped bleeding.

"You should bandage that," he said, unaware that Sylvia's father was watching the scene.

"It's fine, Jake." She pulled her hand from his, too aware that her father had seen Jake take her hand in his, even if only out of concern. "Really."

"It'll get infected," he replied, concerned. "And, trust me, that hurts."

That day, during the dinner hour, it was Jonas as well as Katie who seemed to quietly observe the interactions at the table. They watched as Jake told funny stories and laughed with Steve and Daniel. Occasionally, he would turn to Sylvia, asking her a question or trying to include her in the stories. She resisted, too aware that they were being watched. She tried to keep her expression neutral and her eyes downcast. Yet the more comfortable her brothers were with Jake, the more stress she felt. It was unlike either of them to share such camaraderie with a non-Amish man.

Jonas stood up to leave the kitchen table for the afternoon work. He took a deep breath and exhaled. "Right *gut* food to give strength for finishing the work, ja?" He laughed good-naturedly but his eyes did not crinkle and sparkle like they normally did. "Mayhaps you could help your mother this afternoon, Sylvia. I think we have enough hands in the field and she could use a spare set inside."

Sylvia bit her lip but held back from asking questions about this seemingly rash decision. "Yes, Daed," she said softly.

It wasn't hard to see that she wasn't the only one disappointed. Jake became tense as he sat in the chair next to her. But, like Sylvia, he kept his silence. Daniel and Steve stood up to join Jonas as he began to walk out of the house. For a moment, Jake didn't move. She wanted to tell him to go with them but she knew her mother would hear. It was clear that her parents didn't need more to feed their suspicions. So, she stood up and began clearing the dirty dishes.

Reluctantly, Jake took that as his cue. As he stood to leave, he made certain to approach Katie. "Thank you again, ma'am," he said politely. "Working your fields is sure worth it just to have some fellowship." Katie smiled but didn't reply.

After the men left and Sylvia was finished clearing the table, she stood by her mother at the sink. Katie washed while Sylvia dried the dishes. There was a pit in Sylvia's stomach. How she longed to be outside, working next to Jake. The words from the other night kept racing through her head. Was this something or nothing? To her, she knew that it was something. So it was up to Jake to decide now what it was to him. And then, presuming that he, too, felt that it was something, they both had to make a decision. It was a decision that meant significant change for both of them.

"I'll only be saying this once," Katie said, interrupting her daughter's thoughts. "Watch carefully where you walk, daughter. There are many roads that do not allow for turning around."

Sylvia tried to steady her breathing. She felt resentment swell inside of her chest but pushed it away. Her mother was only doing what she felt was best to protect her child, to protect her family, and to protect her church. But Sylvia couldn't help feeling resentment toward the intrusion in her life. After all, she reminded herself, she wasn't a baptized member of the church and, therefore, could make her own decisions. That was the point of *rumspringa*...to experience some of the world in order to make decisions about joining the church. In her mind, she had the right to travel down any road. If there was no U-turn allowed, that was a consequence that she was willing to accept.

There were no more words between them while they

164

finished the afternoon chores.

Chapter Seventeen

It was the next morning when her father made the big announcement as Sylvia was clearing the breakfast dishes. "I'll be hitching up the buggy now," he started. "Sylvia, you should pack your things for visiting a spell with Emanuel and Shana."

Sylvia stood where she was, the dirty plates in her hands, hovering over the sink. She could hardly believe her ears. She turned around and saw him staring at her, his gaze steady and hard. She looked at her mother but Katie was staring at her hands, which were folded neatly in her lap. Both Steve, Daniel, and her two younger brothers seemed just as surprised. They looked back and forth from their father and mother to Sylvia. It was unspoken but obvious. Something had happened for Sylvia to be sent away so quickly and without any discussion. Sylvia suspected that they knew but she knew the suspicion alone didn't prompt such a hasty action on the part of her parents.

Her youngest brother, never one to be too shy, looked at his father. "What did Sylvia do?"

"Samuel," his mother reprimanded.

"Must've been right awful to be sent away," he mumbled.

"Samuel!"

Sylvia felt the color flood to her cheeks. She felt humiliated and sinful, as though she has truly done something wrong. However, without questioning her father, Sylvia hurried upstairs to her room, reluctantly packing a satchel. But her head began to pound, confused at what was happening.

This was unlike her parents, she knew that. Nothing was done last minute or without some discussion. In her heart, she knew this had to do with Jake Edwards. They had sensed his feelings toward her and hers toward him. Her mamm had warned her clearly enough but her daed must have decided it was not enough. So, her parents were separating Jake and Sylvia, giving them distance in the hope that the flame would flicker and die. Sylvia fought back tears, knowing that she had no way of telling Jake where she was going or how to find her. And, if her instincts were correct, her parents would instruct Steve and Daniel to not disclose that information.

The ride to Emanuel's farm seemed to take hours. She stared idly out the buggy window, her mind racing with thoughts. She knew that he would be looking for her after the singing on Sunday. What would he think when she wasn't there? Would he think she didn't care? No, she scolded herself. He knew better than that. How long was she supposed to stay with Emanuel and Shana? Weeks? No, she told herself. Likely it would be months. Shana wasn't due for a while yet. The bulk of the help would be needed after the baby came. How would she survive that long without Jake?

When Shana opened the door, she seemed surprised to see her younger sister-in-law standing before her. Emanuel, on the other hand, greeted her as if he was expecting her. Shana didn't question her husband but gave him a curious look before she welcomed Sylvia with a warm hug. "It's always a pleasure to have you," she said. "The children will be quite pleased and I can always use the extra pair of hands." She wasn't due for another six weeks but her two other children, Noah and Hannah, could certainly wear her out.

No one needed to tell Sylvia which room was hers. She

always stayed in the upstairs bedroom that was in the back. It was small but closest to the children's room. The children shared a room for the time being. It was easier for Shana plus they were young enough where it didn't bother them. After the new baby was weaned, there was bound to be a rearrangement of sleeping quarters.

Sylvia stared at the small room for a moment. A simple bed was pushed against the outer wall and there was one window in the rear with a small, narrow dresser underneath it. With a sigh, she unpacked her satchel, hanging up her two dresses on the pegs that stuck out of the wall. She placed her undergarments and stockings into the drawers. She didn't wear stockings during the warmer months of spring and summer but she wasn't certain how long she would be staying.

She spent her days helping Shana with the housework in the morning and Emanuel in the fields after dinner. She appreciated their kindness during this time but no one spoke about the real reason she was there. Emanuel seemed to look at her with sympathy in his eyes but he didn't broach the subject. That wasn't his way. Besides, Sylvia knew that he had fought his own battles when he had decided to court Shana, something that he did despite his parents' very strong lack of approval.

Sylvia could remember how somber her parents had been when he had announced his decision to marry her. For Katie and Jonas, it was as if the decision was a sign of their own parental failings. But, they had eventually accepted Emanuel's decision and embraced Shana, supporting their son's marriage to the Englischer woman. Of course, when Emanuel and Shana both decided to take the kneeling vow and had joined the Amish community, a weight was lifted off of both of her parents' shoulders.

Shana tried to draw her out one evening as they sat in the reading room. Shana was sewing some clothes for the children while Sylvia mended some linens. "Something weighing heavy on your mind, Sylvia?"

"No more than usual," Sylvia said casually.

"You know that you can talk to me," Shana said slowly. "You had wanted to talk a while back after church, ja?"

Sylvia shook her head, "I can't..."

"It's the widower, isn't it?" Shana said.

Sylvia raised her eyes and looked at her sister-in-law. There were tears threatening to spill from her eyes. "Was this how it was with you and Emanuel? Is this how you felt?"

Shana took a deep breath, hesitating before she responded. She wanted to say the right thing but she wasn't certain what that was. "Well...I'm not sure what you are feeling but I know that I kept thinking about him, wondering what he was doing, feeling lost when he wasn't around."

Sylvia nodded, swallowing back the tears. "Yes, yes that's it. I feel lost and so very alone."

Shana sighed. "I don't know what to tell you, Sylvia. You had asked me if it was hard for me to leave my world for Emanuel. The life is very different, you see. As much as I try, it can still be hard." She watched Sylvia's reaction to her words. "But we can't choose who we love, you know. Sometimes it just happens."

"I can't stop thinking about him," Sylvia whispered.

Shana smiled. "Yes, I can see that. Sometimes when you are apart, that makes it worse."

It was later that afternoon when Emanuel asked Sylvia if she wanted to ride to the market with him. Shana had a list of things that they needed to buy from the store. She agreed, knowing that it would do her some good to keep busy. The more she moved, the quicker time passed. Distractions helped her mind focus on other things and she welcomed them. So, when she saw Emanuel getting the buggy ready for the ride to the market, she hurried outside to help him with the horse's harness.

The market was a good distance from Emanuel's farm. It was one that she hadn't visited before. She wandered through the aisles, looking at the rows and rows of packaged goods. Emanuel pushed the cart and loaded it with flour, sugar, and other daily supplies. In one aisle, an Englische woman and her daughter stared at Emanuel and Sylvia. Emanuel nodded politely as he passed them and Sylvia shrank next to him, trying to disappear from their stares. She never could understand why Englischers found Amish so fascinating. After all, she reasoned, we are people, too.

She began to wonder about the Englischer way of life. What was so different about it, she thought. Electricity, cars, fancy clothes. But underneath the layers of store bought things and fancy surroundings, they loved and lived just like the Amish. Was being worldly so sinful after all? True, there were distractions from worshipping God but wasn't that the purpose of the church? To help the lost find their way?

"Ready?" Emanuel asked.

She nodded and helped him carry the boxes of groceries to the buggy. As he drove the horse and buggy back toward the farm, Sylvia sat looking out the side window. The acres and acres of green pastures and growing crops flowed like waves along the road. Cars raced by the buggy, some slowing down to look at the plain box-like buggy as the horse pulled it down the road. Whenever they passed another buggy going in the other direction, Emanuel would nod or wave if he thought he knew the driver. Sylvia leaned her head against the buggy door and shut her eyes. The rhythm of the buggy lulled her into a state of relaxation that she hadn't felt in a while. No, she thought, being worldly wasn't a sin but she wouldn't change her Amish upbringing for anything. Like Jake had said, there was a peace about her and she didn't want to lose that feeling.

The following Sunday was a church Sunday at a neighbor's farm. It was a long three hours and Sylvia found herself fighting the urge to fidget. Her mind wandered far away from what the bishop was preaching. During one song, Shana had to nudge her to stand. She flushed and tried to feign interest in the songs that flowed from the community of worshippers. The only saving grace was that Sylvia was able to help Shana with the children during the service. Noah fussed a little and, at one point, Sylvia carried him outside and walked around the farm, showing him the baby cows and fuzzy yellow chicks. He chased the chicks, trying to catch one but to no avail. She laughed at his attempts, glad for the distraction.

During the fellowship hour after the service, Sylvia helped the women serving the men and then served the women. When it was her turn to eat, she slipped away. Her appetite was gone and she felt that too familiar choking feeling in her chest again. She wandered behind the barn and disappeared into the mule shed where it was quiet and no one would look for her there. She needed to think and to get herself pulled together.

"I thought I saw you slip in here," he said.

She spun around at the sound of his voice. "Jake!" She had to remind herself to act proper, despite wanting to run into his arms and weep against his shoulder. She looked over his shoulder to see if anyone was nearby. "What are you doing here?"

Jake walked into the mule shed and leaned against the railing. "I ran into your brother. I asked him where you were." He reached out and pulled the ear of the nearest mule. "He hesitated, didn't want to tell me." He looked at her. There was a sadness in his eyes. "I suspect they all know, yes? Steve finally relented and told me where you had been hidden. I drove out today and looked for a Sunday gathering. Figured I might find you nearby and, while I was walking by, I saw you wander this way."

"Steve told you?" She was surprised. If her father had ordered them to silence, she couldn't imagine how or why her brother would have gone against his wishes.

"Truth is that I told him...I wanted to see you," he said without looking at her. "No, that's not it. I needed to see you."

"I see," she said shyly.

"You doing alright?"

She nodded, choking back the tears that threatened to surface. There were too many people around. She couldn't risk a scene by crying.

He leaned closer to her and lowered his voice, even though no one was around. "Could we meet later? Go somewhere for a while?"

"I...I don't know," she stammered. She had never thought about sneaking out of the house. She knew other Amish youth did it but that was never anything she had contemplated. Meeting Jake at her parents' farm was entirely different than going somewhere with him. "I wouldn't know how," she said, her voice barely a whisper.

He traced her cheekbone with his finger. "I hate to be the one to remind you that you are, indeed, an adult. You simply walk out the front door."

She laughed, despite herself. "It's not that easy, Jake."

He held her chin in his hand and, just briefly, lowered his lips onto hers for the softest of kisses. "Find a way. I'll be waiting at the end of the lane at nine. Take as long as you need. I have something for you..." He leaned down, brushing his lips against her cheek before he straightened up and took a step backward.

"Jake..."

He reached out and touched her hand. "It's been a long few weeks, yes?"

She nodded, not trusting her voice.

"Go back to your people, Sylvia. Try to smile and think about later tonight. We have much to talk about, I suspect." Without caring if anyone could see them, he lifted her hand to his lips and kissed it. She shut her eyes and surrendered to the tears. He gave her an encouraging smile as he reached out to wipe the tears from her cheeks. "None of that, dear Sylvia." Then, he backed away and headed toward the doorway. "Until later, yes?"

Sylvia watched him leave. A few minutes later, she heard a car engine start and heard it drive away. She stayed in the mule shed, thinking about what had just happened. He had found her. He had actually taken the time to find her, tucked into the winding roads of Lancaster County. And he was coming back tonight for her. She knew that she would be waiting for him. More importantly, she knew that she would go with him wherever he took her.

Chapter Eighteen

Shortly after Shana and Emanuel retired, Sylvia slipped out of the front door. She shut it quietly behind herself and hurried down their driveway. It was only quarter past nine. She was certain he would still be there. The night was dark and the moon was just over the horizon, looming larger than usual. The cicadas sang their evening chorus in waves throughout the fields. She had always loved the cicadas, listening to them when she slept as a little girl. Tonight, however, she felt as if they were singing just to her as she walked down the driveway, marching her along, keeping her company, guiding her to where he would be waiting.

In the pale white glow of the moon, she saw him standing by the mailbox. Seeing him waiting hit her like a lightening bolt. There was no more doubt; there were no more questions. She found herself running toward him, the pain of the past weeks of separation vanished as he greeted her with arms wide-open. She fell into his embrace, collapsing against him. She didn't care that he held her tightly or that he pressed his lips passionately against hers. She was beyond caring. The loss of time apart had led her to this moment. Indeed, the more they were separated, the more she realized how much she loved him.

So, as they stood at the end of the driveway, she felt herself melt into his arms, folded neatly against his body. They fit together like two pieces of a puzzle, the perfect fit. That was when the tears came and she began to cry.

He pulled back and wiped her tears away. He didn't ask what they were for or why she was shedding them. He already knew. He had parked his truck further up the road and he lifted her into his arms, carrying her to it. She pressed her face against his neck, sobbing quietly. She didn't know where he was taking her and, for once in her life, she simply didn't care. So it didn't surprise her when he took her back to his farm.

It looked different at night. There were no lights burning so everything was dark. The light from the moon cast long shadows on the floor. Outside the windows, there was a blue tint to the fields. Sylvia had never been in his house at night. She felt out of place as Jake led her inside. But, to her surprise, he didn't stop in the kitchen. It felt as if she was floating above, watching the scene unfold. She felt a complete disconnect with her body when, without so much as a word, he took her hand and slowly led her upstairs. She hesitated for a moment but, when he turned to look at her, his eyes meeting hers, she followed him, knowing that whatever was to happen was God's will.

He led her to the bedroom and, when he opened the door, she gasped. The room was lit with glowing candles. He beckoned her to come forward into the room, pulling lightly at her hand. He motioned for her to sit down while he closed the door behind himself. When she finally sat down on the edge of the bed, she noticed the bouquet of white carnations on the dresser. In the center of the bouquet was a single red rose. He reached for it and knelt before her, handing her the rose. Not knowing what else to do, she took it and held it awkwardly in her hands. It was different than the roses that grew at her mother's farm. It was more delicate and sophisticated.

"It's beautiful," she said softly.

"Sylvia," he started. He waited until she looked at him. "We come from different worlds, I know that. But we have to find a way to merge them."

Her heart pounded inside of her chest. She wasn't used to this. It wasn't real. She had to blink, wondering if she was dreaming. "Jake?"

"This isn't going to work, not the way that it is right now." He wrapped his hands around hers. "I can't be separated from you anymore. And, if your reaction tonight is any indicator, I think you feel the same way." The flames from the candles flickered and cast dancing shadows around the room. It felt as if the room was spinning ever so slowly like a carousal. He cleared his throat and squeezed her hands gently. "Sylvia, when we talked that night at your father's farm, you said that this was either something or nothing. I want to assure you that this is, indeed, something."

"And then that means..." she started softly.

"Yes, that means that we have to make a big decision. Are you willing to make a big decision, Sylvia?"

"I...I don't know, Jake. What is the decision?"

Jake took a deep breath, hesitating just momentarily before he spoke. "I want you to marry me," he said.

The words sounded foreign to her. They rang in her ears. "Marry you?" she repeated.

"You don't have to answer me right now. I know that there is a lot to consider. But I want it out there, on the table. That is my intention and my promise to you." He pressed his hand against her cheek. "But you have to know where I want this to go. I have to know that you want it, too. That's the only way we can begin to figure it out."

"I...I don't know what to say," she whispered.

"Typically this is the time when you would say yes or no

but, like I said, you don't have to answer me right now," he replied, his tone light and teasing.

Her head felt light and her breath was shallow. She felt as if she was floating overhead, watching the scene unfold beneath her. She was removed from the two strangers that she watched, too aware that one of them was herself. How her life had changed in the past few months. If only she had not been standing on that hill of growing wheat back in March. And then, she felt a surge of strength. Thank God that she had been standing on that hill of growing wheat back in March.

"Yes, Jake," she heard herself say. The words were like a foreign language, escaping her lips for the only time in her life. She had never thought to hear herself say such a thing and certainly not to a man like Jake Edwards. Jake Edwards with the handsome brown curls, bright blue eyes, and well built body. He was so unlike any of the Amish men with a charismatic personality and devilish charm about him. "Yes, I will marry you!"

He looked surprised. It took him a minute to digest what she had said. He laid his head down in her lap, his arms wrapped around her waist. She felt him sigh, a happy, contented sigh. He must've worried that she would say no. She placed her hand on his head, letting her fingers touch his curls. He is to be my husband, she thought. Lifting her eyes up, she gazed at the ceiling and said a silent prayer to God that the path she had chosen was the one to which He intended her to follow. If only she knew more about what He wanted from her. But, clearly, this man at her feet needed her. Whatever had happened to him in the past had brought him here to find himself and, in doing so, he had found her.

He lifted his head and stared at her, slowly getting to his

feet. He reached for both of her hands. "Will you stay for a while? We can talk, we can relax and just be together."

"I will stay for a while," she said.

"We have a lot to figure out." He stretched out next to her on the bed, reaching out for her hand. When she stretched out beside him, he reached back for her hair, gently prying the pins out from the bun once again. When her dark brown hair cascaded onto the bed, he smiled. "You are beautiful, Sylvia Lapp." She blushed and looked away. She had never considered herself beautiful and was taught to not even think in such ways. "And even more so when the color floods your cheeks," he teased.

She pressed her hands to her cheeks. They did feel warm. She smiled. "You embarrass me."

"Get used to it, for if telling you that you are beautiful and special and loved embarrasses you, you will be embarrassed for many years to come."

She met his gaze again. "Will you join the church?"

He shook his head. "I am not Amish, Sylvia. You know that. But there is nothing wrong with us living among your people. They used to be my people, I suppose. Way back in my family. But I can't pretend to be something I'm not. I can go so far as joining a Mennonite church. They are willing to take both of us. It's apparently not unheard of, you know." He paused. "We could be married as soon as you'd like."

"Who will tell my parents?"

He took a deep breath. "I suppose I will talk to them."

"I suppose that's best," she agreed. She didn't want to be there when he told her parents. The distress that they would feel, losing one of their children to the fancy world, would be heartbreaking to witness. She had seen how poorly they had responded when Emanuel had temporarily left the People. It had been a very sorrowful time in their house.

"I love you, Sylvia. I have from the moment I first saw you on that hill," he whispered.

She bit her lip and met his gaze. "I think I fell in love with you, too...that day at the market when you saved me."

He shut his eyes, remembering. "Ah yes," he said. When he opened his eyes, he reached over and pulled her closer to him. With his hand on her neck, he held her tight, lowering his mouth onto hers. "Sylvia," he whispered. "I will continue protecting you for the rest of your life," he murmured before he pressed his lips against her lips, letting the passion flow between the two of them.

The glow of the candles in the room, the beautiful flowers, the emotion of the moment. Sylvia didn't stop him from kissing her. She felt him pull her closer to his body until she was tucked neatly in his arms. His lips were soft and tender against hers. She felt a glow throughout her body as she realized that she had just promised to marry this man, this glorious man who held her in his arms and began to kiss at her neck. She felt shivers down her spine and the glow began to expand. No, she didn't want him to stop in the least.

But he did. He stood up and pulled her to her feet. She stood before him, her hair cascading down her shoulders. He brushed it with his finger so that it fell behind her back and down to her waist. In doing so, his hand gently touched her shoulder. She shivered, just enough to make him smile. He left his hand on her shoulder while he ran his other hand down her back, caressing her.

Without knowing it, she shut her eyes. She concentrated on his touch, enjoying the gentle pressure. She wanted to feel his fingers on her skin. She burned for his flesh upon hers. So, when his hand drifted down and carefully began to unbutton each button, she didn't stop him. Nor did she resist when he slid her dress down, off of her shoulders and pushed it down by her hips. She didn't fight him or hold back. Instead, she released herself into the moment. She let him continue to undress her, diving forward to give way to the physical demands that the past months had placed on her body and soul.

There was a moment, just one, when she thought about stopping him but, as he searched her face for approval or refusal, she gave a slight nod to her head and, with that, she ventured into the realm of intimacy that was to be shared only by man and wife. In fact, she realized when he had broken through any last resistance, it was the moment they indeed had become man and wife.

After they had made love, Jake held her in his arms, protectively shielding her from any feelings of guilt or remorse. In truth, she felt nothing but glory at the fact that she was to marry this wonderful man. He stroked her bare shoulder and kissed the top of her head. His touch sent shivers up her spine.

"You know that I love you, Sylvia," he spoke into her loose hair. But she heard him. Oh yes, she thought, I do, I truly do. She felt tears come to her eyes, but this time it was tears of joy. "What's that?" He leaned forward, wiping the tears away. "No tears, please. I didn't hurt you, did I?"

She shook her head and tried to smile. "No, that's not it. I'm just happy. Happy and scared at the same time."

Pulling the sheet up to cover her bare shoulder, he tucked it under her chin. "I feel the same, Sylvia. I wasn't expecting this, either." He ran his hand along the sheet, covering the length of her body. He rested it on her hip. "But no tears. Not today, not ever. What we both just experienced was magical, Sylvia. And that's because there is no shame or sin in loving one another. Do you understand that?"

She nodded.

"You are truly beautiful, dear Sylvia. And we will tell your parents as soon as you are ready. In the meantime, I can arrange a simple ceremony with the Mennonite church. You tell me when and that will be when it happens. I want you here with me, and the sooner, the better." He kissed her cheeks as he spoke. "This is where you belong...in my arms, each and every night...all night. You tell me when you are ready and I will make it happen, dear Sylvia."

"Now," she whispered.

He laughed softly. "Now? I don't think any minister would be happy if I woke them up now to marry us!"

She curled against him. "But God can marry us."

For a long moment, he was still. She wondered if he had fallen asleep. But he answered the question for her when he jumped off the bed, reaching for her hands and pulling her to her feet, the sheet draped around her shoulders. "That's exactly what we can do. We can marry ourselves before God!" She felt the color flood her cheeks as she realized that she was standing before him, wrapped in the sheet from his bed. He didn't seem to notice as he held her hands in his and stared into her face.

She tried to hide her embarrassment. "Jake! We aren't even wearing clothes!"

182

"Isn't that how He made us?"

She did laugh at that. "But…"

He silenced her by gently placing a finger against her lip. Then, his expression somber and calm, he said, "Standing here on this 21st day of July, I confess before God that Sylvia Lapp is my one and true wedded wife, in sickness and in health, for better and for worse, from this day forward until death do us part." He paused and waited. When she didn't say anything, he raised an eyebrow.

She felt that floating feeling again, as if she was hovering over the scene, watching herself. Was this really happening to her? Or was she dreaming one of the movies? But as she stared at him, watching her, the glow from the candles casting dancing shadows across his handsome face, she heard herself whispering, "I confess before God that Jake Edwards is my one and true wedded husband, in sickness and in health, for better and for worse, from this day forward, until death do us part."

With tenderness that she had never experienced, he leaned down and kissed her. The kiss was genuine and true, a moment of unity and love. With his hand placed on the small of her back, Jake pulled her tight against him. His skin felt warm against hers. The heat made its way through her and she wrapped her arms around his neck. The tenderness gave way to passion and she felt him lift her into his arms, taking the few steps toward the bed and laying her down. He hovered over her, careful not to put too much weight on her. He brushed the hair away from her face and gazed into her eyes. "Now," he said. "You are truly my wife."

This time, when he made love to her, she indeed knew that there was no shame or sin for, indeed, they were married in the eyes of God.

Chapter Nineteen

By the time Jake brought her back to Emanuel and Shana's farm, it was almost four in the morning. They parted at the end of the driveway, the sun not having yet begun its ascent into the morning sky. Jake held her closely, caressing her cheeks and staring down into her face. They didn't speak, just held each other and gazed into each other's eyes. For that moment, Sylvia felt as though nothing else mattered in the world but the man standing before her. The thought of being apart from him pained her. She wondered if he felt the same way when he finally sighed and glanced toward the house. He nodded and leaned down to brush his lips against hers.

"I shall see you tonight, ja?" he asked.

"Tonight?" She'd be so tired, she knew it. Neither had slept and they both had full days ahead of them. But, on the other hand, she couldn't imagine not seeing him. She wanted to be with him, to stay close to him. The thought of being apart, even if only for a few hours, pained her. "Ja, tonight."

She managed to hurry inside and upstairs before anyone awoke. As she lay in bed, resting and thinking about what had transpired the night before, she couldn't believe that she had professed her eternal commitment to Jake Edwards before God. She felt gloriously alive, aware of all her senses. She remembered being in his embrace, feeling his love, and she flushed, biting her lip and shutting her eyes. Jake was right...how could something so wonderful and magical be a sin? But it didn't matter. They were committed to each other and, soon, she would live with him on the farm. All of this would be behind her.

When she emerged that morning, she smiled at the children and greeted Shana with a warm hug. Shana laughed at her sister-in-law who was normally so quiet and shy. "What in the world?" She hugged her back. "You must have slept well last night. I know you haven't been doing so since you arrived here."

Sylvia pulled away. "Why would you say that? I always sleep fine here." She set about getting the table ready for the morning meal. "But last night was a good night, ja." She tickled Noah under his chin. He giggled and grabbed at her leg. She laughed and hugged him back.

By midday, Sylvia found that her mind was in a whirl. She wondered what Jake was doing, where he was, and whether he was thinking about her just as much as she was thinking about him. Her distraction was increasingly apparent. She found herself staring out the window and smiling to herself. Once she even caught herself laughing, remembering Jake as he told her funny stories about his childhood as they lay together, entwined in each other's arms. She had never shared so much with any one person nor had she learned so much about anyone. It was as if a door had opened, a door that she knew could never be shut again.

"Where are you, Sylvia?" Emanuel asked when she was outside helping him with the barn.

She looked up at him. "I'm sorry, Emanuel. Did you say something?"

He leaned against his pitchfork and rested his chin on his folded hands. There was an odd seriousness about her brother's expression. "You aren't here right now, are you?"

"I'm sorry, brother," she said with downcast eyes.

186

"Daed told me about the Englischer," he said softly.

"Daed told you *what* about the Englischer?" she asked, shocked that such a topic would have been discussed. What could there have been to discuss?

Emanuel sighed and walked over to his younger sister. He put his hand on her shoulder and graced her with a kind and understanding smile. "I want to tell you, Sylvia, you will decide what you need to do but it won't be easy. Whether he joins the community or you decide to leave, you will both have challenges before you."

"Emanuel!" she exclaimed, her cheeks flooding with color.

"Rely on God. He will not lead you astray. As Daed always says, pray for stronger shoulders, not lighter burdens." He squeezed her shoulder. "I would not have changed any of it, Sylvia. Make certain that you feel the same way." And then, he turned back to work, leaving Sylvia in an emotional turmoil.

Part of her wanted to tell him; he had given her the perfect opening. But that was not the Amish way. Her courting period was her own business and not something that was casually shared. Her intention to finalize her marriage to Jake before a church was also her decision and not one that required permission from her parents, family, or friends. So, she kept her silence and bent her head to focus on work.

By the time the evening unfolded, Sylvia found herself energized and anxious, waiting for Shana and Emanuel to retire for the night. She took the two little ones up to bed, tucking them in with a hug, kiss, and soft song. She stood back and watched them sleep, Noah with his thumb stuck into his mouth, Hannah with both of her arms over her head. At just over one year old, Hannah still slept in a crib so Sylvia made certain the side was raised and latched before she quietly retreated out of the door, carrying the kerosene lantern with her.

Shana and Emanuel were seated around the kitchen table. Shana was working on some more mending under the lantern that hung over the table while listening to Emanuel read from the Bible. Sylvia hesitated at the doorway and listened to the passage.

"'Do you not know? Have you not heard? The LORD is the everlasting God, the Creator of the ends of the earth. He will not grow tired or weary, and his understanding no one can fathom. He gives strength to the weary and increases the power of the weak. Even youths grow tired and weary, and young men stumble and fall; but those who hope in the LORD will renew their strength. They will soar on wings like eagles; they will run and not grow weary, they will walk and not be faint.'" Emanuel looked up, sensing Sylvia's presence. "Join us, Sylvia."

She sat at the table, opposite Shana. "I did not mean to interrupt," she said meekly.

"You weren't interrupting," he replied. "I was reading that passage for you."

"For me?" she asked.

Shana looked up from her mending, one of Noah's jumpers. She set it on the table and reached her hand out to take Sylvia's. "If anyone knows what you are going through, both of us do. You can talk freely to us, Sylvia. Mayhaps that's why Daed wanted you to come stay here. Instead of being *ferhoodled* at their house, you could lean on us for advice and support."

"So you can soar, Sylvia," Emanuel added with an understanding smile.

She shook her head. "I don't understand."

"How serious is this?" Emanuel asked boldly.

"I...I don't know how to answer that."

Shana took a deep breath, glancing at Emanuel before plunging forward. She had never been one to hold back what she was thinking. "Has there been any discussion about marriage, Sylvia? And, more importantly, within the church or not?"

Sylvia couldn't look at either one of them. She never expected to have them confront her. That just wasn't done. *Strength to the weary.* The words echoed in her head. If she confessed, would they try to talk her out of it? *Understanding that no one can fathom.* She shut her eyes and took a deep breath. "Yes and I don't know." She looked up, gaining strength from speaking freely. She felt liberated. "We have committed ourselves before God but not before a church," she admitted. "We want to wait until your baby is born, knowing that you will need help. Then we were going to talk to Daed and Mamm." There was a silence. Sylvia suspected that they hadn't expected that response but they did not show any emotion or surprise.

Finally, Emanuel stood up and walked away from the table. He stood at the counter for a few moments, both Shana and Sylvia watching his back. He was thinking, trying to come up with advice for his younger sister. He couldn't criticize. It was less than five years ago when he, too, had been faced with the same decision. But with Sylvia it seemed so different. She was young and innocent. The Englischer was older than her and more worldly. What was the likelihood of conformity on his part?

Emanuel exhaled loudly and turned around. "If that is your decision, Sylvia, I don't think you should wait until Shana is back on the mend. We can make due. Mayhaps sister Sarah's eldest daughter can come help or one of the neighbor girls. A commitment before God..." he hesitated, trying to imagine his youngest sister taking on such a monstrous task. "*Ach vell*...in the eyes of God, you have already taken that step, ja? And a wife should be with her husband..."

Shana nodded her agreement. "Emanuel speaks wisely, Sylvia."

Sylvia looked at both them but there was nothing further to be said. She chewed on her lower lip for a minute, realizing that everything seemed to be going too fast. "I'm not certain I understand..."

"You should go home, Sylvia," Emanuel said. "If you have made that commitment, you need to tell Daed and be done with it."

Shana covered Sylvia's hand with own again. "Their disappointment will go away, Sylvia. The night that Emanuel told them that we were going to wed, I thought your mother's eyes would haunt me forever. But she was more supportive than I thought possible during the wedding and our first year together. She's stronger than you think...and sees more than you can ever hope to hide."

Emanuel laughed, "I'll say."

Even Sylvia had to smile. "Ja," she agreed.

Later that evening, she wandered down the lane to wait for Jake. He wasn't there when she arrived so she hung back in the shadows. She listened to the night and closed her eyes for just a minute. It sounded like her Daed's farm. The night air was warm and there was not a large breeze. She rubbed at her neck, hoping that she wasn't too sweaty. When he finally pulled up, it was a little past nine-thirty. He jumped out of the truck and greeted her with an embrace.

"I couldn't wait to see you," he said, holding her tightly. She loved being in his arms. He seemed to pull her into him, his arms protectively holding her. He was so much taller than her that she felt like child being dwarfed in a warm bear hug. Often, he stooped down a little which made it feel even warmer.

"Oh Jake! I have such *wunderbaar gut* news!" She told him about the conversations with Shana and Emanuel. He laughed and spun her around. "To have the support of the family, even just two of them, means so much to me," she gushed.

He pressed his hands against her face, holding her delicately and staring at her. "I told you that God wanted us together and would find a way." He lowered his lips down to brush them lightly against hers. When he pulled back, he tilted her chin so that she was looking up at him. "Sylvia, I will go speak to your father tomorrow."

"Tomorrow?" Again, she had that surreal feeling. She wondered if all young brides felt this way.

But Jake insisted. He wanted to shield her from the reaction and protect her from any emotional distress. Then, to her disappointment, he bade her an early good-night, telling her that she needed some sleep as did he. She could tell that he was tired by the drawn look in his face. After all, he teased her, they would have plenty of time to spend alone together for the rest of their lives. But this night, when he said good night, there was a difference. This night, he walked her up the driveway to the door of the house, rather than watching her from the end of the driveway. And he had been correct. Despite the energy that flowed throughout her body, she fell asleep within minutes of lying down.

Chapter Twenty

The first morning in Jake's house, she woke up in his bed to find him still sleeping. It was almost five and the sun was cresting over the horizon. She leaned on her arm and, with her free hand, traced a line down his back. The morning light caught onto the simple gold band on her finger and she stopped, lifting her hand to stare at it. It felt uncomfortable, wearing something around her finger like that. But Jake had insisted, slipping it onto her ring finger just after the ceremony.

When she questioned him with her eyes, he kissed her cheek. "It's just a little something from my world that I'd like you to consider," he had said.

His breathing pattern changed and she could sense that he was waking up. She sank back into the pillow and clutched the sheet around her, watching and waiting for her husband to wake at last. "Is it that time already?" he groaned, rolling over slowly. When he opened his eyes and saw her watching him, he cleared the sleep from his throat and reached out with a hand to tousle her loose hair. "Good morning, dear Sylvia," he said.

"Good morning, dear husband," she replied.

"Did you sleep well in your new bed? Or rather, what little sleep you had?"

She burrowed her head against his shoulder, suppressing an embarrassed smile. "It is rather early, isn't it?"

"That isn't what I meant," he said, tugging at a strand of her hair that had fallen over her shoulder. He held her close to him, his hand rubbing her bare back. "Who was it who wanted cows anyway?" he teased. But after a few minutes, he took a deep breath and exhaled. "Well, like them or not, they need to be milked, yes?" He tossed the sheet back, exposing her nakedness in the budding morning light, which, despite the intimacy from the night before, caused a blush to color her cheeks. "And as much as I'd prefer to stay here with you..." He swung his legs off the side of the bed.

She sat on her knees behind him, her hands caressing his shoulders. "I should like to help you, Jake."

He leaned his head back so that his cheek was pressed against hers. With his eyes shut, he breathed in her scent. It was always a clean smell. Fresh and clean. He smiled at her smell and her touch. "Yes, I should like that, too, dear Sylvia." He forced himself to stand up and moved about in the darkness to get dressed. "And then, this morning, I shall take you out for a post-wedding breakfast. Let someone else wait on both of us so that we can talk and enjoy ourselves."

"Breakfast out?" she asked. She had never heard of such a thing. Someone else making their breakfast? "But I thought I could make our first breakfast here. I wanted to do that for you," she added.

He finished putting on a white t-shirt and ran his fingers through his hair. It still looked slept on and messy but in a rugged sort of way. The curls flopped over his forehead, one hanging over his left eye. "Well, since you put it that way, I think that's a fine idea, too," he conceded. He leaned down to give her a quick kiss, pausing to smooth back her stray hair from her face and smile into her eyes. "My pretty Sylvia," he said. "I took the liberty of buying you some new dresses. They're hanging in the other bedroom. If you don't like them, we can take them back. I'll meet you downstairs for a nice cup of honeymoon coffee." And he left her alone to ponder his words.

New dresses? Bought? She had never worn a store-bought dress. She wondered what was wrong with her other dresses, the ones that she had packed and brought with her. But just as quickly as she thought the question, she knew the answer. Her old dresses were Amish and, despite having been raised that way, she had made the decision yesterday before the Mennonite church that she would never be Amish again.

So, curiosity got the best of her and she wandered into the back bedroom to see what these store bought dresses looked like. Carefully, she opened the door. It creaked, the hinges in desperate need of being oiled. She peered inside but everything seemed exactly as she had left it the last time she had been there with some of Jake's unpacked cardboard boxes lined up against the side of the wall. She shut the door and hurried to check the other bedroom.

When she opened the door, she couldn't believe what she saw. Boxes upon boxes were piled on the bed. Some had pretty white bows on them. Others were tied with ribbon. In all of her life, she had never seen so many boxes and she wondered what they were. She looked at the pegs hanging on the wall and, true to his word, she saw several dresses hanging on hangers. Two were sleeveless and floral with tapered waists and decorative buttons down the front. One was a paisley print with slightly ruffled sleeves. She reached out to touch the material. It was soft and cotton, not the normal polyester that her dresses had been made from. She had never worn something so pretty and he wanted her to milk cows in this? She bit her lower lip and hesitated, not wanting to disappoint him. She finally chose the simpler of the two floral dresses.

When she went downstairs, she felt different. She wasn't wearing her prayer covering and the soft cotton was light against her skin. She had never worn a sleeveless dress and she felt too aware of her bare shoulders. But the look in Jake's eyes made it worthwhile. He set down his coffee mug and whistled, low under his breath.

"Now, Sylvia Edwards," he said as he walked toward her. "That's a beautiful dress!"

"To milk the cows?" she asked, laughing as she lifted the edge of the skirt so that it fanned out. "It seems awfully....fancy."

Jake caught her in his arms and pulled her close. Nuzzling at her neck, he whispered, "You see fancy, I see beautiful." He gave her a warm kiss. "And that's a work dress, dear Sylvia. Did you see those other boxes?"

"Whatever is in them?" she asked.

"I bought you a few things...I figured you wouldn't feel comfortable shopping so I did it myself. To spoil you just a little." His joy radiated from himself. She had never seen him so energized. Reluctantly, he released her from his arms and went to the counter to finish making her coffee. "Now, warm yourself up and let's go greet our herd for the morning milking."

She didn't say anything but she felt uncomfortable, alright. Shopping for things? Things for her? She wondered what he had purchased and why. She had plenty of things. And, while she knew that she wasn't going to be an Amish woman and would have to conform a little to the non-Amish ways, she certainly hoped that he didn't expect it to happen overnight. But she would never say that to him. His eyes glowed and he was so joyous and happy. How could she begrudge him such

196

happiness?

"*Danke*," she said as she took the steaming mug of coffee.

Was this what it was like to be Englische, she wondered. Did men and women share so much? In many ways, she supposed that she could learn to like it. He was spoiling her with fresh coffee and so many gifts. It would take some getting used to, she knew that for a fact. But she also saw that he was truly pleased to do these things for her and that was something that she enjoyed seeing...his pleasure.

It was warm already when they went outside. It was going to be a hot week. The barn was full of flies and the cows were complaining from full udders. Neither Jake nor Sylvia needed to tell the other what to do. He did point to where the buckets were stacked next to the stools. But, they both proceeded to work, side by side, washing the cows' udders with clean, soapy water before milking their small herd of cows. The sound of the steady stream of milk against the metal buckets filled the room. The cows mooed their appreciation at the relief. Occasionally, Sylvia would stop to swat at a fly or to push a stray hair from her face. But, otherwise, it was business as usual.

She loved milking the cows, listening to that tinny sound and the cows chewing whatever cud was left from the previous night feeding. When the bucket was filled, she started to carry it to the storage container but Jake jumped up and took the heavy bucket for her. So, she took his place with the cow and finished tugging at her udders.

It didn't take as long to milk the twelve cows as it took to milk at her father's. When they finished, it was six-thirty.

Jake told her to go along inside and start preparing breakfast while he fed the cows their breakfast. They could muck the manure later when the cows were done feeding and ready for morning pasture time. She could feel his eyes on her back as she walked around the cows and retreated out the door toward the house.

So much had happened in the past week. She could scarce believe it as she walked into the kitchen. Only this time, she smiled to herself, it was *her* kitchen. True to his word, Jake had spoken with Jonas in private. Sylvia didn't know when that meeting would take place as she didn't see or hear from Jake until almost five days later. Those were the longest days of her life. After the evening meal, she would sit on Emanuel and Shana's porch, her eyes searching the road in the hopes of seeing a truck pull along and slow down.

By the fourth day, she couldn't eat or sleep. Her energy was sapped and she felt tears fighting their way to the surface. Where was Jake? What could possibly have happened? She wondered if he had changed her mind and she found herself, once again, fearful that she had made a mistake. Now that Shana and Emanuel knew, there could be no backing out for Sylvia.

But the next morning, there was a knock at the door during their breakfast. Emanuel looked up, wondering who it could possibly be at this early hour. But when he opened the door, it was Jake standing there, his hat in his hand and a nervous smile on his face. He greeted Emanuel with a warm handshake, "You must be Sylvia's brother, Emanuel. Jake Edwards. Glad to finally meet you." He looked past Emanuel and found Sylvia, sitting at the table, almost trembling from keeping her emotions in control. "If you don't mind, I'd like a word with Sylvia," he said.

Emanuel took a deep breath. "Was just headed out to the barn. You make yourself at home, Jake."

Jake hesitated then shook his head. "No, it's something that both you and your wife might want to hear, too."

At this, Emanuel raised an eyebrow and caught Shana's eyes over Jake's shoulder. She was smiling to herself, probably thinking back to their own courtship days. "By all means, Jake. Come on in."

When he entered the room, he greeted Shana with a polite nod and smile. As always, his presence seemed to fill the room. He was taller than all of them with broad shoulders and a charismatic personality. Shana could see that at once. But there was also something innocent and pure in his demeanor. Having grown up Englische, she had a different perspective to pull from than Emanuel and Sylvia. She was often distrustful of the Englischers. But not this one. She immediately liked him.

Jake headed to where Sylvia sat. He knelt before her and took her hands in his. He kissed them and stared up at her face. "I told you that I would talk to your father. And I did, Sylvia. I can't say that he was happy about this but I can tell you that he didn't seem very surprised. We spent some time together, sorting it out. And I can promise you that there are no hard feelings from your parents. I told them that we would join the Mennonite Church. I told them that I would never take you from your family. And I told them that I would do all that I could to be a good Christian husband for you, leading as plain and simple a life as I could possibly provide, being that I'm not Amish."

Sylvia felt the tears winning the fight. "And I'm not

shunned? He's not too terribly disappointed?"

"Well, I wouldn't go that far but I think Katie and Jonas had some good preparation from this," Jake said, making light of the moment by winking at her. "And why would they shun you? You never took the baptism so there is nothing to shun."

Shana cleared her throat. "What are the plans, Jake?"

"It's up to Sylvia. Whenever she is ready, I will arrange for the minister." He reached out to wipe away one of her tears. It glistened on his finger. "Under the circumstances, I suspect it would be alright if we married privately, no fanfare or fancy dinner. I don't think our dear Sylvia would be up for something like that."

And so it had been settled. The following Saturday, a minister came to Emanuel's farm and, under the noon sun, Sylvia became Mrs. Jake Edwards with only her family as witnesses. Shana seemed the most moved during the ceremony, perhaps the only one that could truly understand the turmoil that Sylvia was going through...and the challenges that faced them both in the upcoming months. There was a light dinner before everyone parted in time to get home for evening chores.

By the time that Jake brought Sylvia back to his farm, it was almost four o'clock. He had taken her first to a nearby park so that they could walk, hand-in-hand, alone along the edge of a river. They sat under the shade of a large tree, dipping their legs in the cool water, Sylvia leaning against him as he stroked her arm. For a long time, neither spoke. They listened to the running water, the calming music helping to soothe them as they both tried to grasp the enormity of what had just happened. For Sylvia, she felt a conflict of emotions...unsure of what she had committed to while loving Jake with all of her heart. For Jake, he felt the weight of insuring that Sylvia was protected as much as possible and trying to keep her life as plain as he could.

Jake had done the evening milking while Sylvia wandered through the house, staring at what was now *her* new home. It felt familiar to her, which helped. Yet, it didn't quite have that home feel to it. She noticed that it needed a good cleaning...the dirt and dust had accumulated since she had been there last. For a while, she stood by the window, staring outside at the barn as if willing Jake to emerge. But he didn't. So she decided to venture outside and look at the vegetable garden they had planted together almost two months prior. The weeds had sprung up, choking some of the plants. She noticed that the tomatoes were too tall and needed to be thinned. She had a lot of work to do to catch up on her chores, she realized.

"There you are," he had said as he walked up the hill toward their garden plot. His eyes roved over the rows of weeds, plants, and brambles. "Looks like we know what one of our first projects will be," he teased.

She nodded. "Needs some tending, that's for sure."

He put his arm around her neck, resting it across her shoulders. "There's lot of things that will need tending to around here, Sylvia," he had said. "But right now, I can only think of one thing..." He nuzzled at her neck. "You."

If she wanted to protest, the thought quickly dissipated when she realized that not only were they married now, but they were standing on their own farm with no one else around to witness such a public display of affection. So she turned toward him and put her arms around his waist. *Husband,* she thought and one of those familiar waves coursed through her body. She wondered if all newlyweds felt this way and, immediately, she pushed the thought far away. Impossible, she had told herself. There was no way anyone could ever feel the love that she and Jake felt for one another.

Standing on the edge of the weedy garden patch, she had lost herself in his kiss. For the moment, she forgot everything except this exceptional man who stood before her, blessing her with his love. She didn't protest when he lifted her into his arms and carried her to the house. He paused as he fumbled for the door and kicked it open with one foot. "Allow me to carry you inside, Mrs. Edwards," he had said. But he didn't stop in the kitchen. No, he headed for the stairs, setting her down gently so that he could guide her upstairs to the bedroom where they spent the rest of the evening.

Now, the morning after as she made her first breakfast for her husband, she remembered his love and smiled to herself. She had never known much about the behind-doors life of a married couple. It wasn't as if anyone really talked about it beyond the basic facts that sexual relations were saved for marriage and resulted in children. She hadn't known that there could be pleasure in the process...pleasure and emotion and an intimacy that made her want to curl up and never leave Jake's side.

"Mmmm ummm!" he called out enthusiastically when he walked through the door. "Something smells delicious!" He walked over to where she stood by the stove and gave her a quick kiss before retreating to the sink to wash up. "Eggs, bacon! Why, Sylvia, you are spoiling me!"

After they had eaten and Sylvia cleared the plates, they

202

sat outside on the front porch, drinking a cup of coffee and planning their day. It was Sunday and there wasn't much they could do around the farm, being a day of rest. Off-Sundays were usually spent visiting with family and friends and, for the unmarried folk, attending singings. Jake leaned against one of the porch posts, one leg stretched out along the porch while the other dangled, almost touching the ground. "Much prefer just spending the day with my wife," he said casually. "Perhaps we could ride into town?"

Sylvia bit her lip. She didn't want to ride in the truck. It was Sunday. But how to tell him without sounding ungrateful or demanding? "Or a nice walk while it's still not too hot?"

"Ah," he said. He caught the gentle pleading of her tone and realized his mistake. Graciously, he conceded. "Walk it is! I can show you the property. I don't think we have walked that yet, have we?"

She was grateful for his tact and understanding. "Thank you," she said softly.

He reached his hand out for hers and brought it to his lips, kissing the back of it. "It'll take time, I suppose...for both of us," he acknowledged.

So they walked around the perimeter of the property, hand in hand. He told her stories about his grandfather, what little that he knew about him. He told her that he had always heard about the farm, knew that it was in the family but never dreamt of living on it until after the accident. It had taken him over five years to finally do it.

"All I knew was that my life was going too fast and I wasn't appreciating it," he said in a matter of fact tone. "I needed a change...to find myself."

"And you have, ja?" she asked.

He wrapped his arm around her as they walked and kissed the top of her head. "And much more. Ja!" he teased.

He had big plans for the farm. He wanted to breed the horses but also to farm the land. Sylvia listened to him talk about planting winter wheat in October. He also planned to plant corn next spring. He had learned a lot from Steve. Even using the mules had been an exciting part of the experience. He had found that he had liked using them to harvest the corn. Sylvia was relieved to hear that he would not be using gas-powered equipment. While she knew that she, too, would have to make concessions, she didn't want to lose the essence of her spirit in the process.

After they shared a quiet lunch together, Jake retreated to the barn for a little while, giving Sylvia some time alone to unpack her hope chest and make the house her own. For years, she had been working on linens and tablecloths and even a special quilt for her wedding bed. She smiled as she unpacked each item and remembered the hours she had spent making them. After she covered the kitchen table with the pretty white tablecloth that was embroidered along the edges, she escaped outside to cut some fresh flowers to place in the center of the table.

Back upstairs, she covered their bed with the pale blue and white quilt that she had stitched two winters ago by the kerosene heater in her parents' kitchen. By the time she was done, she began to feel as though she could eventually think of the small farmhouse as her home.

"Ah, pretty as a picture," he said as he leaned against the bedroom doorframe, his arms crossed across his chest.

She had just finished making the bed, the quilt spread out and wrinkle free. She stood up and smiled at him shyly, "Do you like it?"

"Of course I do," he replied. "But I referring to you." He laughed when the color rose to her cheeks. He liked to tease her and make her blush. Her innocence enchanted him. "Perhaps now would be a good time to look through some of those packages in the back bedroom," he suggested, reaching his hand out for her to hold.

For the next hour, he sat in a ladder-back chair watching as she opened up the packages. There were more dresses and button-up sweaters as well as some pretty straw hats. There was even a plain white nightgown in the softest fabric she had ever touched. In another box, there was a fancy new hairbrush, comb, and mirror set. She had never seen so many new things, each one taking her further away from her upbringing and making her realize that her future was going to be quite different. When the last box was opened, she sat on the edge of the bed and stared at everything that he had bought for her.

"I don't know what to say," was all she could muster.

He watched her thoughtfully, not responding right away. She ran her hand over the nightgown. The neckline was cut in a V and there was a long slit up the side. It was beautiful, she couldn't help but admit that. However, she didn't need or want beautiful things. And the dresses. If the work dresses he had purchased for her were pretty, these other dresses were much fancier. Where would she wear them?

"These must have cost so much money," she finally said. "I...I don't need so many things, Jake."

He nodded in agreement. "You're right. You don't."

She looked up at him, confused. "Then why?"

Nonchalantly, he shrugged his shoulders. "Why not?" He stood up and walked toward her, reaching for the pretty straw hat that was resting inside a box next to her. Gently, he placed it on her head. "A husband can spoil his wife, ja?" He tilted her chin so that she was forced to look at him. "It's just one of the ways that I can show you how much I love you." He leaned down and kissed her. "And, you must admit that it would raise a lot of eyebrows when we go places together if you dress Amish but you are traveling with an Englischer man."

There was truth to that statement. She nodded her head and looked around at the many different things that he had purchased for her. She couldn't even remember her father ever buying anything for her mother as a surprise. It just wasn't something that Amish did. But she had married out of the church. There were many compromises that she would undoubtedly have to make in the future. This was just one of them.

"*Danke*, Jake," she said. "This was most kind and thoughtful."

He laughed and gave her shoulder a playful squeeze. "Maybe. Or maybe it was selfish...Perhaps I just don't want to be chasing tourists away from you for the rest of our lives."

That afternoon, she helped him with the barn chores. Together, they cleaned the manure, fed the horses, and milked the cows. She liked working alongside Jake. Unlike her father's farm, Jake talked to the cows, hummed a song, or even made little jokes to her. Chores were jovial and fun instead of silent and tedious. He even helped her carry the heavy milk buckets

206

and seemed to always be smiling at her, watching her when he thought she wasn't paying attention. She pretended not to notice but her heart fluttered in her chest knowing that his eyes were upon her. His adoration humbled Sylvia. She hoped that she was worthy of such devotion and love.

Before she knew it, it was time to clean up and start supper. She looked up at Jake and he nodded toward the house. "I'll be in after I turn out the cows," he said.

She quickly hurried to the house, trying to think about supper. She hadn't planned anything. She wasn't used to being in charge of the kitchen for all three meals. That was something she'd have to figure out quickly in order to get into a routine. What on earth was she going to prepare for this man?

Looking through cabinets and the refrigerator, she was thankful to find some fresh vegetables, potatoes, and thinly sliced ham. It would have to do, she realized. But the next day was Monday and they'd have to go to the market so that she could stock up on proper food for the week's meals.

The table was set and a kerosene lantern lit up the room when Jake came back inside. He hesitated for a moment but didn't reach for the light switch. The glow from the kerosene lantern flickered against the walls, making shadows dance in the fading light from the retreating sun. He washed his hands and sat down, letting Sylvia serve him for their first supper together.

"It's all I could find," she apologized as she set down his plate before him. "If we could, perhaps we might go together to market tomorrow?"

"That we can do," he said agreeably, waiting for her to sit. "I suppose teaching you how to drive the truck is out of the question," he said after they had bowed their heads for a silent blessing.

"Drive the truck?" she gasped, practically choking on her first bite of food.

He sighed. "Well, I suppose it wouldn't hurt to get you a buggy or cart then. We do have these lovely horses, don't we? They could use the exercise and you would be a wonderful advertisement. People will see this beautiful woman with this beautiful horse and, since they can't have the one, they might want the other!"

She laughed. "You are incorrigible!"

After supper, he helped her clear the dishes from the table. There was a peaceful quiet in the room. It filled her with happiness. It felt strange to know that, once again, she would be spending the night at Jake's home...her home. Yet, when he smiled at her as he set some more dishes by the sink, everything just felt right.

While she washed the dishes, he disappeared into the next room. She could hear him fiddling with something but she wasn't certain what it was until he returned to the kitchen. He took the dish towel from her hand and set it on the counter. "Come Sylvia. This can wait," he said, leading her into the sitting room.

He had lit another kerosene lantern, this one not as bright as the one in the kitchen. The room glowed and there was a gentle hissing noise coming from the lantern. However, he turned his attention to the old piano where he had place a small radio.

"I want you to dance with me," he said as he turned a knob and soft music filled the room.

"I...I don't know how to dance," she said. Truth was that she had never even thought about such a thing.

"It's easy," he said, taking her into his arms. He wrapped one arm around her waist so that she was tucked up against him. "Just follow my movements, Mrs. Edwards," he murmured into her ear.

She leaned against him while he moved slowly to the music. At first, she felt uncomfortable. She had listened to music before during her *rumspringa* and with some of her friends at volleyball games. Steve even kept a battery-operated radio in his buggy before he joined the church. But dancing? That was something Amish just didn't do.

Yet, as he held her tight, she shut her eyes and tried to relax. She could feel the muscles beneath his shirt and his arms were wrapped protectively around her. The too familiar waves of anticipation began to flow through her body and she felt her pulse quicken. She lifted her arms and placed them over his shoulders, just like she had seen in the movies. Her cheek was pressed against his chest and she felt his chin resting on top of her head. They fit together so neatly, like interlocking pieces of a puzzle.

"Isn't this nice?" he asked softly.

"Umm," she replied, not wanting to break the spell of the moment.

He ran his hands up her back. "And this is only the beginning," he whispered. She could feel him loosening her bun until her hair flowed freely down her back. She was getting used to his fascination with her hair. He tugged gently at it, tilting her head back so that he could draw his lips across her neck.

"It's been a long day, Mrs. Edwards. What do you say about retiring early this evening?"

Even in the fading light of the sunset, he could see her cheeks turn pink at the suggestion. But she didn't argue as he turned off the lantern, leaving the radio on to sing them goodnight as he led her upstairs for their second night as husband and wife.

Chapter Twenty-One

To Sylvia, their first week of marriage seemed to pass too quickly. Time did not stand still on Jake's farm. Their days started before the sun crested in the sky. They worked together, side by side, from five in the morning until seven-thirty. During that time, they milked the cows, fed the horses and mules, and filled the water troughs in the fields. They would turn the cows back out after the milking then take time to clean the horses' and mules' stalls. It wasn't demanding work and she enjoyed working in his company. By seven-thirty, she would hurry into the kitchen to put some fresh coffee on the stove and begin preparing for breakfast.

During the late morning, Jake often worked with the horses. He would spend hours grooming them and lunging them in a small paddock behind the barn. Sylvia would spend that time *redding* the house and gathering any clothes that needed to be washed. She had decided that she would do laundry on Tuesdays and Fridays, spreading the work out across the week so that there wouldn't be too much to do in one day.

After lunch, she spent time baking in the kitchen. She made fresh bread each day that week, loving how the smell welcomed Jake when he came in for an afternoon coffee. Then, she would spend the rest of the day helping him in the barn unless he had to run an errand into town. She wasn't comfortable riding in his truck and, with the exception of the market, tried her best to avoid doing so. The quick errands seemed frivolous to her, aided in part by the ease of turning a key in the ignition.

True to his word, he bought her a used open top wagon. It was large enough to carry plenty of groceries or even supplies from the farm store. It arrived on Friday while she was hanging up the laundry to dry in the sun. A man drove up the driveway, his own horse pulling the carriage while another buggy followed behind. Sylvia peered over the clothesline, her heart skipping a beat when she realized that the men were unhitching the wagon to leave it. Jake hadn't told her. Instead, it was just one more of his endless string of surprises.

They spent the rest of the day trying to harness one of his older and calmer horses to the carriage. The two men who had sold Jake the carriage stayed around to help. Sylvia watched helplessly as the men put the harness on the horse and tried to hook her up to the wagon. She was resistant at first, stamping her hooves and dancing back and forth to avoid the weight of the harness. But the men were persistent and it took about five tries before the horse gave in and accepted the strange contraption behind her. The men worked with Jake, showing him how to drive the horse and even turn the wagon around, being careful not to cut the circle too tight.

"Shouldn't take too long to make her bombproof," the one man said to Jake. "She's a fine looking horse. Seems high quality."

Jake rubbed his jaw as he stared at the horse. "The buggy is for my wife. How long you think until the mare's safe enough for my wife to drive?"

"Give it a week or two," the man said. "Stick to back roads for a while. And it wouldn't hurt if you rode along as the grounds man, especially in the beginning."

So, for the rest of the week and all of the following, Jake

spent as much time working with the mare as he could. He was concerned that he felt comfortable turning over the reins to Sylvia. He wanted her to have mobility, to be able to visit with her friends and family. But he wanted her to be safe, above all else. Finally, when he felt confident enough in his own ability to control the horse as well as in the horse's calm nature when pulling the wagon, he invited her to ride in the wagon with him.

It was a beautiful day with crystal blue skies and fluffy white clouds. The sun shone overhead and, while it was hot, there wasn't too much humidity in the air. After lunch, they harnessed the horse to the wagon and Jake helped her climb up to sit on the padded seat. He climbed up and sat next to her. He glanced at her and raised an eyebrow. "Ready for this?" She hid her smile, realizing that he was nervous. She wondered if he was nervous about the horse or his own skill. But she said nothing, just lightly touched his knee to reassure him that it would be fine.

The wagon lurched forward and the horse started trotting right away. Jake did his best to slow her down until they had reached the main rode. He pulled on the right rein, forcing her to turn to the right. "I thought we might take a quick visit to your parents. We haven't seen them in almost three weeks already."

Three weeks, she thought. Had it flown by that quickly? "Seems hard to imagine that so much time has passed," she replied.

"Time flies when you're having fun," he teased, nudging her softly with his elbow.

She felt relaxed by his side with the wind on her face.

The sun warmed her and she took a deep breath. Yes, she thought, time sure does travel at a different pace these days. She couldn't help herself from leaning toward him so that her arm brushed against his. He glanced down at her and smiled, appreciative of even that small gesture that said so much without any words.

When they arrived at her parents' farm, Sylvia took a deep breath. It felt strange driving down the lane with Jake by her side. Indeed, her parents had not been happy with the news. In many ways, Sylvia was thankful that Jake had spoken to her father privately. By the time Sylvia had returned to the farm just before her wedding to Jake, the shock had dissipated enough so that her mother was able to congratulate her, despite the sorrow in her eyes that said otherwise.

When Jake stopped the horse and wagon in the driveway, he leaned over to help Sylvia get down. She waited patiently for him to tie the horse to the side of the barn before they walked, together, toward the house. Jonas sat inside, enjoying a hot cup of coffee after his noon meal with Katie scurrying to wash the dishes. They both looked surprised to see Jake and Sylvia walk through the door but they gave them a genuine welcome and invited them to sit at the table. Sylvia hurried to her mother's side, grateful for the opportunity to help her while Jake sat at the table next to his father-in-law.

"Well, well," Jonas said lightly but Sylvia could see the strain in his face. It was not easy for him to greet his daughter with her fancy husband from the world of the Englische. "Was wondering when you two would get to visiting us. Thought you forgot about us."

Jake laughed. "Not at all, Jonas. But your daughter sure has kept me busy...Been working with one of the horses to drive her new wagon."

Jonas raised an eyebrow. "A new wagon, you don't say?"

"Didn't think she'd take a shine to learning how to drive my big pickup truck," Jake teased with a wink in Sylvia's direction.

"Can't say I blame her," Jonas replied. He set his cup down on the table and glanced out the window. "What do you say you show me this horse of yours? Steve told me they were good quality stock."

After the two men retreated outside, Sylvia continued helping her mother, quietly waiting for her mother to say something. Anything. But, as the silence grew, so did the awkwardness of the moment. Both women were stuck in their own thoughts, wondering how to break the barrier and move forward. Already Sylvia could sense the distance and it pained her, knowing that her choice had created this separation between herself and her mother. But the choice had been made and, despite feeling sad at the loss of this relationship, she knew that she wouldn't have changed it for anything in the world.

Finally, Sylvia cleared her throat. "Getting along well at Jake's farm," she said softly. "It's different though."

"*Ach vell*, t'is to be expected, I suppose," her mother replied.

"Quiet," Sylvia said. For a moment, neither spoke again. The dishes clattered as they neatly stacked them after they were dried. Sylvia lifted them into the cabinet for her mother. "I wish I had spent more time cooking with you," she offered.

"Ja, I can see that," Katie said.

"It's difficult to plan all of those meals."

Katie turned around, facing her daughter. For the first time, Sylvia noticed how tired her mother looked. She was shorter than Sylvia and her hair was pulled back so tightly into a bun that the part down the center of her head had stretched into a wide patch of baldness. There were bags under her mother's eyes and grey hair sticking out from under her prayer cap. Sylvia wondered if her marriage to Jake had aged her mother or just the passing of time, unnoticed until she had been away for so long.

"Your sisters are coming over this Friday afternoon for an applesauce canning. Suppose you might want to join them," her mother said, offering a touch of an olive branch. "Applesauce works for a *gut appeditt* and farmers have that."

She was staring at her daughter, seeing her with new eyes. The dress that Sylvia wore was a plain blue Amish dress. She had insisted on wearing that to her mother's, despite Jake's raised eyebrow. But, despite the Amish dress, even Katie could see the change already in her daughter. She had been exposed to the world, to a relationship with her new husband that had clearly spoiled her for the plain life.

Katie knew that, no matter how much Sylvia tried, she would stray further and further from the simple upbringing that both Katie and Jonas had provided. Even if Sylvia didn't know that yet, Katie was quite certain that this marriage would not end the same way as Emanuel and Shana's...with a kneeling vow and embracing the Amish way of life.

"That would be right *gut*," Sylvia said, her eyes downcast as she recognized how much she wanted to be there with her sisters. To make applesauce all afternoon meant talking and laughing, sharing fellowship with her sisters. She looked forward to being a part of that community once again.

"*Danke*, Mamm."

"Now, let's go see what canned goods I might have to spare. Can't have you starving your new husband, ja?"

When Sylvia walked out of the house, she had a box filled with glass containers of canned vegetables and bags of frozen food. Her mother had also sat down with her, going over some simple recipes and cooking plans so that Sylvia could organize a routine for the cooking. Through the sharing of such information, Sylvia felt the barrier slowly thaw. She was grateful for the time that her mother spent and the knowledge that she passed along. And, when it was time to leave, she could only smile her appreciation at her mother as Jake took the box from her and set it carefully in the back of the wagon.

He reached out and touched Sylvia's arm. "Ready, Sylvia?" he asked softly.

"Ja." They waved their good-byes, no hugs or kisses. Jake helped Sylvia get into the wagon, making certain that she was settled before he walked around to the driver side and got into the wagon beside her.

"I'll pick you up Thursday morning, then, Jonas?"

Jonas nodded and waved, stepping back from the wagon as it began to move. "That'd be right appreciated, Jake. We'll go check out that auction in New Holland." Her parents both stood in the driveway, watching as Jake slapped the reins on the horse's back and started down the driveway. They both waved as the wagon rolled away.

Sylvia waited a few seconds until they had pulled away. Then, she looked up at Jake. "Auction? You're picking up my father to go to an auction?"

Jake nodded. "Need some equipment for the fall

217

plowing. Your father offered to help me out." He winked at her. "Being so much wiser than I am about farming and all, his advice would be greatly appreciated."

She couldn't hide the smile. She knew that Jake didn't really need her father's help. But that was a wonderful *gut* way to break the ice and rekindle the friendship. By asking her father for help, Jake had found a way to create a thread between her new life and her old one. She was overwhelmed at his thoughtfulness and reached out to hold onto his arm as she leaned her head against his shoulder.

"*Danke*, Jake."

Perhaps it was the way she said it, with genuine appreciation, that made him slow the wagon down. He pulled over to the side of the road. Once the horse was stopped, he held the reins in one hand so that he could lean over toward her. The seat creaked under his shifting weight. Ever so gently, he took her chin in his hand and tilted her face up toward his. He searched her face, his eyes sparkling. Then, with the softest of pressure, he brushed his lips against hers and whispered, "You're welcome, Sylvia."

Back at the farm, after he unharnessed the horse and put the mare back in the stall, he carried the box inside for Sylvia and helped her unload the box of food. He kept her company while she unpacked it, showing him the different cans and bags of food as she set them on the counter. She was pleased with the contribution that her mother had made toward their pantry. It was truly a gift from the heart. When Sylvia told Jake about the Friday applesauce gathering, he seemed happy for her and told her, "I told you it would all work out." Then he kissed her on the top of her head and excused himself to the barn to work with the horses and get

218

ready for evening chores.

For the first time in weeks, she felt truly at peace with herself. Yes, she thought, indeed everything would work itself out. Her parents would accept her decision, she would live a happy life, and Jake would be a good farmer.

She took the canned goods into the pantry that was under the stairs to set the jars on the shelves. She hadn't been in there but once before when Jake had taken her to the market right after they were married. The shelves were basically bare but she was quick to organize the glass containers on them. Before she was done, she felt a sense of accomplishment. After Friday, she would certainly have enough jars of applesauce to carry them through the winter and spring. And their own garden was growing some nice beanstalks. She would be able to can those vegetables before long. Soon, the pantry would be filled with food from their own land.

Yes, she thought. Everything was working itself out, indeed.

Chapter Twenty-Two

When the seasons began to change, it was time to plow the fields for planting the winter wheat. Since the field hadn't been plowed in years, the field had to be mowed first. Jake had purchased a larger mower and a plow for the mules to pull through the fields. Sylvia helped him with the task, walking ahead of him to clear any branches or rocks from the path of the mower. After the field was mowed, they had to collect the clippings, some of which could be used for bedding for the animals. Then it was time to begin plowing. Since Jake hadn't done this alone before, Sylvia was able to work alongside, helping to direct him and move the mules through the unbroken soil. By the end of September, the field was layered in pretty rows, waiting patiently for the seeds to be planted.

Their days had fallen into a predictable routine that gave Sylvia great comfort. Once a week, they would ride together to the market to pick up supplies. Sometimes they would stop at her parents on the way back. The visits were short but kept Sylvia grounded. She knew that her mother was still not fully accepting of her youngest daughter's decision but the tension had diminished a little more with each visit. And, despite the disappointment in Sylvia's decision, Jonas seemed to get along well with Jake, genuinely enjoying his company as did Steve and Daniel. It seemed that they all laughed easier when Jake was around.

The first week of October, when Sylvia and Jake stopped by the visit, Katie and Lillian were sitting around the kitchen table with a pen and paper. Apparently, Steve had finally shared his plans to have the church publish the announcement about betrothal to Emma. The wedding would be held at the Lapp farm during the first week of November on a Thursday afternoon. While Katie had suspected his upcoming wedding for many months and had grown extra food in the family garden, there still was a lot to do in preparation.

Sylvia found herself eager to help, especially since she had not had the benefit of a proper Amish celebration to welcome her own marriage to Jake. It would be wonderful *gut* to finally get to properly introduce her husband to her community, even if she was never going to officially be a part of it again.

It was about this time when a letter arrived at the farm. Sylvia had picked up the mail from the mailbox. It was usually bills that were addressed to Jake. During their two-month marriage, Jake handled the finances and Sylvia never questioned him about it. Despite his large acquisitions, he never complained about money or the expense of running the farm. Sylvia never even thought to ask. Growing up Amish, her parents had never discussed finances in front of the children and Sylvia always presumed that her father handled that aspect of the family. So it was natural that she merely left the small piles of bills on the counter to let Jake respond as needed.

But this letter was different. It was handwritten and addressed directly to Jake. There was a return address from Connecticut but she couldn't make out the name. She held the letter in her hands, examining it with curiosity. The handwriting looked like a female might have written it, with the letters having such fancy curves. Who would have written to Jake? Well, she thought to herself, if it's important, Jake will share it. She tried not to think twice about the letter and left it on the counter where she always left Jake's mail and went about the day.

It was laundry day so she carried the basket of dirty linens, towels, and clothes out to the barn to use the washing facility. The air was cooler than it had been in weeks passed. She found that she enjoyed the autumn much better than the summer. The leaves were just beginning to turn colors and the air had a crisp feel to it in the mornings. A perfect day for hanging laundry to dry in the sun.

"Sylvia."

She turned around, startled by Jake standing behind her. She hadn't heard him approach. It wasn't unusual for him to sneak up on her. Sometimes he would catch her unaware in his arms, nuzzling her neck and whispering his never-ending love into her ear. Other times, she would find him watching her and, once the familiar blush covered her cheeks, he would laugh at her, teasing her with his eyes.

This time, he stood on the edge of the porch, leaning against the post and staring at her. His lithe body was stretched out, his one boot crossed over the other. His arms were crossed over his chest and he held the letter in one of his hands. Whenever she looked at him, it always caused her a moment of breathlessness. The power of his presence never ceased to overwhelm her. Yet, something was different. The expression on his face was taunt and serious.

"Jake? Is everything OK?"

He pursed his lips for a moment, his eyes falling onto the letter. He seemed to re-read the letter before clearing his throat to answer her. "I have to go home."

The word struck her as if he had raised a hand to her. *Home?* she thought. The word had rolled effortlessly off of his lips. He hadn't thought twice about using the word. She frowned. "What do you mean? This is your home," she said, her voice sounding stronger than she felt.

He took a deep breath and rolled his eyes. "I mean to Connecticut."

"Whatever for?" She had never thought about his past beyond what little he had shared with her. She had never asked questions...had never thought to ask questions. In her world, Jake was living in Leola, Pennsylvania and he was her husband. Any world or life from before his move to Leola simply did not exist. But suddenly, she realized that she had been mistaken. She began to feel her pulse race.

"I have some unfinished business that needs my attention, Sylvia."

"Unfinished business?" The words rolled off of her lips but she didn't understanding what he meant. She felt light-headed and faint.

"In Connecticut and in New York," he replied. His voice was strained and she could see the muscles tensing in his jaw.

What type of business could he possibly have back in Connecticut or New York? He had said that he had left his business behind. Now he was telling her that he still had ties to his old life? Business ties meant the possibility of Jake needing to leave Pennsylvania and the cozy life that they were slowly creating. Business ties in another state severed the strength of his roots to Leola. Business ties created a cause for alarm. Suddenly, the past two months of tranquility and peace evaporated.

"I'm going to have to leave you here to tend to the farm," he said, his voice very matter-of-fact. There was no room to question his directive.

Sylvia chewed on her lower lip. Alone on the farm? To tend to the cows and the horses? She had never been alone before. There was always someone around...her parents, her brothers, her sisters. Alone had meant a long walk through a field but not for days on end. "For how long, Jake?"

He shrugged his shoulders. "Can't say. A week, I suppose. Maybe just a few days. Can't tell until I get there."

A week? Sylvia steadied herself against the clothesline. "I see," she managed to say.

He walked down the porch steps and came to her side. "Are you alright, Sylvia? You look pale."

She nodded but let him help her toward the porch and into the kitchen. When she was seated at the table, he stood next to her. Beads of sweat were on her forehead, despite the cool temperature of the day. He hurried to the sink to get her a glass of cool water. When she took it from him, she looked up with concern in her face.

"You never spoke of having ties back there, Jake," she said softly.

"You never really asked, did you?" he replied, his tone more abrupt and short than she was used to hearing. There was a hard look on his face when he sighed and ran his fingers through his hair before pulling out the chair next to her and sitting down. "Look, Sylvia, there are some things that I haven't shared with you, things that I just can't talk about yet."

"I see." She digested what he had said as quickly as she could. Then, when it dawned on her what it meant, she frowned. "Do you not trust me?"

He shook his head and reached for her hand. "That's not

it, Sylvia."

"How can you not speak to me if something is bothering you?"

A dark cloud passed over his face. He took a deep breath and shut his eyes. "I can't bring that part of my former life into our world, Sylvia. I told you that it is an ugly world out there. I meant it."

"Does this have to do with your first wife?"

"Partially, yes." He kissed the back of her hand. "Don't fret. I'll return in no time, dear Sylvia."

Knowing that he was not going to share any more information with her, she obediently acquiesced. No point in being argumentative, she thought to herself. "Everything will be fine here, Jake. I'm sure that I can handle the chores. If it gets to be too much, I can always ask Steve or Daniel for help, ja?"

Even as the words slipped past her lips, she wasn't certain that she believed it. How would she ever be able to survive alone? But that was what good Amish wives did...supported decisions made by their husbands. Only she knew that, technically, she was no longer Amish and Jake certainly never had been. She only knew that she had to do what she had been raised to do.

He pressed his hand against her cheek and the softness returned to his expression. "If anyone can handle it, you can, dear Sylvia."

"When will you leave?"

He glanced at the clock on the wall. "Tomorrow morning. Right after chores." He stood up and reached his hand down to help Sylvia to her feet. "You just take it easy while I'm gone. Don't try to do too much." He kissed her forehead as if she were a child. "Now, let me go see what needs tending to in the barn before I leave. I want to make certain that you have everything that you need until I return."

Sylvia hesitated. It was all well and good to tell her to take it easy but that didn't get the cows milked, animals fed and watered, and stalls cleaned. And, just as important, if he left tomorrow, how would they get the wheat planted? Was that something she should attempt to do? But she didn't ask. They had some time to plant the seed but, if the window began to shrink, she would have to attempt to do it herself. She just prayed that Jake would return within the week timeframe. In fact, she prayed that Jake would not be enticed by the world he had abandoned.

She had never considered that he would leave her alone on the farm, that he would return to Connecticut or New York. She had taken it for granted that, once married, he would stay with her in Leola, never seeking to leave the comfort of Lancaster County. She fought the empty feeling that grew in her core. She had to believe in God that he would return and their lives would continue as they had for the past few months.

Chapter Twenty-Three

Sylvia sat on the front porch, watching the sunset behind the barn. She was exhausted and she was thankful that the evening chores were finished. All she wanted to do was to crawl into bed and sleep. Her body ached, her hands were callused, and she felt weak from all of the work that she had done in the past days. Every day, she had risen at five to take care of the animals. It took her much longer since she had to do it by herself. By the time she was finished with milking, feeding, and cleaning, it was almost nine o'clock. There were mornings when she was too weary to make herself a decent breakfast. It didn't make sense to cook for one, she reasoned. So, a simple piece of toast and cup of black coffee satisfied her until noon.

After breakfast, she would tidy up the house. But, being that it was just her living there, she didn't have as much to clean. It was amazing how much cleaner the house was when only one person lived in it. She tried to keep to the same schedule that she had before Jake had left. She did laundry on Tuesday and Friday, baked bread on Monday, Wednesday, and Saturday. The only difference was that on that Sunday, she stayed by herself in the house, reading the Bible and resting as much as she could.

By the time that the first week rolled into the second week, she was in despair. She had not received any letters from Jake and, without a telephone, there was no way to get in touch with him. Even if she could, she wouldn't know where to call. The isolation concerned her, especially as each night rolled into a new day without any word from her husband.

She was embarrassed to visit with her parents. They would be alarmed if they knew that Jake had left her alone with so much responsibility. They might even insist that she return to their farm. It was unheard of for an Amish woman to be left alone on a farm for such a long period of time. But Sylvia didn't want to stay with her parents. She had promised Jake that she would hold the farm together, take care of the animals, and be there when he returned. But the days dragged on and the nights were increasingly lonely. She even cried herself to sleep one night and woke up, ashamed of herself for being so selfish for wishing that Jake had never left.

By the middle of the second week, she knew that she would have to visit her parents' farm. She had promised to help with the preparation for Steve's wedding. And she needed help with the wheat planting. She was afraid to wait much longer and needed advice from her father. So, knowing that she could no longer avoid visiting her parents, she finished her morning chores on Wednesday before setting out on the road, walking toward her parents' farm.

The air was crisp and cool. She was glad that she had worn a heavier shawl as the dark clouds in the sky promised no Indian summer for that day. The weather matched her mood. She had hoped Jake might return early. To tell her parents would be very hard for Sylvia. She could imagine their reaction and it pained her. To be newly married and have her husband leave her alone? It was shameful. Perhaps she should have insisted on going with him.

"Well hullo Sylvia!" Steve called out from the mule shed. He jogged a few paces to catch up with her. "Haven't seen you for a while. Thought you and Jake might stop down last week."

She bit her lip but didn't say anything about Jake.

"Promised Mamm that I'd help with your wedding."

"A week from Thursday, ja!" he said, smiling proudly. He accompanied her to the house and opened the door for her. "Sure am glad you came over. Mamm needs the help," he said.

Inside, Lillian and Katie were sitting at the table, making long lists of what was needed for Steve's wedding celebration the following week. They looked up and saw Sylvia. For a moment, they seemed relieved. But, as Katie stood and approached Sylvia, drying her hands on her apron, her expression changed.

"You ill, Sylvia?"

She shook her head. "No, Mamm. Just tired."

Katie took her arm and moved her toward the sofa that was in the back of the large kitchen. "I can see that. Sit for a spell. Where's Jake?"

Sylvia tried to avoid the question. "I walked over. While the weather's so nice," she explained.

"I see," Katie said but her voice didn't sound convincing.

Lillian came over and sat next to Sylvia. She, too, had a concerned look on her face. "Well, we can always use the help. But you can relax for a few minutes. You look winded."

"And pale," Steve added.

Katie shooed him out of the kitchen, telling him to leave the women to the women's work. Begrudgingly, he did as he was told. Once he was gone, Katie turned her attention back to her daughter. "Been busy on the farm, ja? Planting that wheat?"

Sylvia tried to smile. "I need to speak to Daed about that. But that can wait. I wanted to find out how I could help with the preparations for Steve's wedding celebration." She took a deep breath. "Just let me know where to start."

It felt good to spend time at her mother's. Lillian was always cheerful and good-natured. She seemed to have countless amounts of energy. And her stories about the children were entertaining and helped to distract Sylvia from her troubles and concerns. She was amazed that Linda had just started her first year of school. It seemed like just yesterday she was running around barefoot in the yard as she chased the spring kittens. But she was almost seven now and that meant school. Lillian's other children were napping so that had given her time to help her mother-in-law.

When it was time for dinner, Jonas came into the kitchen, stomping his feet as usual. He greeted his daughter with a friendly smile. "I heard the wind blew in a little bird from down the lane," he teased. He went to the sink to wash his hands. As he dried his hands, he turned around and saw Sylvia for the first time. A look of concern crossed his face. "You looking tired, Sylvia. You getting ill?"

Katie looked at her husband and frowned. "Think she's working too hard. Never heard of a man who had his wife work alongside him so much."

Both Jonas and Sylvia looked at her. It wasn't like Katie to speak out against someone and her words seemed too harsh. And with that, Sylvia knew that she could never tell her parents about Jake's unexpected trip to Connecticut. Certainly her mamm would not understand nor would she approve. The pit in Sylvia's stomach tightened and she felt ill. She just prayed that Jake would return in time for Steve's wedding. There would be too many questions if he didn't.

She left her parents' farm in the early afternoon,

heading back along the road. A few cars passed her as she walked. As each one passed, she caught her breath, hoping that perhaps...But they were just cars. None of them were Jake's truck. She scolded herself. After all, he had said a week and it had only been ten days.

It was the next morning that Sylvia knew she could no longer avoid the inevitable. If she waited any longer, the winter wheat would not be planted. She needed to get that seed in the ground, even if it meant doing it by herself. She knew that she would be busy the following week, baking food for her brother's wedding. The time to plant was almost gone and she couldn't wait any longer for Jake's return.

So, as soon as she had milked the cows, she hurried out to the fields and looked at the empty rows of plowed dirt. Somehow, she thought, she needed to do this one thing. She tried to suppress her anger and hurt that Jake had not returned on time nor had he written to her. But she knew that there was nothing she could do about it. Typically, she had helped her father and brothers with the planting. She had never seen her father do it alone. But this time, Sylvia knew that she had no choice unless she confessed to her parents that Jake had virtually abandoned her.

The sun was barely rising over the ridge when Sylvia headed into the mule shed. She stared at the two mules and took a deep breath. "*Ach vell*, girls," she said. "I need your co-operation today, ja? It is just the three of us and we have a long day ahead."

She spent the day spreading manure along the plowed rows, using the mules to pull the manure spreader. It was hard work to fill the spreader with a shovel and, by the end of each day, she was sore and her hands were callused. On Friday, she drove the plow along the rows to create deeper furrows. By Saturday, she managed to walk the ten acres, manually tossing wheat seeds into the furrows. And, as the sun was setting that night, she had just finished filling in the furrows so that the wheat could grow. The work was hard but she was thankful that she was able to do it. It kept her mind from the fact that Jake's absence would soon be more than two weeks.

The following week, she spent her time at her own home cooking as much as she could to help her mother. Even though the wedding would be held at Emma's house, with so many people attending, there would be a great need for coleslaw, bread, pies, and cooked beans. Sylvia was thankful that Jake had left her some money so that she could buy any supplies that she needed at the market. She hoped and prayed that Jake would return in time for the wedding but as the week wore on, she became more concerned that he would not make it.

As she kneaded the bread, she felt tears springing to her eyes. How would she explain his absence if he didn't show up? Had he forgotten about Steve's wedding? The more time that she spent alone, the more her mind crafted new, creative reasons why he would not return.

It was the morning of Steve's wedding. She woke up early, feeling ill. Jake was not there and she found herself embracing the fact that he was not going to return that day. She'd have to face her family and their questions. The shame was almost too great a burden. They would blame her for having married outside of the faith. They would think poorly of Jake. It would certainly strain their relationship with her husband. She went through the motion of milking the cows and graining the horses before she turned them out for the day. She was tired. No, she thought, I'm exhausted. All she wanted to do was crawl back into bed. But she knew that she had to rely on her faith to get her through this day.

The wedding service would begin at 8:30 in the morning so Sylvia hurried through the morning milking and feeding. She decided that the stall cleaning could wait. After all, she needed to get cleaned up and dressed before heading over to Emma's parents' farm. She put on her burgundy Amish dress and prayer *kapp*. She was too tired to care if anyone raised an eyebrow that she still wore Amish clothing. She held her head high as she loaded the wagon full of the food she had made and slapped the reins on the horse's back to start the thirty minute drive.

When she arrived, she was thankful that some of the Amish youths were standing by, eager to help her carry the boxes of food into the house while one of the men took care of her horse. The sun had barely risen over the horizon and the sky was a beautiful rosy orange. Sylvia took a deep breath and headed into the house, knowing that the questions would certainly be asked as to why her Englischer husband had not accompanied her. All night, she had tossed and turned, wondering how she would answer. Finally, she had determined that the truth was the best. She would acknowledge that he had left two and a half weeks ago and had yet to return.

In the crowd, Sylvia looked for her family. Her mother and father were seated near the front of the church room. Shana stood in the back of the room with Noah, Hannah, and five week old baby, Isaac. Sylvia squeezed her way to stand next to her sister-in-law.

"*Wie gehts*," she whispered into Shana's ear.

Shana stared at her sister-in-law for a moment as if trying to place something in her mind. Her eyes seemed to be staring at her, seeing her in a different light and, for just a brief moment, Sylvia was fearful that her expression gave away the angst that she had been feeling. But, when Shana smiled, Sylvia was relieved. There would be no questions just yet.

Instead, Shana's face lit up and she reached for Sylvia's hand. "Oh Sylvia! It's so good to see you! It's so exciting, isn't it?"

Sylvia nodded, suddenly feeling the urge to cry and confide in Shana. But she knew that this wasn't the time nor the place. "Ja, I'm so happy for Steve and Emma. I wish them many blessed years."

Shana frowned for a moment then leaned closer to Sylvia so that no one could hear. "I mean about the baby."

Now it was Sylvia's turn to frown. "What baby?"

Shana's expression changed from genuine delight to surprise. "Why, yours! You are expecting, ja?"

For a moment, the room seemed to spin around. Pieces of the puzzle came whirling together. What she had thought was exhaustion from working so hard was the onset of a pregnancy. She had woken up ill for so many days but thought it was because of Jake's disappearance. She had barely been able to eat anything but thought it was because of being too tired to cook. Yet, as she thought about it, she had not lost weight but, in fact, she had gained it. And her monthly course had not come for months. In fact, she suddenly realized, she hadn't had it since before her marriage to Jake.

Sylvia gasped and clutched at Shana's arm. "Oh," she exclaimed and several people turned around to look at her.

234

Shana laughed, trying to be quiet but found it difficult, given the realization that Sylvia hadn't known. She shook her head and patted Sylvia's arm. "I suppose I am the first to congratulate you," she whispered then, with one last smile, she turned her attention back to the sermon that would be held before the ceremony to wed Steve and Emma.

The sermon seemed to drag on for hours. Sylvia stood by Shana's side, trying to digest what her sister-in-law had just told her. Was it possible that she had been so preoccupied that she didn't even notice the changes to her own body? Clearly she had gained enough weight that Shana noticed right away.

Sylvia tried to count backwards and realized that she was probably just over three months pregnant. A baby, she thought. She wanted to be happy but it was hard without Jake by her side. Would she be forced to have this baby alone? Would Jake ever return? Why hadn't he at least written to her? The questions raced through her mind and she knew that, if she didn't sit down soon, she might just collapse from the shock.

There was a break in the sermon when Bishop Peachey took Steve and Emma into another room to talk about the responsibilities of marriage. During that time, the congregation sang several songs. Leah managed to work her way over to Sylvia and gave her a hug. They were standing at the back of the room, near the door in case Shana's baby cried. Leah held Sylvia's hand and smiled.

"It's so *wunderbaar gut* to see you!" she whispered. "You simply disappeared, Sylvia."

Sylvia nodded, leaning supportively against her friend. "I suppose that's what happens when one marries outside the church," she replied, her voice soft and sad.

Leah looked around. "Where is this fancy Englischer you married?"

Sylvia fought the tears that came to her eyes. She was about to reply when Shana pinched her softly, reminding her that, even if it wasn't Sunday, they were supposed to be singing and worshipping with the rest of the guests. Leah smiled and waved her hand at Sylvia, returning to her place a few rows ahead of where Sylvia stood with the other women with young children.

There was a cold breeze coming in from the door near where they stood. It was a welcome relief as the room was increasingly warm. She felt tired and leaned against the wall. She was so thankful that she was standing and not seated on those hard benches. Sylvia tried to sing along with the rest of the community of guests. The song was sung slowly in High German. She knew the words from years of listening to them but she was having a hard time singing them. Her attention was elsewhere. Her hand rested on her belly. Yes, indeed, she could feel the swell beneath her fingers now. She couldn't believe that she hadn't known...hadn't even suspected.

Someone laid a hand on her arm. Her thoughts interrupted, she turned her head, wondering who was trying to get her attention. She didn't want to get reprimanded again by Shana. But when she turned, she found herself looking up at the tall man standing next to her. She gasped and reached out, the tears suddenly spilling from her eyes.

"Jake!" she whispered hoarsely.

Again, several people turned around, frowning at the disturbance. Sylvia didn't care. Part of her wanted to hug him while the other part wished she could tell him what she really thought. The conflict of emotions flooded through her and it was all she could do to stand there silently.

But Jake put a finger to his lips, slipping his arm protectively around her waist. She stared at him, concerned because, despite the handsome black suit that he wore, he looked thin and pale. But she didn't care. The anger and disappointment that she had felt seemed to disappear. He had returned. He had remembered Steve's wedding, knew how important it was to Sylvia that they attend together, and he had returned. The pain of the past few weeks vanished so easily now that she was filled with such joy and relief at Jake's sudden appearance at her side.

It wasn't until after the ceremony when the crowd began to gather for the celebration common meal that Sylvia had a chance to escape outside with Jake. He shut the door behind them and, when he turned, he reached for Sylvia and pulled her into his arms. She melted against him, the sob that had been building finally escaped from her throat. She couldn't speak but cried against his shoulder. He let her cry, holding her tightly and rocking her gently to calm her sorrow.

"I'm so sorry, Sylvia," he whispered. "You have no idea what I have been through, where I have been, and how I have fought to get back here."

She wiped at her eyes and looked up at him. "You didn't even write," she whispered.

"I didn't even write," he acknowledged with guilt in his voice.

"I thought you had abandoned me," she confessed.

"How could you think that?" he asked firmly.

"You said you'd be back in a week," she said. "I was so worried, Jake. I didn't know what to do."

The door opened and several men filed out. They glanced at the couple standing by the door. Jake smiled at the men and turned to Sylvia. "I'll explain later. For now, let's go enjoy ourselves. It's your brother's day and an important one for us, too." He looked around, certain that no one was looking before he leaned down and gently placed a kiss on her forehead.

Inside, Steve and Emma were seated at the corner table. They were served first and many of the guest gathered around the worship area while the first group of guests sat at the benches, eating food after filing past the buffet table. Emma's mother and sisters were busy insuring that the food on the tables remained filled so that no one would be hungry.

That evening, Steve and Emma would stay at her parents' house in order to help clean up in the morning. Later, they would visit the houses of family and friends for the next several weekends then live at her parents' house until Steve was able to set up their own home. It was rare that newly married Amish couples had their own home right after their wedding, although some young men were able to save up and buy a farm for their new bride. Sylvia knew that Steve had bought the farm near Emanuel's but it wasn't ready for them to move in yet.

Jake led Sylvia back to where Shana stood. He greeted his sister-in-law with a friendly hello, uncertain about how much Sylvia's family knew about his disappearance. But Emanuel greeted him with a warm handshake and smiled at his sister. It was apparent that Sylvia had not told her family. For that, he was relieved. He wasn't up to answering questions just yet. He just wanted to forget about his trip and immerse himself into the peace of his new community.

Jake never left her side during the time they spent at the wedding feast. She was grateful for his support, especially since she knew that they had a lot to talk about that evening. She felt as if a weight had been lifted from her shoulders. Her faith in the Lord had brought Jake back to her.

Despite not knowing the story of why he had been gone for so long or why he hadn't contacted her, she found herself happy. Her husband was home and was safe. And, of course, now that he had returned, she couldn't wait to share her wonderful *gut* news about their expecting a baby. Everything would be set right, she knew. It was, indeed, an important day for all of them.

Chapter Twenty-Four

When they left Emma's parents farm after the wedding celebration was dwindling, Sylvia drove the horse and wagon home and Jake drove his truck. It was fortunate that no one saw so that she didn't have to answer any unwanted questions about why they had arrived separately. She could imagine her parents' reaction and was careful to avoid them during the meal. Had they recognized that she had arrived alone? Did they notice how Jake looked, so tired and pale? No, she thought, it's best to avoid those questions until she, too, had some answers.

They left as soon as guests started to say their goodbyes, careful not to be the first to leave in order to pay their respect. But both were itching to escape, to return home and be together at last. Yet, it was important for Jake to meet some of these people, the friends of Sylvia's youth and relatives from throughout the church district.

During the fellowship time, Sylvia was pleased to see Jake introducing himself to people, charming those that he met, including her friends Leah and Millie.

Millie had taken her aside and whispered, "He's like a movie star, Sylvia!"

Sylvia had blushed but didn't have any comments.

Leah seemed less impressed. "But is he a godly man?"

Sylvia remembered how Leah had been concerned about the relationship she had with the Englischer when she was working for him. She knew that tongues were wagging and people were staring. It must have been hard for her parents, to have their non-Amish son-in-law attending the wedding, a reminder of what Sylvia had done. By not joining the church, Sylvia had caused a lot of hardship for her parents. And, to have decided against joining in order to marry such a man?

Sylvia didn't care. If only they knew how wonderful he was to her, how he treated her at home, she thought. How could she have settled back into the rote routine of Amish life, married to someone like Adam Knoeffler? No, she thought. Jake had shown her another side to life and love that, once she experienced it, had ruined her for a life as an Amish wife. Yes, indeed, she had already forgotten about the pain and hardship of the past weeks.

She simply couldn't wait to be alone with him, couldn't wait to tell him the news. Shana had kept smiling at her during the fellowship time, knowing the secret and knowing that Jake didn't know. When Jake and Sylvia had walked to the bridal table to congratulate Emma and Steve, she was so grateful that he was by her side. The pressure was gone and she felt as if the weight of the world was lifted from her shoulders. She had believed in God and He had provided.

When the horse pulled her wagon into the driveway, she wasn't surprised to see Jake waiting for her outside. He helped her down from the wagon, his hands lingering on her waist. He didn't say anything, but just stared down at her for a long moment. She thought that he might kiss her, right then and there. But, instead, he cleared his throat and told her to go wait for him inside the house, that he would take care of the horse. She did as she was told, relieved that she did not have to make such decisions anymore. Her husband was back and he would take care of her.

She sat at the table, waiting for him to enter the house. She was nervous, wondering what he would say to excuse the time away. She felt ashamed of herself that she had thought he had left her for good, returning to the worldly ways of his Englische past. How could she have doubted him? She laid her hand over her stomach, gently rubbing it as she realized that she would also have to tell him about their baby.

She wondered about what his reaction would be. Would he share the happiness that she felt? Or would he be upset that it had happened so quickly? She began wondering what had happened to him. Where had he been? What news was he going to tell *her*? She suddenly realized that, despite her own happy news, his could certainly not be as welcoming.

When he walked in through the kitchen door, he paused, standing in the doorway and staring at her. His eyes looked hallow and vacant. Sylvia didn't move but waited for a reaction from him. Would he be upset about the wheat? Did he have something terrible to tell her? She held her breath, waiting to know what direction the rest of the day would take.

"Sylvia," he said slowly, taking a step toward her. He seemed to hesitate as he stared at her. "I know that we need to talk but I need you," he said, his voice low and hoarse. He walked toward her and reached for her hand. "I need you," he repeated.

"I'm here for you," she replied, letting him pull her to her feet.

"That's not what I mean," he murmured as he embraced her and lowered his lips to her neck. She smelled sweet and clean, just the way he remembered. He gently removed her prayer *kapp* and set it on the table. It looked pretty on the oak table, the strings coiled naturally from where Jake had set it down. "Come," he said as he led her toward the stairs, not bothering to turn on the light in the fading afternoon sun.

She let him lead her upstairs and undress her. She stood before him, naked and frightened. Whatever had happened had upset him, she thought. But he was seeking comfort in her arms and that was good enough for her. She let him remove her hairpins, her hair flowing down her back, just the way he liked it.

His hands wandered over her body, stopping just momentarily at her stomach. He paused, looking at her with an unspoken question in his eyes. It was clear that he recognized what she had so obviously missed. Sylvia paused, then, with her eyes downcast, she nodded. He lifted her chin with his finger, staring into her eyes as he exhaled loudly, a contented sigh, and lowered his mouth onto hers with a passion that indicated his own grief from his extended and unexpected absence.

The sky was not completely dark as they lay in each other's arms after having shared an intimate reunion. Jake tucked the sheet and blanket around Sylvia's shoulder. He leaned on his side, running his free hand down her arm. He sighed, his mind whirling with all of the things that he wanted to tell her. But, as his hand travelled down her side, he brushed against her stomach. "When did you find out about the baby?" he asked.

She placed her hand on top of his. "I didn't realize it, Jake. I feel so foolish. It was Shana who noticed and asked me."

"A baby," he said, his voice soft and gentle. There was something peaceful in the way that he said the words.

"Our baby," she said.

"When...?"

Sylvia shrugged her shoulders and frowned. "I don't know. I must be three months along. Late April...May, I suppose." A silence fell between them. He continued to gently rub her stomach, her hand still pressed upon his. The room was growing darker and they both knew they would have to get up to take care of the evening chores. "Are you pleased?" she asked shyly.

He answered her by kissing her gently on the forehead. "Who wouldn't be pleased? It's the right order of things," he said. "A baby will make everything different...better than it already is, yes? And you will be a magical mother, I'm sure."

The words were genuine but there was something heavy behind his tone. Sylvia noticed it immediately. Her husband had not returned to her with the same sparkle in his eyes that had been there when he had left. She took advantage of the moment to ask what was truly on her mind.

"Jake? It worries me what happened..."

He rolled onto his back and covered his eyes with his arm. "What didn't happen?" he answered in response. He took a long moment to collect his thoughts before he continued. "I had to return to the city, Sylvia. It was hard. Really hard."

"Why, Jake?"

"When Jennifer died..." he began. "Well, let's just leave it as I had to meet with lawyers and financial people. There were issues regarding her death that I really don't want to discuss. Going back there, to the place where it happened, well, it was more than difficult." There was a long pause. He didn't want to proceed but did so cautiously. "I was sick, Sylvia. Worn out and plain sick. I wound up in the hospital."

"Jake!" His revelation frightened her. The hospital?

244

"That's why I didn't write to you. And, of course, I couldn't call. I had to deal with reliving everything, especially when I had to return to New York City. I never wanted to go back there, not after what happened. The stress left me sick, Sylvia, both emotionally and physically." He sighed. "All I could think about was coming home to you but my body couldn't take the strain of the decisions that I had to make, the meetings, the craziness of that city."

"I don't understand," she admitted. What was he saying?

"I never wanted to return there. The noise, the people..." he said as he quickly sat up and turned his back toward her.

She wanted to go to him, to comfort him, but she suspected that he needed a moment to clear his head. She could tell that he was conflicted. So many questions swarmed through her mind but she waited, obediently, for him to take his own time to tell his story.

"After having lived out here for so long, there is a bit of a shock when you return to that place. It's like comparing hell with heaven. Having survived the one, I only wanted to return to the other." He ran his fingers through his hair and sighed. His bare shoulders heaved under the weight of his feelings. "You can't imagine it, Sylvia. And, for that, I'm thankful." He stood up and reached for his clothing, stepping into his pants before he turned to her and gave her a hint of a smile. "It's not important. I'm fine now and I'm back." He reached out to stroke her cheek. "And I feel so much better now that I'm with you and on the farm. Now, if I'm not mistaken, we have some evening chores and then I want to hear about everything that happened while I was gone."

Sylvia didn't press him further. She knew that, when he

was ready, he would share more with her...if he felt that it was important. For now, she was just happy that he was home. With love and tenderness, she knew that she could continue to nurse him back to health...emotionally, physically, and spiritually. From his reaction and his hesitation to share with her, she knew that whatever was troubling him was powerful deep but any type of solution to his woes resided in the fact that he was back where he belonged.

Chapter Twenty-Five

Sylvia sat with the group of women, their fingers moving expertly among the material as they quilted. She was wedged between Lillian and Shana for which she was thankful. It was awkward, sitting among the women, knowing that they regarded her as an outsider. There was talk about the church and people that she knew but Sylvia felt left out, as though she was hearing about the lives of complete strangers.

She didn't see her family as much as she would have liked and life on the farm had taken a turn. She spent a lot of time alone, inside the house, especially given that it was winter and so cold. However, Jake spent most of his time in the barn. He was quiet and aloof. Whatever had happened during his trip had set him backward to a place where he hadn't wanted to return and one that Sylvia was finding increasingly difficult to understand. Coping with the change in her husband along with the change in her lifestyle was creating its own vacuum of stress on her life.

"Your stitches look fine, Sylvia," Lillian said quietly. "So small and petite. Have you been practicing at home?"

Sylvia nodded. It was true. She had been sewing a lot at home, fixing Jake's clothing as well as her own but mostly sewing small quilts and linens for the baby. If nothing else, it helped to pass the time that she spent alone. She had found solace in the simple act of creation. It kept her from worrying which was something she had been taught to avoid. To worry meant that she doubted in her own faith in the Lord. Keeping busy kept her from thinking too much about what was at the root of Jake's deep reflection.

"Lots of practice for clothing your own family, ja?" Shana asked, her voice soft so that the other women couldn't hear but Lillian could. She stressed the word family just enough so that Lillian understood the hidden meaning.

"Oh Sylvia!" Lillian whispered. "How *wunderbaar gut!* I wondered but I didn't want to ask, of course. Jake must be very excited."

Sylvia smiled but didn't reply, her eyes wandering to the other women, a silent reminder that others were near. Excited? She wondered about that herself. He seemed to treat her with more gentle care and concern, true. But he was always attentive to her needs, never failing to help with carrying things for her or to help with more labor-intensive chores. There was nothing that he could do differently to show that he loved her and cared about her. But she didn't know if he was excited about the baby. Apprehensive might be a better word, she thought. It was almost as if he didn't want to believe in the baby, as if he didn't have faith that it was real.

The other women were laughing about something and Sylvia looked up, wondering what she had missed. She always enjoyed their teasing and joking during the quilting time together, but, today, her mind was elsewhere.

The holidays had come and gone in a fast-paced blur. For the first time, she had not celebrated with her family. Shana and Emanuel had taken pity on her and invited Jake and Sylvia to their home. It was a distance away so they were made the trip in Jake's truck. Steve and Emma joined them as they were staying at Emanuel and Shana's home. The arrangement worked nicely as Steve helped Emanuel with farm work while Emma provided extra help to Shana who had just had her own baby two months prior to their wedding. Since Steve was

248

waiting for the closing on the farm he purchased near to Emanuel's, it also afforded him opportunity to visit with the owners and learn about his new property.

The holiday meal was a joyous occasion and the small kitchen of Shana's house seemed cozy enough. The children bought life and laughter to the fellowship while everyone took turns holding the new baby. But, for Sylvia, it was bittersweet as she was well aware that she had not been included in the celebration at her parents' home. Her older sisters and younger brothers had shared fellowship with their parents, their families filling in the gathering room. And, of course, Jonas Junior would have been there with Lillian and their children. At best, there would have been upwards of seventy or eighty people crowded into the house for food, song, and celebration. For the first time, Sylvia was not there. It hadn't felt like the holidays and that had left an empty feeling in Sylvia's core.

Now that the holidays were over and the depths of winter were upon them, the days seemed to drag on. The sun rose later in the day and set earlier in the evening. The darkness suited her mood. She didn't care for the winter cold and missed the warmth of the summer sun on her face. She missed working outdoors and helping Jake in the barn. He woke early and worked by himself, insisting that she keep warm inside the house. But that meant that the milking and animal care took twice as long in the morning and early evening. It also meant that he was tired so, every night, shortly after supper, he retired to bed. She realized that she rarely saw him during the day and they only spoke during meal times.

So, Sylvia had been glad to hear about the quilting and was especially glad that Shana had joined them. She was spending a few days at Katie and Jonas' while the work at her own home was not as busy. Yet, with the other women so nearby, Sylvia knew that this wasn't the time or the place. With a big sigh, she realized that there never seemed to be a good time or place anymore. She was either completely alone or she was in a crowd of people where intimate conversation was impossible. Even at the Mennonite church that she and Jake frequented, she felt as though she was a stranger. Different people, different sermons, and different songs. The culture was too different for her own comfort.

Later that night, she prepared the evening meal. The kitchen smelled of fried pork chops, creamed corn, and fresh biscuits. She had set the table for the two of them, always putting her place setting to the right of Jake. Every evening, she hoped that there would be a glimmer of that spark in his eyes when he came through the door. Tonight was no different. So, with bated breath, she waited to hear his footsteps on the porch steps and then crossing the porch to the front door. The door squeaked and a gush of cold air came into the room.

He greeted her with a warm smile as he took off his coat and gloves. "Sure is cold out there tonight."

She hesitated before approaching him, reaching to take his outer garments. "Go warm up by the heater and I'll take care of these, Jake."

Without another word, he walked over to the kerosene heater and pulled the kitchen chair over to it. Rubbing his hands before it, he did his best to regain warmth. With the door shut again, the cold air quickly dissipated. "Today was your quilting, wasn't it?" He shifted the chair back to the table. "Did you have a nice time?"

A nice time, she thought. What is a nice time these days?

She wanted to tell him the truth, that she had felt like a stranger among those women. They didn't look at her the same way, they spoke differently around her, and they regarded her with caution and a level of distrust. She was the outsider and it had hurt. But there was no benefit to sharing this with him. Perhaps he would think that she wanted him to feel sorry for her and that tiptoed too close to manipulation and even a touch of pride.

"It was quite nice," she heard herself say. "Shana was there."

"And how are you feeling?"

The question was always the same. He asked about her day first and how she was feeling second. She smiled as she dished food onto two plates. "Are you asking about the baby?"

"Well, I suppose at this point, I consider you both one and the same," he replied, an unsettling emptiness in his voice.

Setting his supper on the table at his place setting, Sylvia sat down next to him. "I think we are both feeling fine tonight."

After the silent blessing over their food, Jake began to eat while Sylvia sat quietly for a moment, watching him. He glanced at her, surprised to see her eyes upon him. Setting his fork down, he wiped his mouth with his napkin and met her gaze. "Seems like we're going to get some snow in the next day or so. We should probably head to market tomorrow and stock up. Once the snow falls, I don't want you on the road in a wagon, buggy, or truck."

"I can make a list after I clear the supper dishes," she said, too aware of his protective proclamation. She wouldn't act against his wishes and she understood his trepidation about poor weather and an accident. But she wasn't certain she appreciated the gruffness with how he spoke to her. "It would be nice to go out together tomorrow. It's been a while, ja?" He didn't respond but turned back to eating his supper. "Jake?" she asked cautiously. "Mayhaps you'd feel better if you talked about what's eating at you so."

He took a quick, short breath and sat back in his chair. For a long moment, he stared at her. His eyes seemed to study every feature of her face as if trying to memorize them. When he was done, he gave a short shake of his head and forced a small smile. "Nothing's eating at me, Sylvia. Just worry."

"Worry?" she asked. "What could you be worried about, Jake?"

"What could I be worried about?" he repeated. Reaching for her hand, he held it. Both of their hands rested on the table and he caressed the back of her hand with his thumbs. "Let's start with you."

"Me?" she asked, her voice high pitched and unable to hide her surprise. All along, she had been fighting the urge to worry about Jake. Despite her upbringing, she couldn't help but find herself concerned. Yet, at the same time, he was worried about her? She found that incredulous. He had nothing to worry about when it came to her. The sun rose and set on her love for Jake Edwards, even during this trying time. "That's rather unnecessary," she added softly. "To worry is to show that you don't trust in God."

"I don't think you understand," he said as he withdrew his hand from hers and picked up his fork. He poked at the food on his plate. "If anything happened to you, Sylvia..." The words lingered between them because he couldn't finish the sentence.

"It's not up to me, Jake, but up to God. However, I have no fears about having this baby," she reassured him. She knew that was only partially true. Every first time mother had trepidation about childbirth. The idea of the unknown, both during and after, was certain to scare any woman. But Sylvia was raised to know that children would be part of her life and she was eager to have her own. God would protect her, if that was His plans.

Jake shook his head. "That's not it, Sylvia."

"Then what is it?" she asked gently.

"Sometimes we cannot control things. I promised to take care of you, to protect you. But maybe there are things that I cannot do. Maybe I will make it worse, exposing you to the outside world so much. You've sacrificed so much for me. I know it can't be easy."

If she was an arguing type of person, she might have countered his claim. But, she wasn't. Besides, there was truth to what he said. It hadn't been easy. Getting used to the not-quite-Amish lifestyle was difficult, indeed. Whenever they went places, he liked to drive. She was uncomfortable with driving, unless it was a long distance. She often stayed home instead of joining him to avoid the overuse of the truck, a luxury that shouted of the way of the Englische. The house had electricity and the bright lights hurt her eyes at night. She was always lighting the kerosene lamp but Jake would flip the switch when he walked into a room. But the worst part had been the separation from the community.

There were times that she would be invited to local gatherings at her family's house. But it wasn't as frequently as before. While Amish sometimes shunned wayward members of the church, she had never joined. Yet, in many ways, she felt as though she were shunned, having fallen outside of the fold. She felt lonely. To make matters worse, Jake's somber mood since his return left her feeling even worse...she felt alone. "God doesn't give us more than we can handle," she finally said.

While she appreciated Jake's awareness of the sacrifices she had made, she was more concerned that he was not back to his jovial self. He seemed distracted and disturbed. The trip back to Connecticut had set him back. Sylvia wondered if there were simply too many memories from his first marriage, reminders of the accident, which had caused this distance between them. All she could do was pray that God would help lead Jake out of the darkness that seemed to envelop him.

Chapter Twenty-Six

It was February when she faced the empty bedroom. It was time to start preparing for the baby but she dreaded cleaning out the room. Jake was so busy with working in the barn that she didn't want to ask him for help. She was too aware that he rarely spoke about the upcoming birth of their first child and he certainly didn't have the foresight to plan for a room. But Sylvia didn't mind. Her days had become so routine that she welcomed the change. In addition, Lillian had volunteered to help her.

Of course, now that she stood in the doorway, she wasn't sure where to start. She had picked the smaller of the two rooms to be the baby's. While the baby would sleep in their bedroom until it slept through the night, she still needed a changing table and place for its clothing. The only problem was that the smaller bedroom was filled with boxes that held some of Jake's things. He must have brought them when he had moved but had never emptied them.

"There you are!" Lillian said as she walked up the stairs. "Baking bread, I smell. What a wonderful *gut* welcome to your home."

"Nothing like fresh baked bread and jam on a cold winter day," Sylvia said as she greeted her sister-in-law with a smile. "It's right kind of you to help. I know you have your own chores."

Lillian peered over Sylvia's shoulder into the room. "Oh my," she exclaimed. "We do have our work cut out for us, don't we?"

They spent the next hour, seated on the floor as they rooted through the boxes. Some of the boxes contained clothing. Sylvia and Lillian sorted through them, making piles in the hallway of what they felt should be donated and what was wearable. One of the things that Sylvia loved about Lillian was her ability to laugh and talk, making any occasion cheerful and celebratory. From the first day that Jonas Junior had brought his new bride to live on the Lapp farm, Sylvia had always felt close to Lillian and enjoyed spending time with her. Today was certainly no different.

It was just after ten when they took a break to retreat downstairs for a warm cup of coffee and slice of Sylvia's fresh bread. They sat at the table, looking out the window toward the barn. The door was open just enough so that Sylvia could see the lights were on but she didn't see Jake moving around. She figured that he'd be working on the stalls right about now. The sky was grey and there was a hint of snow in the clouds.

"Can't wait until spring finally comes," Lillian said.

"At least we didn't have much snow this year, ja?"

Lillian laughed. "Not like last year. But the children are quite sore about that. They were looking forward to sleigh riding!"

Sylvia laughed with her. "I can imagine."

"I bet Jake's anxious for spring, too, ja?"

Her question caught her off-guard. It wasn't like Lillian to ask questions of a personal nature. Sylvia wondered why her sister-in-law had shifted the conversation. "I imagine so," she answered cautiously.

"First time planting spring crops and you said two of the horses were going to foal in the spring, if I recall. Should be exciting," Lillian continued.

"Ja, exciting," Sylvia added, lifting her coffee cup to her lips and watching Lillian carefully.

Her sister-in-law took a deep breath and glanced at Sylvia. She smiled but it wasn't her normal smile. It seemed forced. "Speaking of exciting, you sure haven't looked very excited recently, Sylvia. I know it's none of my concern or maybe I'm just *ferhoodled*. But I was wondering if everything is OK?" She set her cup down and reached out to touch Sylvia's hand. "You just look so sad, sister."

Try as she might, Sylvia couldn't help feeling the tears well into her eyes. She glanced down at the floor, blinking rapidly in the hopes that they wouldn't fall down her cheeks. But, it didn't take long for the first one to trickle down. She raised her eyes, knowing that she couldn't avoid Lillian's concerned gaze. It was time to confide and confess.

"It's been hard, Lillian," she started. "I miss so many things. Mamm's cooking, the church services, the fellowship."

"I know, Sylvia. We all know it must be hard," Lillian said, comforting her with her soft words.

The tears streamed down her cheeks now. "And then, there's Jake..." She hesitated to share everything but she needed to speak to someone, to hear a different opinion, to get some advice. "Ever since he disappeared, he just hasn't been the same."

It took a moment for Sylvia's words to sink in. Lillian frowned and tilted her head. "Disappeared? What do you mean that he disappeared?"

"It was just before Steve's wedding. He received a letter and was gone the next day. Returned to where he came from.

He said he'd be gone for a few days but it was almost three weeks. I didn't hear from him and had to plant the winter wheat by myself. Did all of the chores alone...milking, cleaning, mucking."

"Sylvia!" Lillian gasped. "You should have come to us! We would have helped. You should never have undertaken that alone!"

"I tried to ask for help. But, when I did, Mamm made a comment about how Jake makes me work too hard. I was embarrassed." She paused, hearing her own words. "Yes, I was so embarrassed that, just two months after I left the fold, I had been abandoned. I'm so ashamed, Lillian, but my pride truly got in the way." She dabbed at her eyes with the corner of her apron. "Of course Jake came back, showed up at Steve's wedding. I was so happy to see him...relieved that he had returned."

"Why did he leave?"

Sylvia shrugged. "I never thought to ask for details. He said he had unfinished business to tend to in New York City and Connecticut." The tears were in control now but she still felt heavy-hearted. "He hasn't been the same since, Lillian. I'm so afraid that he thinks he made a mistake."

"Mistake?"

Sylvia nodded. "Moving here and marrying me. He rarely talks to me, spends all of his time in the barn. I'm so afraid of what would happen if he decides that he doesn't like this life."

"Oh Sylvia," Lillian said. "I'm so sorry." She looked genuinely upset. One of the key comforts in an Amish woman's life was that her husband was her life mate. There was no such thing as a mistake in marriage. She couldn't even begin to imagine how Sylvia felt. Those were foreign emotions to Lillian and she could only sense the tip of the grief that Sylvia was experiencing. "Perhaps you should talk to him?"

"I've tried. Believe me, I've tried. I do whatever I can to make him happy. I'm adapting to the little things that make our lives non-Amish. But it's so hard, Lillian. And when I broach the subject, he seems to shut down. He says that he's worried for me. That's the only thing that I can get out of him. But I don't think he means about the baby."

"Worried? I wonder about what."

"If he'd only talk to me," Sylvia added quietly.

Lillian took a deep breath and sighed. "You just have to have faith in the Lord, Sylvia. Jake loves you. Anyone with eyes and a heart can see that. Whatever is bothering him will come out sooner or later. But it seems that it will be on his time, not yours."

Having talked about the situation with Lillian, Sylvia already felt a little better. She realized that she had been holding too much inside. She missed the Jake that she had fallen in love with but she knew that he was still there. Lillian's words rang in her ears, that Jake, indeed, loved her dearly. She had no choice but to wait for him to share his burden with her. "Ja, time will mend the wound, I suppose."

After finishing their coffee, they returned upstairs to continue working on the rest of the bedroom. Lillian carried several boxes of items that they felt should be donated downstairs and left them on the porch. In the meantime, Sylvia sat beside another box, one of the last remaining boxes in the room that needed to be unpacked and sorted through. They had cleared out six boxes but two remained.

When she lifted the lid, she was surprised to see that it did not contain clothing but papers and files. She glanced through the box, shifting through the stacks of envelopes. She started to put them back when her eyes noticed a bank statement sticking out of a file folder. Without thinking, she lifted it by the corner and glanced at it. It was dated a few months ago. She had never thought to ask about their financial situation. That was just something that men handled, at least in most Amish households. But when her eyes shifted across the paper, she felt her heart start to pound when she saw the amount of money in the bank account.

"Sylvia?"

His voice startled her. She turned her head to look at the doorway. But there were no words that came to her lips.

Jake stood there, his face pale as he saw her kneeling before the box. "I came to see if you needed anything else bought down. I saw Lillian lugging boxes," he said slowly, his eyes lingering on the paper in her hand. "I didn't know you were clearing out a room already for the baby. You should have told me."

"Jake, what is this?" she asked, holding the paper for him to see.

"You weren't meant to see that," he replied. His voice was low and his words spoken in a crisp, even tone.

She felt angry and hurt. "You thought you should keep something like this from me, Jake?"

"It wasn't intentional."

"Not intentional?" She struggled to get to her feet. He reached out to help her but she cringed from his touch. "Where

260

did all of this money come from, Jake?" Clutching the paper, she waved it at him. "Is this new life of yours just a hobby? A game to you?"

"Sylvia..."

She shook her head, defiant for the first time in her life. "No. I have been patient with you for months. You left me alone, you ran off somewhere with no explanation. You returned to me a changed man, an empty shell. I've been struggling to understand, to help. But you have shut me out. You took me away from my own world and abandoned me in yours, Jake. Now this?"

"I fail to see why this is such a big deal," he stated.

"Where did all of this money come from?" she repeated.

"A settlement."

She looked at him in disbelief. "A what?"

He took a deep breath and leaned against the doorframe. "A settlement. A legal proceeding."

"I don't understand," she said, her voice returning to her normal tone. But she still felt the stress of the situation. "You were given this money?"

"Yes."

"Given this type of money?" She couldn't believe it. Who gives away millions of dollars? "Why?"

"It was from her accident," he said softly.

"From a car accident?"

There was a moment of silence. Then, Jake walked over to the box on the floor and ruffled through it. He pulled out something that looked like a newspaper and turned back to face her. The expression on his face was so sorrowful that

Sylvia felt her heart skip a beat. He seemed to apologize with his eyes as he said, "I never meant to expose you to this, Sylvia."

"Expose me? To what?" His evasiveness was taxing her nerves and, for the first time, she felt anger at him.

He handed her the newspaper. It was the front page of the New York Times. "I never said it was a car accident. You just assumed that," he stated.

He watched as her eyes scanned the newspaper. There were photos on that page. He knew exactly which ones she was looking at since he had stared at that newspaper many times before in complete disbelief. While it had happened years ago, it still seemed just as surreal. And the memories were just as raw. Now, as he watched Sylvia, he knew the moment that the realization sunk in.

When she looked up at him, he nodded. "Yes, Sylvia. It's true. And I was there when it happened."

"You were there?" She thrust the paper back at him as if it was burning her hands. Her own face was pale and her eyes wide with shock.

"I told you that I worked on Wall Street. She did, too. Only I worked in a different building. When I heard about what happened, I ran as fast as I could to where she worked. But there was too much smoke and debris. I couldn't get close enough. But I was standing there when it collapsed. I saw the whole thing happen, Sylvia." He shut his eyes as if trying to erase the memory. "I couldn't save her. You have no idea how helpless I felt. How helpless I still feel when I think back to that horrible morning. What I saw that day haunts me. It took me a long time to forget, if you can ever forget something like that."

He opened his eyes and looked at her, registering the shock on her face by what he was telling her. "I told you the world is an ugly place and I told you that I never wanted to go back to that city. Now you know why."

Yes, she knew the world was ugly. She didn't know how ugly, but she knew that the church sheltered them from being overly exposed to it. The rules that the bishops, elders, and deacons made and enforced insured that by creating a safety net around the community.

"So you came here to escape that ugliness. Why did you go back, Jake?"

"There were some legal issues with the settlement. Being there brought everything back. I had to actually drive by the site. Life just seemed to sweep the debris away and go on, rebuild...forget. As much as people say they will never forget, they have. It's cliché at this point. No one cares, not really. That's why I came here, Sylvia. To find myself and try to make sense of this tragedy." He raised his hand to his brow and rubbed his forehead. "Then I met you. You were the peace that I wanted to find. You helped me find it. How could I not fall in love with you? How could I not want this? But then I had to go back and it sent me into a tailspin."

"I don't understand," Sylvia whispered.

Jake took a deep breath. "There are simply too many memories, too many emotions. It was like déjà vu, you see. Right before it happened, we had only just gotten married. We had a promising future that was stolen. And, now, all I can think about is how I could promise to protect you and a baby when I cannot control the dangers of the world."

"And now you push me away?"

"I didn't mean to push you away."

She looked down at the bank statement again. The paper felt dirty and worldly. It was full of sin and evil. "This money is no *gut*, Jake," she stated simply. She reached out and handed it to him. "You have to know that. Money doesn't help with forgiveness. Maybe it just makes it worse. No wonder you are so *ferhoodled*." She waited until he took the paper. "You can't hide from what happened by coming to your grandfather's farm and playing farmer while pretending to be Amish, Jake. You will never find that peace. We are not a pill that can be swallowed to make the pain go away. You either want it or you don't."

He flinched at her words. "What are you saying?"

"You can't take the good but leave behind what you think is bad." She started to walk past him. She was upset and needed to get some fresh air. But he reached out for her arm. "Jake, I really need to think about this. I need some time alone."

"I'm not trying to take the good and leave the bad," he said. "I'm not pretending to be Amish. I told you that I would not join the church."

"You've brought a great deal of worldliness into my life. How would I ever have been able to return to the People?" she asked sadly. "I see now why the church doesn't want us exposed to your world."

He released her arm and she walked down the stairs. In just a few minutes, he had exposed her to the most horrific evil that she could imagine. She knew that the images on that paper would stay with her for a long time to come. But, what was even worse was the fact that, in just a few short months, he had changed her entire life.

Chapter Twenty-Seven

Sylvia had no choice but to leave the house. If nothing else, she just needed time to clear her head. She needed to make sense of what Jake had just told her. So, when she bumped into Lillian at the bottom of the stairs, Sylvia fought back her tears as she asked Lillian if they could finish the room another day. Lillian nodded, not asking any questions. Clearly, she had overheard at least some of the conversation between Sylvia and Jake from the bottom of the stairs when she went to rejoin her sister-in-law.

"And I think I'll join you for a visit with Mamm," Sylvia whispered before collecting her black jacket and waiting by the door, her eyes downcast as she waited for Lillian. Together, they walked across the field in silence, Sylvia's mind whirling with too many thoughts and ideas and Lillian knowing that Sylvia needed time to think.

Tragedy, she thought. An amazing tragedy. But the Amish weren't immune to tragedy. They looked at it with sorrow but knew that it was God's will. Tragedy was met with forgiveness. If Jake couldn't find forgiveness, he'd never find happiness. And she knew that part of the reason why he didn't want to return to the Amish roots of his ancestors was because he couldn't find that forgiveness. If only he would consider giving himself to God, she thought unhappily.

When Lillian and Sylvia arrived at her parents' farm, Katie was clearly surprised to see her youngest daughter. They hadn't seen much of Sylvia during the winter months. But, now Katie immediately saw that there was a problem. Sylvia looked tired and asked if she might lie down for a while. Katie glanced at Lillian, as if seeking an explanation, but her daughter-in-law only averted her eyes. The story was not hers to share. If Sylvia wanted to confide in her mother, she would do so when she was better rested.

So Sylvia climbed the stairs and went to her old bedroom. It felt wonderful *gut* to sink into her old bed. She wrapped the blanket around herself and, with her hand on her stomach, she sank into a much needed sleep that, thankfully, was not haunted by the images that Jake had shown her.

When she woke, she was surprised to see that the sky was dark. Without having a clock in the room, she had no idea what time it was. She sat up and looked outside the window by her bed. As she had predicted earlier, it was snowing. For a long time, she sat on the edge of the bed, her head in her hands as she tried to digest everything that she had learned.

She was upset about the excessive wealth and the details of his first wife's death but not so much as she was upset by the fact that he had neglected to tell her these things. Instead, he had withdrawn into himself, shielding himself from emotion by pushing her away. But her biggest concern was that, perhaps, his commitment to the farm was a fleeting fancy, a whim to seek that peace and to forget the evils of the world. But that would all be in vain. She knew that he needed to find God and seek forgiveness in order to properly heal.

With a deep breath, she braced herself to go downstairs and face her family. She wasn't certain if she wanted to confide in them, given her mother's comments in the past about Jake. Since she wasn't certain what she felt, how could she expect them to guide her? Plus, she didn't know if it was best to shield them from the facts. Her own eyes were open to the Englischer world. Did she need to do that to them, too?

She entered the kitchen. Her mother looked up from the chair where she sat, the Bible open on her lap. Apparently Katie had taken advantage of the quiet to read the words of God. Her mother had always taken great comfort in reading Proverbs in times of great stress. Sylvia leaned against the doorway, smiling sadly at her mother. There was no use denying that her mother suspected that something wasn't going well in her youngest daughter's life. With a deep breath, Sylvia moved to the seat next to her mother. She didn't speak for a few minutes, waiting for her mother to close and set aside the Bible.

"Well, daughter," her mother began. "I suppose you came home for more than just an afternoon nap."

Sylvia couldn't look her mother in the eyes. "Ja," she admitted. "I suppose."

"You cannot run away from your problems," her mother started slowly. "You made some choices and now you have to rely on God to lead you through whatever waters are troubling you."

"Mamm, I just don't understand why he didn't tell me before about everything," Sylvia said. "There are so many wonderful *gut* things about Jake. I don't want you thinking poorly of him if I tell you that he's truly lost and needs to find salvation but he won't find it without God."

With a simple nod of her head, Katie acknowledged that she understood what Sylvia was saying despite the limited amount of information that was being shared. "And if he doesn't find salvation, daughter? What happens then?"

"I don't think he'll ever find the peace and forgiveness that he seeks for himself."

Katie placed her hand on the Bible and sighed. No one who witnesses pain or suffering in their own children is immune from the same, especially a mother. "I'm not right certain what to say to guide you, Sylvia. No matter what happens, you have chosen Jake and you need to help him as best you can. These problems need to be resolved in your own home. Coming here for a respite only delays the resolution."

Sylvia frowned. "I know that, Mamm."

"In times of need, there is only one place to turn and that is the Almighty."

Sylvia knew that, too. But, without the comfort of the church and People, she didn't feel as if she had the ear of the Almighty. Had she taken the kneeling vow, she could have turned to the bishop or elders for guidance. The community would certainly have provided her with support and prayers. Without them, she felt afraid to reach to God. Perhaps He would turn a deaf ear to her needs just because she hadn't taken the vow. But she knew that she had to try.

"Yes, Mamm."

"Now, I'm suspecting you need to go home and make a supper for your husband, ja? I'll ask Daed to take you. No use walking on the roads with the snow and all," her mother said.

But her father wasn't to be found. He wasn't in the barn nor was he wandering in the fields. Instead, Katie found Daniel with the younger boys in the hayloft, getting ready for the evening feeding. She instructed Daniel to take Sylvia back to the farm. They were surprised to find that, despite not being on the farm, Jonas' buggy was still parked in the horse shed. Twenty minutes later, Sylvia entered her house, her heart heavy. Jake's truck was not parked in the driveway which was covered with a solid inch of snow. There were no traces of tire prints. She knew that the evening milking needed to be tended to so she hurried into the barn and got to work on the evening chores.

It was close to seven when he returned. She was sitting at the table, reading the Bible, when he arrived. He stood in the doorway, the cold drifting in and setting a chill to the air in the room. Shivering, she placed her bookmark in the Bible and shut the book before she lifted her eyes to meet his. Neither spoke but he stepped into the room and shut the door behind him. His footsteps were heavy as he crossed the room and sat next to her at the table. The clock on the wall ticked and the silence seemed the ring in her ears. She needed him to speak, to explain, anything to make this situation better.

"I'm going to need some time, Sylvia," he finally said, his voice breaking the silence. "I need some time to sort this out."

She wasn't certain what he meant but she didn't dare ask him. What exactly was he going to "sort out", she wondered.

"I'll get back to where I was, I promise you that." He hesitated. "But I just need a little bit of time. Can you give me that? Can you do that for me?"

Was he actually asking her for patience and time? Did he think that she would turn her back on him? She frowned and met his gaze. "Jake, I am your wife. I will do whatever you need me to do. You take whatever time that you need." She ran her fingers over the leather cover of the Bible in front of her. "You once told me that you wanted to find the peace that you see in me. If that is truly what you want, then you might want to spend some time with this." She pushed the book across the table toward him. "This peace that you seek can be found amongst these pages, Jake."

He looked at the book and, for just a moment, reached out to leaf through the pages. But, he seemed discouraged and shut the book. "I'm not a good Bible reader," he confessed.

She smiled at him and reached for the book, bringing it back so that it was before her. "Mayhaps we can read it together. Mayhaps that would be *gut* for your heart and your soul, ja?"

Jake didn't respond right away. He stared at her, his eyes focused on her face as he rubbed his chin. He was thinking, she could see that. And, as she watched, she saw a light begin to shine in his expression. It started in his eyes but traveled down his face. And, when he took a deep breath and smiled back at her, she felt as if something had just happened. Whatever it was, she could sense that it was important to him.

"Mayhaps, dear Sylvia, that is just what we both need, ja?" he replied, the teasing tone in his voice reminding her of her Jake, the Jake that had left the farm back in November but had yet to truly return.

Chapter Twenty-Eight

Ever since the night of the revelation, the snow had come with an unusual fierceness. While beautiful on the fields, it was taxing on the nerves. Snow meant cold and ice, which made work around the farm more difficult. The days had been bookended by prolonged night skies that lingered well into the morning and arrived early in the afternoon. With snow covering the ground, Sylvia had spent most of her time indoors with the exception of helping Jake with the morning and evening milking. By nine in the morning, Sylvia would be finished with cleaning the kitchen from breakfast and working diligently on her house chores. She found herself baking more and more during the winter months. She felt the need to create food, smell the bread in the oven, and feel the warmth of the stove.

The winter had never been her favorite season, despite the beauty of the snow. However, this year was different. In years past, she had been able to go sleigh riding with her friends and brothers or ice skate on the pond behind the Smuckers' farm. This winter, she was married and expecting her first baby within the next few months. There was no room for sleigh riding or ice-skating. In fact, despite the valiant efforts that Jake had been making, he was still overprotective of her taking the horse and cart or even walking to visit with her parents. Under the snow, there was indeed a layer of ice that made the roads more dangerous that she had seen in past years.

So, she was surprised to hear two buggies pull into the driveway. She hurried to the window to look outside, curious as to who would be visiting on such an overcast and snowy day. The buggies stopped by the barn, the horses shaking their heads and their breath steaming in the cold winter air. She was surprised to see Bishop Peachey, the minister who headed up her parents' church district, emerge from one of the buggies. With his long white beard and deeply sunken eyes, he was a man who intimidated, even before he spoke.

But it was the other two people who emerged from the other buggy that surprised Sylvia even more: her father and Jake. She hadn't seen Jake's truck this morning and just presumed that he was gone to town. But now, he had returned with her father and the bishop. The combination of the three men startled her. It was an unlikely grouping.

Sylvia hurried back to the sink to wash the flour from her hands. She had been making bread when they had arrived. Quickly, she wiped down the counter and shook out the rag in the sink. It wouldn't do anyone any good to see her kitchen in such disarray. By the time she had cleared some of the countertop, she heard them walking up the porch steps, stomping the snow from their feet and clapping their arms against their sides to fight the cold.

"Sylvia," the bishop said, greeting her with a solemn nod when he walked into the room.

"Bishop! What a *wunderbaar gut* surprise!" As soon as she said it, she wondered if it was true. She looked questioningly at her father and Jake. But their expressions remained stern and serious. What on earth, Sylvia wondered, could have made Bishop Peachey travel to her and Jake's farm in such weather? She hoped that nothing serious had happened, that they were not coming to her with bad news. For a moment, she panicked about her mother. Could something terrible have happened at her father's farm? Why were they here and looking so serious?

The bishop didn't waste any time. Taking off his hat, he held it in his hand. "Sylvia, your father came to me on behalf of your husband."

His words surprised her. Her husband? Why would Jake want to speak with the bishop? And, perhaps even more important, why would Jake enlist the help of her father? For what? She frowned as she digested the words.

"Your husband has come to me, seeking salvation for both himself and for you."

Salvation? She was confused. Jake had certainly started to seem more relaxed in the past few days but to seek out the bishop, asking for salvation? Whatever did he mean, she wondered. "For sure and certain, I don't understand."

The bishop gestured toward Jake. "Your husband has come to me, seeking permission and the blessing of the church district to study for his kneeling vow. As you are certainly aware, it is not often that Englischers' feel moved by the spirit of *Gott* to seek baptism into our faith and agree to the commitment of our ways." The bishop paused as if giving homage to the seriousness of the decision. "Jake will need to go through a Proving and learn many things, Sylvia. He will need the help of everyone in the community. But, you must know that none of this can happen without your blessing and your consent to follow your husband to the ways of the People."

The words that came forth from the bishop's mouth caught Sylvia off-guard. She had to repeat them to herself, her mind unable to comprehend what the bishop was saying. Jake wanted to take the kneeling vow?

Sylvia looked at Jake, surprise on her face. "Jake? Is this true?"

He nodded once but did not speak.

Sylvia looked at her father who stood silently besides Jake. His silence was out of respect for this momentous decision that both Jake and Sylvia would have to make. However, she could see the glow in her father's eyes. Now she understood. For the past few weeks, Jake had been spending a lot of time away from the farm during the day. He must have been spending time with Jonas, seeking advice and guidance on this very important matter. "I would like nothing more than to take my kneeling vow alongside my husband," she said carefully to the Bishop. "But only if this is his true wish, to follow the way of the People and the Lord."

The bishop cleared his throat, pleased with Sylvia's response. Her obedience to her husband was commendable. "There will be a lot of work ahead of both of you. Jonas has agreed to instruct Jake on the Dordrecht Confession of Faith and the Ordnung. I'm certain that you, too, will help to guide your husband. The formal instructional will be conducted during the summer months and, upon acceptance from the congregation, you will attend the autumn baptism." At this point, the bishop turned his attention to Jake, leveling his eye at him. "During this time, son, you will be expected to behave as though you are already part of the community. *Verschteh?*"

Jake took a deep breath and, once again, nodded but remained silent.

The bishop seemed satisfied. "I find this a very important day for you both, Jake and Sylvia. He that seeks the Lord will truly be rewarded. I'm quite pleased with your decisions and support your commitment. I hope that you both prove worthy of the redemption that you seek." With that, the bishop turned to Jonas, asking him in German if he wanted a ride in his buggy to return to his farm. Jonas followed the bishop out of the house, leaving an amazed Sylvia staring at his back. She waited until she saw them leaving in the one buggy before she turned her attention back to Jake.

"Jake?"

He stood before her, looking lighter and happier than he had in weeks. No, she corrected herself, months! He walked across the floor to stand before her and reached his hand out for hers. When she gave it to him, he squeezed it gently. "I thought about what you said and realized that you are right," he said. "I can't straddle the fence any longer."

"Why didn't you talk to me?"

"This was a decision that I had to make on my own, Sylvia," he explained. "I came here seeking peace. Instead, I found you. We have a life together and will spend many happy years on this farm, I know that. But I still want that peace. If that means releasing the past and following in the footsteps of my ancestors, I'm good with that."

"It's not just about the lifestyle, Jake," she reminded him. "It's also about the faith and beliefs."

He lifted her hand to his lips and kissed the back of it. "I know that. God, how I know that." There was a smile on his face, a genuine smile that she hadn't seen in months. "The past few weeks, you have been sharing the Word of God with me every night after supper. I have been listening, Sylvia. I have listened and I do believe. I don't come to this decision lightly. You know that I was opposed to it. But, after I made up my mind, I asked your father for guidance and we spent several days talking about this. When I confirmed my decision, he went to the bishop on my behalf before making proper introductions. I had several meetings with him, too. Then, it was decided that this was an appropriate course of action."

She couldn't believe her ears. Only in her dreams could she have imagined that Jake would travel this path. He had been so adamant from the very beginning that he would never join the Amish church. She knew that such a leap of faith and commitment of life was unusual for Englischers. Her sister-in-law was one of the few who had successfully done it. Now, standing before her, her very own husband felt moved by the Spirit. He was willing to take the kneeling vow and make the commitment with God, Church, and community. And, from the look on his face, she knew that he was truly at peace with this decision. Perhaps, she wondered, fighting the baptism was what had been holding him back all along.

"This won't be easy for you," she said, her voice soft and gentle.

"It already isn't," he said, looking over his shoulder at the window. She followed his gaze and saw a horse and buggy still standing in the driveway. "I had to sell my truck."

Despite the seriousness of the moment, Sylvia caught herself laughing. "Oh Jake. How will you survive?"

He signed and shook his head. "With the help of the good Lord...and my dear wife, I reckon." But there was a sparkle in his eye, a wonderful glowing sparkled that showed her that, indeed, her husband had returned to her at last.

276

Epilogue

Despite the hard winter that had covered Lancaster County with late season snow, it was an early spring. By April, the ground had thawed and started to dry out. Sylvia looked out the window, smiling as she saw the beams of afternoon sun streaming through the trees, the hint of leaf buds sprouting on the tips of their branches. The cows were in the pasture and Jake was working with one of the horses. Just last week, he had sold two of the horses to local Amish boys who were just starting their courting years. They wanted a fancy new horse to go along with their courting buggy.

Courting years, she thought. Was it only last year that she had met this man? So much had happened in such a small amount of time. She rested her hand on her swollen stomach, feeling the baby move beneath her touch. It would be at least another few weeks before they were blessed with their first child.

Sylvia shook her head in amazement, wondering what would have happened had she not been standing on the hill of wheat on that fateful day when she had been worshipping the good Lord's gift of spring? Now, she was thanking Him for so much more. He had given her the gift of love and understanding, of patience and courage.

Now that Jake was in the full swing of giving his life over to God and the way of the People, she had seen a remarkable change in him. The old Jake was back. He sparkled and glowed when he spoke to her. His touch was loving and caring, never distant or removed. He still teased her, loving to see the color flood to her cheeks but she wouldn't have changed that for anything in the world. There was something magical about this wonderful *gut* man, she knew. Even at the Sunday church services, he carried himself with such a presence that others noticed and seemed drawn to him, like a moth to a flame.

Yes, she thought. Life has a way of changing things, presenting us with challenges and obstacles. But she knew that God never gave them more than they could handle.

She stood at the window, smiling to herself as she gave thanks for the blessings He had bestowed upon her. And when Jake rounded the corner of the barn, the straw hat upon his head and the hint of a beard growing on his face, she felt a joy warm her insides. If she had ever doubted the way of the Lord, she knew that there was one lesson more that she needed. To doubt in the Lord was to question His power and her own faith. Nevermore, she said to herself, watching her husband saunter toward the house, a happy swagger in his step and a smile on his face when he saw her watching him. And she walked toward the door, eager to greet him as he walked through it.

ABOUT THE AUTHOR

Sarah Price's ancestors emigrated from Europe in 1705, settling in Pennsylvania as the area's first wave of Mennonite families. Sara Price has always respected and honored her ancestors through exploration and research about her family's history and their religion. At nineteen, she befriended an Amish family and lived on their farm throughout the years. Twenty-five years later, Sarah Price splits her time between her home outside of New York City and an Amish farm in Lancaster County, PA where she retreats to reflect, write, and reconnect with her Amish friends and Mennonite family.

Find Sarah Price on Facebook and Goodreads!
Learn about upcoming books, sequels, series, and contests!

Made in the USA
Lexington, KY
24 October 2012